Praise For The Author

"I love the way this man writes! I adore his style. There is something about it that makes me feel as if I'm someplace I'm not supposed to be, seeing things I'm not supposed to see and that is so delicious."
REBECCA FORESTER, USA Today Bestselling Author

This book "is creative and captivating. It features bold characters, witty dialogue, exotic locations, and non-stop action. The pacing is spot-on, a solid combination of intrigue, suspense, and eroticism. A first-rate thriller, this book is damnably hard to put down. It's a tremendous read."
FOREWORD REVIEWS

"A terrifying, gripping cross between James Patterson and John Grisham. Jagger has created a truly killer thriller."
J.A. KONRATH, USA Today and Amazon Bestselling Author

"As engaging as the debut, this exciting blend of police procedural and legal thriller recalls the early works of Scott Turow and Lisa Scottoline."
LIBRARY JOURNAL

"The well-crafted storyline makes this a worthwhile read. Stuffed with gratuitous sex and over-the-top violence, this novel has a riveting plot."
KIRKUS REVIEWS

"Verdict: The pacing is relentless in this debut, a hard-boiled novel with a shocking ending. The supershort chapters will please those who enjoy a James Patterson–style page-turner"
LIBRARY JOURNAL

A "clever and engrossing mystery tale involving gorgeous women, lustful men and scintillating suspense."
FOREWORD MAGAZINE

"Part of what makes this thriller thrilling is that you sense there to be connections among all the various subplots; the anticipation of their coming together keeps the pages turning."
BOOKLIST

"This is one of the best thrillers I've read yet."
NEW MYSTERY READER MAGAZINE

"A superb thriller and an exceptional read."
MIDWEST BOOK REVIEW

"Verdict: This fast-paced book offers fans of commercial thrillers a twisty, action-packed thrill ride."
LIBRARY JOURNAL

"Another masterpiece of action and suspense."
NEW MYSTERY READER MAGAZINE

"Fast paced and well plotted . . . While comparisons will be made with Turow, Grisham and Connelly, Jagger is a new voice on the legal/thriller scene. I recommend you check out this debut book, but be warned . . . you are not going to be able to put it down."
CRIMESPREE MAGAZINE

"A chilling story well told. The pace never slows in this noir thriller, taking readers on a stark trail of fear."
CAROLYN G. HART, N.Y. Times and USA Today Bestselling Author

SHADOW FILES

Thriller Publishing Group, Inc.

SHADOW FILES

R.J. JAGGER

Thriller Publishing Group, Inc.

SHADOW FILES

Thriller Publishing Group, Inc.
Golden, Colorado 80401

Copyright©2018 RJ Jagger

All rights reserved, including the right to reproduce this book or portions thereof in any form whatsoever.

This book is a work of fiction. Any references to historical events, real people, or real places are used fictitiously. Other names, characters, places and events are products of the author's imagination, and any resemblance to actual events or places or persons, living or dead, is entirely coincidental.

Library of Congress Control Number: Available

ISBN 978-1-937888-40-4 (Hardcover)

Cover image by Robert Maguire.
Used with permission.

For Eileen

DAY ONE

June 9
Monday

1

The last customer, a white man, sat at the end of the bar peeling the label off a warm bottle of Coors. A few last swallows were left. Seven empties sat to his right, all with sticky glue where the labels should be. So far he'd paid for each bottle but hadn't tipped. That's why Visible Moon let the bottles sit, to remind him. In five minutes the bar would close and she'd find out if the guy was going to stiff her or make things right.

The smart money was on stiff.

Outside the evening was turning to night.

A twilight glow hung in the west. In another ten minutes it would morph into that total and absolute blackness that can only be found in the desert.

Tehya would be here to pick her up any time now.

The bar wasn't much.

It was basically a crude wooden shell out in the middle of nowhere, just off the main road in northern New Mexico, technically on reservation land. The one and only sign was wooden, small and said Bar in red paint—not The Desert Bar, or Last Chance Bar, or The Running Deer Bar—just Bar. The electricity came from a temperamental generator out back. The water—brownish with a hard mineral edge—came from a well.

Visible Moon wiped the counter down with a wet cloth.

She was Navajo, 22 years old, with long black hair braided into a ponytail. Her cheekbones were high, her skin was dark, her eyes were hazel and her teeth were whiter than white. Most of the men who saw her were ugly and drunk and made passes as if she was attractive.

She knew otherwise.

Tehya was the attractive one.

She cast a sideways glance at the white man, braced for trouble and said, "We close in five minutes."

He turned his head slowly, almost as if being pulled out of a trance, then locked eyes with her.

He pointed to a closed door that led to a back room.

"I've heard about that room back there," he said. "Is what I heard true?"

She knew what he meant.

The room had a mattress.

Sex took place there.

Sex for money.

She wasn't the one who gave it though.

Tehya was.

"It's just a storage room," she said.

"That's not what I heard."

"Then you heard wrong."

She continued wiping the counter.

Underneath it, within grabbing range, was a loaded Colt 45, put there by Mojag the day the bar opened and pulled out three times since but never fired.

The man stared at her for a few intense heartbeats, then put the bottle to his mouth, tilted his head back and drained what was left. He laid the bottle down sideways and spun it. When it stopped, the neck was pointing at her.

The man smiled.

"Looks like you've been chosen," he said.

Visible Moon narrowed her eyes.

"I don't want any trouble."

"Me either."

He pulled a five out of his wallet, waved it slowly so Visible

Moon could see what it was, then folded it into a paper airplane and tossed it at her. It didn't fly and dropped to the floor.

"Now is that back room open?"

She picked up the money and tossed it back on the counter, apprehensive but not scared. The man was too drunk for speed. Visible Moon could have the gun out and a bullet in his chest before he knew what was happening.

With Tehya's help, she'd bury him out in the reservation in some out of the way corner.

No one would ever find him.

"Time to go," she said.

Suddenly a light flickered outside.

A car was coming down the road, still a ways off, but definitely coming.

Tehya no doubt.

Visible Moon exhaled.

Then something happened she didn't expect—the man got off the stool, got his footing and headed for the door. The five was still on the counter.

"You forgot your money," she said.

"Keep it."

Then he was through the door and gone.

She stuffed the money in her bra and walked to the window. Outside, the man started his car, backed away from the building and squealed to the north.

His headlights were off.

Another vehicle was coming from the opposite direction.

The headlights were high and bounced like a truck. The left headlight was weaker than the right. Visible Moon had seen the sight a hundred times.

It was Tehya.

She drove a third-hand 1942 Ford pickup.

The stars were already coming out.

Hundreds of them.

Off in the distance a coyote barked.

Then another.

Within seconds a whole pack was yelping. Visible Moon pictured a jackrabbit scrambling for ten more seconds of life.

It would be lucky to get five.

DAY TWO

June 10
Tuesday

2

Shortly after dark Tuesday night, a mean thunderstorm rolled off the ocean and pounded Havana, Cuba with black, heavy fists. Shade de Laurent watched it for a few heartbeats from the window of her rat-in-the-closet hotel and got comfort from it. Bad weather meant people stayed inside. That in turn meant her chances of being caught were slimmer.

She let the curtain fall back and checked her watch.

Five minutes.

That's when the taxi would come for her.

She wore nylons, high heels and a sexy red salsa dress that showcased a 28-year-old body to perfection. The cleavage was just right. The thighs were just right. The ass was just right. The mocha skin was just right. Visually she could pass for a Cuban.

She knew Havana well.

She knew the streets.

She knew the language.

She knew the haunts.

She knew the people.

She had all the right papers—fake, but perfect in every detail.

Still, even with all that, there was always a risk.

The risk never went away.

Right now it was under her skin, in her lungs and in the quiver of her fingertips.

Headlights flashed against the window.

She took one last look in the mirror.

Her face was nice.

Her eyes were mysterious.

Her hair was long, black and thick.

A horn honked.

She blew herself a kiss and grabbed her purse. Inside was makeup, a thick sealed envelope, a wallet and a six-inch folding knife with a razor sharp serrated edge.

She flicked off the lights and headed outside.

Twenty minutes later a cabbie with a gold tooth dropped her off at Loca, a whiskey-soaked salsa club in the center of Havana with a reputation for attitude. She had been there once, two years ago, and ended up leaving with a man who fucked her silly for two straight days.

Inside, the bodies were thick.

The band was loud.

The dance floor was sardine tight.

The air was smoky.

She wedged through the bodies to the bar, ordered a double-whiskey on the rocks and threw it back. The bartender, impressed, poured her another and said, "On the house."

He wasn't bad looking.

She grabbed him by the collar, pulled him close and licked the side of his face.

"Thanks."

"You're welcome. What's your name?"

"Trouble," she said.

He smiled.

"In that case, I think I've met you before."

"I'll bet you have."

She ended up hugging the wall and watching the dancers. No one had approached her yet but her perfume was in the air and eyes studied her.

She'd dance with the first man who asked her.

It didn't take long.

He was tall, dark and dangerous.

He moved with a manly cockiness and let his hands roam freely over her body. She didn't stop him. In another time and place he would have been a serious consideration for more, but not tonight.

Tonight was business.

She stayed with him for a half-hour, checking her watch with more and more frequency. At exactly 10:13 she said, "Excuse me," and headed for the ladies' room.

"Hurry back, baby. I have big plans for you."

She blew him a kiss and disappeared into the crowd.

Game time.

No one was inside the restroom. Shade entered the left stall, shut the door, pulled her dress up and her panties down, then took a long piss. Before she was done, someone entered the adjacent stall and shut the door. Almost immediately, knuckles rapped on the wall and a woman said, "I'm sorry, but do you have any paper in there?"

Shade slipped the envelope under the partition.

"Is that enough?"

"Yes, thank you."

A small package got passed her way.

She stuffed it in her purse.

There.

Done deal.

Then something happened she didn't expect. The woman said, "Can you pass a little more?"

Shade swallowed.

That was code.

It meant something was wrong.

It meant to take every precaution.

She passed toilet paper under the wall, flushed and left.

Outside she was tempted to hang around and see who came out.

Then she shook her head.

"No."

That was against the rules.

Rules were everything.

They were there for a reason.

Suddenly arms wrapped around her abdomen from behind and strong hands cupped her stomach. Lips nibbled the back of her neck. She knew who they belonged to, the dangerous man, the dancer.

He'd be a good protector.

She'd leave with him.

Right now.

This minute.

She turned and raised her lips to kiss him.

It wasn't him.

It was someone else.

It was someone she'd never seen before, a muscular man with a bad-boy face and a crisp white shirt with the top three buttons undone.

He pricked the point of a knife into her side and said, "Don't do anything stupid."

3

The man's eyes made clear that he'd shove the blade into Shade's gut if she gave him half a reason. He'd be ten steps away before she dropped to the floor. He'd be out the door before the first person screamed. He gripped her arm with a powerful hold and pulled her towards the door.

"Come on!"

She hesitated.

Bad move.

The blade sunk into her skin, not far, only a quarter inch, maybe less, but enough to break through and draw blood.

"Do you want to live?"

She nodded.

"Yes."

"Then don't fuck with me. Do you understand?"

"Yes."

He yanked her again and this time she fell into step.

Think!

Think!

Think!

Once he got her outside, she'd be totally at his mercy. He'd take her somewhere dark and abandoned, strap her down good and tight and then interrogate her at his sick little leisure.

She didn't want to die.

Not like that.

Suddenly the man's step slowed and his grip softened. Shade immediately twisted and pulled away, bracing for the blade but possibly not all the way in.

It didn't happen.

Instead the man stood there, then wobbled and dropped to the floor. A knife was in his back. Suddenly a woman grabbed Shade's arm and said, "Come on! We got to get out of here!"

Shade had never seen her before but recognized the voice. She was the woman from the restroom.

DAY THREE

June 11
Wednesday

4

When a woman walked into Bryson Wilde's office Wednesday morning, his first thought was that she didn't want to be here. She was conservatively dressed in a gray pinstriped skirt with a matching jacket and a crisp white blouse. Her hair was packed close to her head and her lips weren't smothered under ruby-red lipstick. In her hand was an expensive leather briefcase.

She was twenty-nine or thereabouts.

She studied him briefly from the doorway.

Then she said, "I'm sorry, I'm in the wrong place."

Two heartbeats later she was gone.

Wilde walked to the window, pulled a book of matches out of his shirt pocket and struck one, bringing the pungent aroma of sulfur into the air. Then he lit the whole book on fire and watched the street through the flames as he waited for the woman to emerge.

He was thirty-one, six-two with a solid frame, green eyes and longish blond hair that he combed straight back. He wore his usual attire, a long-sleeve white shirt rolled at the cuffs, a gray suit and spit-shinned wingtips. His suit jacket was over on the rack. So was his hat, ashen-gray, which would dip over his left eye when he went out.

He waved the matchbook until the fire went out and tossed the remains in the ashtray.

Hot black smoke snaked towards the ceiling.

His office was in the 1600 block of Larimer Street, on the second floor above the Ginn Mill and two doors down from the Gold Nugget Tap Room. Once the retail heart of Denver, now Larimer Street was an unhealthy mix of liquor stores, bars, gambling houses, brothels and flophouses, occasionally punctuated with the sound of gunplay.

He could afford a better place.

He liked it here.

The woman emerged from the building and hesitated briefly next to the water fountain sculpture, a throwback to the area's better days.

The water no longer ran.

It hadn't for years.

The bowl was littered with crushed packs of cigarettes, candy wrappers and butts.

The woman turned left towards 16th Street and disappeared from view behind an ice truck.

Wilde cocked his head for a moment, deciding.

She hadn't been in the wrong place.

The door lettering wasn't fancy but it was clear: Bryson Wilde – Investigator for Hire.

She'd come to see him then changed her mind.

Why?

He grabbed his jacket and hat and went after her.

She was all the way down by the Daniels & Fisher Tower before he caught her.

"You weren't in the wrong place," he said.

She was about to deny it but didn't.

"Are you in trouble?"

"No."

"That sounds like a yes."

The woman exhaled.

"Not me personally, someone else."

"Come on back to the office," he said. "We'll talk about it."

She hesitated.

"I'd need a hundred percent confidentiality," she said.

Wilde nodded.

"Agreed."

"I'm not talking about ninety."

"You're in luck," he said. "I'm running a special this week, a hundred for the price of ninety."

The corner of the woman's mouth turned up ever so slightly. Then she got serious and said, "If what I told you ever got out, a life could be ruined."

"You're in luck again," Wilde said. "I've already ruined my month's quota."

They turned and headed back.

"What's your name?"

"Senn-Rae Vaughn," the woman said. "I'm a lawyer."

5

Fallon Leigh drove north out of Santa Fe doing full speed in a 1942 Packard that she stole from the parking lot of Jose's Kitchen. Stealing a car wasn't on the agenda when she got up this morning. It was something that happened before she checked in for her waitress shift, while she scouted the parking lot looking for a stray pack of cigarettes sitting on a dash or stuffed up in a visor. A half-filled pack of Camels drew her to the Packard. Then she saw the keys in the ignition.

In the split second that followed, everything in her life got too small.

Her apartment.

Her job.

Her friends.

Her whole screwed-up existence.

Just like that, it was time to leave it all behind, every last stinking crumb of it. It was time to start over. It was time to get fresh. It was time to get out of this stinking cow town before it sunk its hooks irretrievably into her every inch of flesh.

She hopped in, cranked over the engine and headed north.

She didn't look back.

That was an hour ago.

Now miles into her new life she had to pull over, and fast, otherwise her bladder was going to explode right here in the turquoise vinyl of the front seat. The topography shooting by was an endless sea of sagebrush, pinions, prairie grasses and arroyos, with an occasional red canyon or cliff. Traffic was almost non-existent. She wasn't smack dab in the middle of nowhere, but was within a few miles of it.

She was twenty-two.

Her body was strong, taut and perfect.

Her face was built to break hearts.

Her hair was long, fluffy and blond.

Her eyes were the color of the New Mexico sky in early morning, during that magical crossover time when the yellow changed to green and the green changed to blue and you never really knew what color you were looking at.

Her skirt was short and white.

It rode up and showcased shapely tanned legs.

Vogue legs.

Glamour legs.

Denver would be a good place for the next chapter of her life. If things didn't work there then screw it, she'd go to New York. If that didn't work, then Paris. That, of course, assumed that she didn't get sent to prison for stealing a 10-year-old Packard. She'd ditch it an hour outside of Denver and then hitch the rest of the way.

She checked her purse to see how much money she had.

There was a five and two one's in the wallet, so she had that plus whatever change was in the bottom.

That would get her lunch and supper, and maybe even a room tonight at a flophouse.

Up ahead a couple of hundred yards where the road curved tight to the left, a good-sized pinion pine was nestled in a grove of sagebrush on the opposite side of the road. She brought the car to a stop on the right side, being careful not to drop off into a canyon, and left the engine running. She walked across the road, got as hidden as she could behind the pinion and took her panties all the way off.

She checked for scorpions or rattlers or ticks on the ground, saw none and squatted down with her feet wide, as far as she could get them away from the spray.

Then she went.

So, so nice.

"Better than sex," she muttered.

She put her panties on and picked her way back over the terrain.

Something didn't feel right. Just before she got to the asphalt she checked her skirt and found a big wet spot on the backside edge.

Damn it.

She'd be sitting on it.

It needed to come off and dry out.

She took it off then noticed something else wrong, namely that her panties were on inside-out. She stepped out of them, turned them around and was about to step back in when a noise came from her right side.

Loud.

Serious.

A car was speeding down the road.

The driver was a man.

He was staring directly at her.

Leaning forward.

Fixated.

Suddenly he saw the curve in the road and jerked the wheel to the left.

The car flipped three times then disappeared over the edge of the canyon.

6

Shade curled up in a ball and concentrated on the noise. She was in the guts of a 24-foot Island Packet sailboat, awash in heavy ocean seas north of Havana. The thunderstorm raged around her. It was sometime after midnight. The night was blacker than black, except when ignited by lightning. She was lucky to not have gotten washed off getting the vessel out of the marina and motoring it out to sea before taking refuge inside.

The sails were down.

A sea anchor kept the bow pointed into the waves.

She thought she was safe after her contact, the woman from the restroom, stabbed the man in the back. She was wrong. They hadn't gotten two blocks before a gun erupted behind them and the woman fell to the ground.

Shade escaped but not by much.

She never found out the woman's name.

In all the commotion she didn't even get a good look at her.

Not knowing how deep the infiltration went, she didn't return to her hotel room. Instead she made her way down to the marina and stole the boat.

That was three hours ago.

Now, the noise of the storm was deafening.

Whitecaps slammed against the hull.

The wind was frantic.

She was a good sailor and had been in more than her fair share of slop, but this was dangerous even by her measures. She had to get out of Cuban waters before the sun came up.

She snuggled herself good and tight into a life jacket, headed topside, raised the mainsail a third of the way then released the sea anchor. Luckily the storm was coming from the north, which was the direction she needed to go. She kept the bow pointed 30 degrees off the breakers and held the wheel tight.

The wind was almost horizontal.

The rain hit her like needles.

What she worried about, though, was planting the bow under a wave. If that happened a wall of water would wash over the boat. Her grip, no matter how tight, would be no match.

Hold on.

She should have hunted around for rope and tied herself to the wheel.

Too late now.

Her network was disrupted.

Everything she'd worked for was finished.

This was the wrong time to think about it but she couldn't stop.

Who else had died?

How did it all happen?

What had gone wrong?

Who talked?

What did they say?

Who did they say it to?

Suddenly the boat jarred as if it hit a wall. Shade immediately knew what happened. The bow had slammed into the middle of a whitecap instead of riding over. She locked her arms in the steering wheel and braced for the onslaught of water.

7

Senn-Rae Vaughn, the lawyer, looked around the office as Wilde got her a cup of coffee. It wasn't fancy but it had the sounds of Larimer Street sifting through the windows. On a credenza by the windows was a radio turned on just enough to hear what was going on without being a distraction. A song came from it, something jazzy.

A closed door led to a second room.

Wilde tapped two cigarettes out of a pack of Camels and offered her one.

"No thanks," she said.

"You don't smoke?"

"I do, but only when I'm on fire."

Wilde smiled, pushed one of the sticks back and lit the other.

"So what's on your mind this morning?"

The woman hesitated.

"Remember, this has to remain confidential," she said.

Wilde nodded.

"We're past that."

"Yeah, I know, but it's important because if word got out about my being here, I'd lose my license to practice law. That's about all I have so don't want it going anywhere."

"Understood."

He waited.

"Okay," she said. "I have a client. Don't ask me his name because I'm not at liberty to tell you. Let's just call him Mr. Smith."

Wilde blew smoke.

"All right. Mr. Smith."

"Anyway," she said. "Ninety-nine percent of the time, Mr. Smith is as normal as apple pie. The other one percent of the time he has a secret life. He likes to tie women up." She looked away shyly, then locked eyes and said, "Have you ever done that? Tied a woman up?"

Wilde cocked his head.

"That's a pretty personal question."

"Yeah, I know, but I'd appreciate an answer."

Wilde shrugged.

"I might have done something like that on an occasion or two," he said.

"Good."

"Why good?"

"Because it means you'll understand," she said.

Wilde pulled a book of matches out of his pocket and lit it on fire.

"How about you?" he asked.

"What do you mean?"

"Have you ever been tied up?"

"That's not relevant."

"Yes it is."

"How so?"

"Because you asked me," Wilde said. "Fair is fair."

She exhaled and said, "No."

"No?"

"No."

"Is that the truth?"

"Yes. Why would I lie?"

Wilde shook the flames out and tossed the remnants in the ashtray. Senn-Rae watched the smoke for a heartbeat and said, "Mr. Smith was indulging his one-percent side on Wednesday evening of last week when something went wrong. He had the woman tied up in a hogtie position on the bed. He stuck a ball gag in her mouth and went to the kitchen to get a beer. Then his phone rang. He talked for a couple of minutes and when he got back to the bedroom the woman was dead."

"Suffocated?"

Senn-Rae nodded.

"It was an accident," she said. "He didn't intend for it to happen."

"Still—," Wilde said.

"I agree," she said. "You don't have to get into it. Trust me, he doesn't feel particularly good about the whole thing."

"I'll bet she doesn't either."

Senn-Rae's face hardened.

"If you're going to judge him then maybe you're not the right person for this case," she said.

Wilde wandered over to the window and looked down.

He had bills to pay.

"Keep talking," he said.

"Things got worse," Senn-Rae said.

"Not for the woman."

"No, not for the woman, for Mr. Smith," Senn-Rae said. "There was nothing he could do for her at that point. If it would have helped to take her to the hospital, he would have done it. But she was dead. He made a decision to bury her body and that's what he did."

"Does she have family?" Wilde asked.

"I don't know."

"Mr. Smith didn't know either, I assume."

"Correct."

"So he buried her body even though she might have family that wouldn't necessarily look too kindly on such a thing."

"I'm not implying that what he did was right," Senn-Rae said. "All I can say is that he was panicked. He was in a survival mode and he did what he did."

Wilde took one last drag and mashed the butt in the ashtray.

"What was her name?"

"Madison."

"Madison what?"

"Unknown," Senn-Rae said. "She was a prostitute out of Colorado Springs. Anyway, there was no news of her body being found in the paper the next day or the day after that or the day after that. Then, three days after the incident happened, on Saturday night, Mr. Smith's house was broken into. Nothing of value was taken but some personal things were."

"Like what?"

She got a distant look on her face.

"Cuff links, a watch with an inscription on the back, an address book and, worst of all, the ball gag and the rope that was used that night. Yesterday, Mr. Smith got a phone call from someone he didn't know—a man. The caller said he saw Mr. Smith bury the body last Wednesday night. He'd be in touch. Then the line went dead. Mr. Smith went back to where he buried the body and it wasn't there. He's pretty sure that the man who called him took the body after he buried it. He's going to blackmail him. If he doesn't cooperate, Madison's body will be planted somewhere with some of the incriminating evidence. An anonymous call will be made to the police."

"Interesting."

"It's a lot more than interesting from Mr. Smith's point of view," she said. "He called me yesterday to find out how much trouble he was in and to think of a way to help him. I'm coming to you."

"Without him knowing it?"

She nodded.

"He made me promise I wouldn't tell anyone," she said.

"You're breaking that promise."

"I am," she said, "but only because it's in his best interest. What I want you to do is find out who his new friend is."

Wilde chewed on it.

"Suppose I'm successful," he said. "What happens then?"

"Then I tell Mr. Smith that I hired you and what you found out."

Wilde tilted his head.

"Then Mr. Smith kills his new friend."

Senn-Rae leaned forward.

"He'll handle it however he decides to handle it," she said. "That will be up to him."

She pulled an envelope out of her purse and pushed it across the desk.

"That's a retainer," she said. "One thousand dollars. There's more where that came from. I expect you to be honest but if you need more you'll get more. Money isn't the issue."

Wilde stared at the envelope but didn't pick it up.

A thousand dollars.

Four months pay.

Senn-Ray stood up.

She set a business card on the desk and headed for the door.

"I need you to start right now, as soon as I leave."

"Agreed."

She opened the door, stepped through and said over her shoulder, "Happy hunting Mr. Wilde."

Then she was gone.

Wilde lit the cigarette, then bounded down the stairs and caught her at street level.

"Bryson," he said. "Not Mr. Wilde."

"Fine," she said. "Bryson."

"Two more things," he said. "Where did he dump the body and what did Madison look like?"

She whispered the answers in his ear.

Then she left.

Wilde watched her walk away, then ran after her and put a hand on her shoulder.

She turned around.

"You lied to me," he said.

"About what?"

"About never being tied up."

She was about to deny it and then said, "Maybe I picked the right man for the job after all."

"We'll see."

8

The car bounced twice off the canyon walls on the way down and then crashed on the bottom with a terrible sound. Fallon pulled her panties and skirt on. The world now had an eerie silence to it, except for the idling of the Packard. She turned the engine off then got as close as she could to the edge of the canyon and looked down.

The vehicle wasn't visible from where she was.

The canyon, however, wasn't deep—a hundred yards, maybe. Here the wall was almost vertical but down the road a quarter mile or so it was more gradual.

She stood there, deciding.

The New Mexico sun beat on her face.

She wiped sweat off her brow with the back of her hand.

If she went down, she wouldn't be able to help.

She knew nothing about first aid.

The sight would be upsetting.

If the man was still alive, she'd never be able to get him up to the road. About the best she could do would be to go for help. That was problematic in that the nearest place was Santa Fe and she'd have to go there in the Packard, the stolen Packard to be precise.

What to do?

Her instincts told her to leave.

It wasn't her fault.

The man may have been looking at her when he went off the road but that didn't mean it was her fault.

She shut her mind off and ran down the road.

Just go down and help if there's help to be given.

Worry about everything else later.

She picked her way down a steep face with lots of unstable rocks. The vehicle was right-side-up on the canyon floor but the wheels and tires were demolished.

The dirt near the back end was wet.

The gas tank must have ruptured.

She approached with a racing heart, listening for sounds but getting none.

Twenty yards away she shouted, "Are you okay?"

No response.

She called out two more times as she closed the gap.

No response.

Inside, the man was a motionless bloody mess.

Fallon shook his shoulder.

He didn't respond.

She heard no breathing.

She saw no movement of his lungs.

"Hey."

She didn't know how to feel for a pulse, but did anyway, both on his wrist and neck. She didn't detect any vein movements.

A wide gash was on his forehead.

It went all the way to the skull.

Lots of blood had come out of the wound but none was coming out now.

"You're dead," she said.

He looked to be in his early fifties.

Now what?

Suddenly she did something she didn't expect. She reached into the man's back pants pocket and pulled out a wallet.

Inside was a lot of money, enough to keep food in her mouth for months judging by the looks of it.

She searched the glove box.

Inside was a Smith & Wesson revolver, a six-shooter.

The chambers were loaded.

There was also a box of shells.

She grabbed them both and took one last look around.

A briefcase was on the back floor. She muscled it out from behind the seat and tried to look inside but it was locked. It felt like there was paper inside.

Money?

The car key was still in the ignition.

It was one of several keys on a ring. One of them probably went to the briefcase. She grabbed them.

Now what?

Nothing.

She was done.

She took off her skirt, tied it into a pouch and put the keys, gun, bullets and wallet inside. Then she tied the other end to the handle of the briefcase.

There.

Now she could carry it all with one hand.

That would give her a free one to climb up with.

The big trick now was to not slip on a rock on the way up.

Twenty steps from the car she turned and shouted, "I'm

sorry. I really am."

9

Two hours of fight, that's what Shade had to endure before the storm lost its bite and passed over. The chop got replaced with rolling swells. She was able to dry out now that the wind wasn't picking spray off the surface. She had no idea where she was other than somewhere between Cuba and the Keys. She deployed the main sail to full extension and continued north.

She needed sleep.

She needed it badly and she needed it now, but the boat had no autopilot and the wind direction was sporadic, meaning she had no option but to stay at the wheel, either that or shut the sails down altogether and bob.

She'd sleep later.

Right now she needed distance.

The more distance the better.

The sky slowly morphed into a lighter and lighter shade of black, the horizon appeared and then the water became visible, at first just the white churn, then the rest.

The day was coming.

Someone would be in the marina by now. If the boat hadn't been reported as stolen, it would soon. Shade went to the transom to see if the name of the boat was painted on.

It was.

Bonita Wind.

The letters were red and large.

They'd be readable through binoculars.

A motorboat on these seas could close the gap from Cuba in an hour or two if it knew what direction to go. It was unlikely she'd be in American waters at that point.

There was no use worrying about it.

All she could do was continue north and hope for the best.

Hours later, with the sun bright and the air hot, a vessel from the north spotted her waving arms and diverted over. It turned out to be a small navy cutter. A dinghy got lowered and four men motored over.

Shade grabbed the rope when they got alongside and said, "My name's Shade de Laurent. I'm with the CIA."

"Do you have papers?"

"No but I have a phone number."

By early afternoon she was back in her Washington D.C. apartment.

A debriefing meeting was scheduled with Kent Harvin and others for three o'clock.

Until then she'd sleep.

Sleep.

Sleep.

Sleep.

That's what she was doing when a knock came at her door. At first she let it be but it didn't go away. When she answered, a man was there.

He had a message for her.

10

When Senn-Rae left, Wilde dropped the top of the '47 MG/TC and pointed the front end towards the place where Mr. Smith buried the body of his little bondage friend, Madison. Up above was a crisp blue sky overflowing with massive amounts of sunshine.

The car was running good.

That could change at any minute but didn't feel like it would—the sky was too blue. The car was more in the mood for mechanical drama when it was out in the middle of nowhere and the sky was churning with angry black thunderclouds.

Wilde bought it cheap last year from a guy who didn't want to go through another winter without a heater, especially in a vehicle that had the steering wheel on the wrong side. The guy said, "This car will do a hundred and sixty."

Wilde raised an eyebrow.

"No way."

The man nodded.

"It will, but you have to drop it out of an airplane to get it. On the road it's good for only half that. Still, that's eighty and eighty's not bad."

It was a tiny little two-seat death trap.

It had no bumpers.

It had no radio.

It had no back seat.

It had no hardtop.

What it did have, however, was a Moss Magnacharger engine under the hood and tan leather seats that seemed to attract the female figure. It also had British Racing Green paint. There was no better color and never would be.

It also had a name, Blondie—inspired by the vanilla ragtop.

He took Santa Fe Boulevard south and let the miles click by. The buildings got less impressive and less frequent, finally giving way altogether to native topography. Fifteen miles later he came to a narrow unmarked dirt road that mysteriously disappeared to the east into rolling terrain. It was choked with weeds and looked like a firefighting access road long abandoned.

This was it.

He turned left.

The ruts kept his speed to a crawl. The foliage was bent, not obviously but enough to suggest that another car had been here within the last week or so.

No doubt Mr. Smith.

Two or three hundred yards into the journey Wilde found what he was looking for—a small grouping of four or five pinion pines.

He pulled over and killed the engine.

Then he had a bad thought.

Would Blondie start again?

He cranked over the key and fired her up.

No problem.

Okay.

He turned her back off and stepped out.

Would she start the next time? How ironic would it be if he just used up the one start he had left? He almost cranked her over again to check, then decided he could be playing this game all day.

Forget it.

A handful of magpies flew out of the pinions. Crickets chirped. A light breeze gently rustled the native grasses. The air didn't smell like Larimer Street. In fact it didn't smell at all.

The quietness was absolute.

Except for the insects, not a sound came from anywhere.

He headed for the pinions, which were thirty steps off the road. Sure enough, there was a shallow grave. The dirt was loose. Wilde squatted down and pulled enough away to confirm that the hole was empty.

He stood up and looked around.

He saw nothing other than nature.

Then something happened.

A rustling sound came from the backside of a yucca.

Wilde wandered over and found a snake.

It had the markings of a prairie rattler. He stepped closer, pretty sure it was just a bull snake impersonating a rattler. It curled up, raised its head and shook the non-business end.

"I'll be damned," he said. "The real deal."

He let it be and headed back to Blondie. He was just about to get in when he noticed something that wasn't nature. It was the top of a boxcar a hundred yards or so to the south, barely visible over the top of a rolling ridge.

Interesting.

He headed back to Santa Fe, drove south and came to a second road, a broader one that had once been gravel, one that led to an old abandoned switching yard.

The tracks were in disrepair and overgrown.

An old boxcar had been left there to die.

So had a gondola, farther down.

Both were rusted, cockeyed and beyond salvage.

Wilde looked north to see if he could see the grouping of pinions where the grave was.

He could see them, but only the very tops.

If a man was standing there—say, Mr. Smith—he wouldn't be able to see him. He headed up the boxcar ladder to see how visible things were from that vantage point.

A pungent odor suddenly filled the air.

It got stronger as he climbed.

When he got his head up to where he could see on top, he found the source of the stench.

A woman was up there.

A dead woman.

She looked to be in her early twenties although it was hard to tell given what the sun and the insects had done to her.

Wilde got all the way up and walked over. There were no obvious wounds. A hatchet wasn't sticking in her head. Her throat wasn't slit from ear to ear. There were no bloody gunshot holes. Still it was obvious she'd been murdered. That was clear from the way she was dressed—like a pinup model—and the way her body was posed.

Someone had staged her.

Someone knew exactly how he wanted her to look.

Wilde looked to the pinions.

From up here on top of the boxcar he could see the grave.

11

Fallon had one thought and one thought only as she climbed out of the canyon, namely that the dead man's briefcase was full of money. It was the right weight. She could almost smell it.

Money.

Money.

Money.

Where'd he get it? Did he rob a bank? Did he blackmail

someone? Was he up to his eyebrows in a life of crime and twists and shadows?

It didn't matter.

The only thing that mattered was that she had it.

The climb made her muscles burn and her lungs pound but she made it up without a fatal misstep. She caught her breath for a few minutes, then untied her skirt from the handle of the briefcase. She stuck the smallest key on the ring into the lock to see if it fit.

It didn't.

She tried the others.

They didn't fit either.

She looked around for a rock big enough to smash the stupid thing open when she saw something she didn't expect. Her car, parked where she left it a hundred yards down the road, wasn't the only one there.

A second vehicle sat behind it.

It was big, fancy and shiny.

A woman suddenly appeared from behind it and walked in Fallon's direction.

She looked to be about thirty.

Her skirt was tight and ended below her knees. Her hair was long and black, her blouse was fancy and her heels were high. Even at this distance she looked expensive on every level. Her walk was purposeful and strong.

Was she a friend of the dead man?

A lover?

An accomplice?

Fallon checked the gun.

Bullets were in the chambers.

Holding her skirt full of treasures in one hand and the briefcase in the other, she headed towards the woman.

It would be best to confront her head on.

The woman fixated on Fallon's thighs and panties as she approached but it wasn't clear if the stare was sexual or curiosity. They stopped a step short of one another. The woman dropped her gaze to the briefcase for a heartbeat then locked eyes with Fallon.

She was stronger up close.

Fallon wasn't sure she could take her in a fair fight.

"Are you okay?"

Fallon hesitated and then stepped around the woman.

"Yes."

"Are you sure?"

She kept walking without turning around.

"Yeah, thanks for asking."

She heard no footsteps behind her.

Ten steps later the woman said, "Hold on a minute."

Fallon stopped.

Then against her better judgment she pulled the gun out of the skirt, raised her arm towards the sky and fired a bullet. She turned and said, "You never saw me here. Do we have an understanding?"

A pause.

Then the woman nodded.

"Yes," she said.

"Good. Stay right where you are until I leave."

At the car, Fallon wrote down the woman's license plate number and shoved the paper in her purse. Then she fired up the Packard and waved at the woman who watched her with a rotating head as she passed.

The briefcase was on the seat next to her.

"You better be filled with money," she said.

Ten miles later she pulled to the side of the road, got out and slipped her skirt on. No one was around. The air was coffin-quiet. She set the briefcase on the ground and shot it until the lock blew apart.

She heard nothing but looked around one last time just to be sure she was alone.

What she saw she could hardly believe.

A car was heading her way.

Coming fast.

12

Shade read the message that got delivered by a man she didn't know:

> MY DEAREST SHADE, I WISH I COULD TELL YOU THIS IN PERSON AND I WISH I COULD HOLD YOU IN MY ARMS. MONDAY NIGHT AT THE BAR, TEHYA WAS MURDERED. SOMEONE STABBED HER IN THE HEART AND THEN SCALPED HER. VISIBLE MOON WAS WORKING THAT NIGHT AND WE HAVE NOT HEARD FROM HER SINCE. SHE IS GONE. WE DO NOT KNOW IF SHE IS ALIVE OR DEAD. I AM SORRY TO HAVE TO TELL YOU THIS. - MOJAG

She slumped on the couch and closed her eyes. She never liked the idea of Visible Moon running the bar, not for a moment. It was a setup for disaster from day one, out there in the middle of nowhere, filled with drunks, no security to speak of other than the gun under the counter. It was a time bomb with a short fuse. That fuse didn't get any longer when Tehya started showing up six months ago and doing the whole sex-in-the-backroom thing.

Mojag should have never left Visible Moon alone.

It was his bar, not hers.

He should have run the place himself.

He was to blame.

Everything that happened was his fault.

Shade reread the message, crumpled up the paper and threw it against the wall. Then she packed a small suitcase and called a taxi. Two hours later she was about to board a twin-prop plane for Denver. From there she'd take a puddle-jumper to Santa Fe.

She called Kent Harvin, the Assistant Director of the CIA. He was in a bad mood.

What she had to say wasn't about to improve it.

"Something's come up. I'm not going to be able to make the three o'clock debriefing this afternoon."

Silence.

"Unacceptable. Be there."

"I can't."

"That's a direct order."

"I have to go to New Mexico."

"Why?"

"A friend of mine disappeared," she said.

"A friend?"

"Right."

"A contact?"

"No, not a contact, a friend. This has nothing to do with my job."

"Then it can wait."

"I wish it could."

A beat.

"What's your friend's name?"

"Visible Moon."

"Visible Moon. What kind of name is that?"

"It's Navajo," she said. "She's Navajo."

Harvin exhaled.

"Be at the three o'clock meeting. You know better than anyone how much we have riding on all this. We need to know what went wrong and we need to know it yesterday."

The line went dead.

Shade hung up and boarded the plane. Fifteen minutes later it lifted into a blue but turbulent sky and headed west.

She closed her eyes and pulled up an image of Tehya being scalped.

She could see the bloody red mess.

She could hear the sawing of the knife and the tearing of the skin.

She could see the hand holding the knife.

It was a white hand.

13

From the boxcar, Wilde headed to Senn-Rae's office on 16th Street, the bustling heart of Denver. The problem was there was no such address and no such office.

What the hell?

Okay, she wasn't an attorney.

She had no office.

So who the hell was she?

He called her from a phone booth and said, "Your office doesn't exist. What kind of game are you playing?"

"I don't play games."

"Allow me to disagree," he said. "When you give someone a business card for an office that doesn't exist, that's called playing a game."

A beat.

Then, "There's an alley off 16th between California and Champa. Head in there and see what you can find."

The line went dead.

Wilde headed into the alley, saw nothing, kept walking and then turned down a one-lane delivery alley that ran between 16th and 17th. On a steel door was a crude sign, Senn-Rae Vaughn, Attorney at Law. Wilde opened the door and found himself in a tight stairwell. He headed up. The door on every floor was locked except for the last one, the one on the sixth floor.

It led to a lofty, voluminous space with wooden floors and exposed ductwork. The best part was the windows, thousands of them.

Senn-Rae was behind a desk near the wall.

Next to the desk was a large table covered with papers.

Next to that were several gray, metal filing cabinets.

Other than that the space was basically just that, space.

Senn-Rae got up and headed towards him. Gone was the conservative attire, now replaced with beige cotton pants and a pink T. Her hair hung loose and free. Her feet were bare.

"You found it," she said.

Wilde frowned.

"Sorry about the accusation."

"Already forgotten," she said. "This space used to hold fifty people. They sewed clothes back in the day. It's ironic because I can't sew at all."

When Senn-Rae walked into the office this morning, she wasn't Wilde's type. He liked 'em blond, curvy and edgy, Night Neveraux—the femme fatale herself—being the prime example. Now, however, looking like she did, there was something about her.

Her stomach was flat.

Her arms were strong.

Her ass was high and firm.

Her mouth had a certain pout that he couldn't stop looking

at.

"I want to take you for a ride," he said.

She must have detected his thoughts because she said, "Business or pleasure?"

"Business."

She hesitated then grabbed her purse and shoes. "Where are we going?"

"It's a secret." A pause then, "Mostly business."

"Mostly business."

He nodded.

"Right, mostly. It's a good thing you're out of your skirt. You're going to need to climb a ladder."

They drove south. The noise of the tires and the wind was too much to allow anything but occasional talk. That didn't stop Wilde from looking over and watching the woman's hair blow.

Most women tied it in a ponytail or held it in a hand.

Senn-Rae just let it go.

"I haven't been out in the country for years," she said. "This is nice."

"Yeah."

Half an hour later Wilde pointed Blondie's nose east onto a dilapidated road that led to an even more dilapidated switching yard. He stopped thirty feet short of the boxcar and killed the engine.

"We're here."

Senn-Rae looked around.

"And where is here, exactly?"

Wilde pointed to the boxcar.

"That's the ladder I was talking about."

"You want me to climb up that ladder?"

He nodded.

"Why?"

"You'll see."

Wilde climbed up first.

The body was exactly as he saw it last.

He got his footing and watched Senn-Rae's face as it lifted above the edge.

"What's that smell?" she asked.

"Keep coming up."

She did.

Then she saw the body and gasped.

Wilde expected her to head back down the ladder. Instead she climbed all the way up, walked over to the body and studied it.

"Do you know her?" Wilde asked.

"No, why would I?"

Wilde shrugged.

"No reason," he said. "I was just curious."

She turned back to the body and said, "Someone posed her."

"Right."

"Why?"

"Good question."

"She's dressed like a pinup girl."

"Yes she is."

Wilde pointed to the grouping of pinions a hundred yards to the north.

"See those trees over there? That's where your client Mr. Smith buried Madison," he said. "If my brain is working right, the person who saw him do it saw him from right here where we're standing."

Senn-Rae got a distant look.

Then she focused on Wilde and said, "So what you're saying is that the person who's blackmailing Mr. Smith is the same person who killed this woman."

Wilde pulled his hat off and wiped sweat off his forehead.

"That's what I'm saying."

14

The mystery car came down the road at an incredible speed, maybe targeting Fallen, maybe not. It wasn't a cop. She flipped open the briefcase with a racing heart.

Damn it.

Damn it.

Damn it to hell.

It wasn't money.

It was ordinary papers. She ruffled through to see if money was underneath. There wasn't, not a single stinking dollar. She kicked the stupid thing into a rabbit bush and shot it until the bullets ran out.

The silence gave way to the low humming of rubber on the road. The mystery car was getting dangerously close. Fallon would never be able to outrun it, not in the Packard. She ran to the car, ripped open the box of shells and reloaded the gun. Then she fired up the engine, did a one-eighty and headed back the way she came. If the other vehicle was after her it would turn around.

She stepped on the gas.

The cars were only a hundred yards apart, closing at a breakneck speed. Suddenly the other car turned into her lane and came directly at her.

There were two men inside.

They wore hats.

She could jerk to the right.

She had time.

She'd flip, though.

Then the other car would slam on the brakes, turn around

and come for her.

That wasn't going to happen.

She put the full force of her leg into the pedal and kept the hood pointed straight. Then just before impact she closed her eyes and screamed.

15

Wilde took one last look at the dead pin-up girl, headed down the grungy ladder, lit a cigarette and threw the match on the ground. It landed next to another match, not his, not weathered. He picked it up and watched Senn-Rae as her body lowered down the side of the boxcar.

"Our friend smokes," he said, showing it to her.

"There's some of those up top too," she said.

"On the boxcar?"

She nodded.

"I thought they were yours," she added.

Wilde climbed up and found six or eight matches flicked onto the far end of the boxcar. He looked over the backside and saw a number of spent butts on the ground. He climbed down and gathered them up, twelve all told.

"He spent some time up there with her," he said.

Senn-Rae cocked her head.

"Before or after he killed her?"

"Good question."

The butts had no filters.

Wilde lit one, inhaled and said, "Camel." Then he searched the weeds under the railcar.

"What are you looking for?"

"Clothes," he said. "I'm trying to figure out if he dressed the woman here or brought her that way."

Senn-Rae joined in.

They found nothing.

"Check that area back there," he said.

Something small and red caught his attention in the weeds to the left. It turned out to be a book of matches with all the guts ripped out. On the cover was a gold B. He continued the search, found nothing else then showed Senn-Rae what he found.

"B," she said. "I wonder what it stands for."

"Bastard would be my guess," he said.

On the drive back to Denver they talked about whether they should report the murder to the police, perhaps anonymously.

"I think we should," Wilde said. "I don't like the thought of this guy running around loose. Who knows if he already has someone else in his sights?"

"Think it through."

"How so?"

"If they find him before we do, there's probably something about the blackmail scheme at his house. Mr. Smith may well end up exposed."

Wilde wrinkled his brow.

"We can't have that."

Senn-Rae shrugged.

"It's your case," Wilde said. "I'll do whatever you want."

She looked out the windshield.

Then she turned and said, "I need to sleep on it. In the meantime, run down that book of matches. It's probably from a restaurant or bar."

Back at the office, Wilde found Alabama sitting behind the desk with her 24-year-old feet propped up, reading a magazine.

He tossed his hat at the rack and overshot.

Alabama snatched it out of the air and threw it back.

He missed again.

It landed on the desk.

Alabama put it on and dipped it over her eye. "Where have you been all morning?"

He told her about the new case, including the fact that he took Senn-Rae to the boxcar to see the body that had been dressed up like a pinup and posed. "I went up first," he said. "I wanted to see the look on her face when she got up."

"Why?"

"I wanted to see if she was surprised or not," he said.

"Why?"

"Because I had a sneaking feeling that she already knew about the body."

"And?"

"And what?"

"And, was she surprised?"

Wilde shrugged.

"There was surprise on her face but I don't know if it was real or not."

"Interesting."

"Isn't it?"

Alabama studied him. He knew the look and said, "Now what?"

"You like her."

"I like all my clients," he said. "They keep the lights on."

"Maybe," she said, "but with this one you'd be just as happy with the lights off. I can already tell."

Wilde went to deny it.

Instead he pulled the red book of matches out of his pants pocket and tossed it on the desk.

"This is from the scene. Do you recognize it?"

"No. You want me to run it down?"

"Yes," he said. "It's probably from a bar or restaurant, or maybe a hotel. Start with those, the ones that begin with a B."

She swung her feet off the desk, stood up and ran an index finger down Wilde's chest. "I'll be back in an hour. Don't screw anything up until I get back." Halfway to the door she turned and said, "Hey, what's this writing on the back?"

Wilde looked.

Sure enough, there was something written on the back, barely visible, in red ink. He walked over to the window where the light was better.

"It's numbers," he said.

"A phone number?"

"It looks like 616."

"Could be a room number," Alabama said.

16

Tires squealed as the other car swerved at the last second. Fallon opened her eyes, got the front end of the Packard pointed straight and checked the rearview mirror. The other car was off the road, flipping.

She slammed on the brakes.

The Packard fishtailed then ground to a stop.

The air was coffin-quiet, broken only by the passing of oxygen in and out of her lungs.

Her hands trembled.

She bowed her head into the steering wheel still alive, not dead, incredibly not dead.

She got out and looked at the crash, which was a good distance down the road. The car was upside down. The wheels were pointed at the sky, still spinning, not with much strength but spinning nonetheless.

Her blood raced.

Get the hell out of here.

That's what she should do, no question, just get the hell out right now this second. The men in the other car might still be alive. They might have guns.

No sign of movement came from the wreck.

Anyone unhurt would have been out by now.

They were either dead or busted.

What to do?

What to do?

What to do?

She paced, then hopped back in the car, spun it around and headed for the wreck, coming to a stop on the shoulder. She left the engine running, looked for traffic and saw none in either direction. She grabbed the gun and stepped out. The metal was cold and heavy in her hand.

Three giant black birds circled overhead.

"Are you okay?"

No answer.

Déjà vu.

"Hey!"

Silence.

She pointed the barrel at the vehicle and then took one cautious step after another towards it. Inside she saw something she didn't expect—a bloody body, deathly still and unmoving—but no second body.

She spun around.

The other man was thirty yards away behind a rabbit bush, on his back, badly hurt, with pain etched solidly on his face. He was using every ounce of strength he had to force his broken body to get the barrel of a gun raised up high enough to shoot her.

She froze.

The barrel continued elevating.

She watched, transfixed by the slowness.

Shoot him!

That's what her brain screamed but her hand didn't respond.

She turned and ran.

The gun exploded behind her with a deafening solitary crack. She waited for her spine to shut down or her consciousness to fade.

Neither happened.

She wasn't hit.

Something in her brain brought her body to a halt. She turned and stared at the man.

"Go ahead and take another shot," she said.

The gun was still in the man's grip but had dropped to the ground.

"Go on!"

He raised it up.

Fallon stood there.

Motionless.

Waiting.

Her arms were down to her sides but her finger was on the trigger.

"Shoot me!"

The man pulled the trigger.

The bullet passed so close to Fallon's head that she felt the suction of the vacuum.

This is where she expected to kill him.

This is where she pictured herself pointing the cold barrel at his stupid face and pulling the trigger. When she looked into his eyes, though, she saw a line—a line that would change her life forever if she crossed it.

"Rot in hell," she said.

Then she walked away.

Back at the Packard, she shifted into gear and drove down the road. Suddenly the briefcase appeared on her right. It had no money inside. It did, however, have something important enough to cause everything that just happened.

She grabbed it, threw it in the back seat and got the hell out of there.

17

The bar was desolate and alone when Shade pulled into the dirt parking lot mid-afternoon. A sign in the window said CLOSED. A bouquet of withered wildflowers sat on the ground in front of the door. She headed around back, busted a padlock off the door and stepped inside.

The wood creaked.

Stale smoke choked the air.

A large brownish mark stained the wooden floor midway between the bar and the entrance, once blood, since diluted with a mop.

That's where Tehya must have been scalped.

Two bullets were embedded in the walls, but they were from last year. There were no new ones.

A door led to a backroom. The back wall was crammed with shelves of cleaning products, generator gas, staples and whatnot. A mattress was on the floor, covered with a thin white sheet. A box of rubbers sat where the pillow should be.

Shade laid down, felt erratic springs on her back and closed her eyes.

She hoped to feel Tehya's spirit.

She got nothing.

Shade was half Navajo, not full. Her mother, Prairie Aspen, was full Navajo. As to her father, she didn't know anything about him other than he raped Prairie Aspen one moonless night and that's how Shade got created. He might be white, he might be Mexican, he might be something else. The rumor was that Prairie Aspen's man, Deh-Keya, hunted him down three days later. He took him out to a remote part of the reservation and then spent a week killing him.

Prairie Aspen would never talk about him.

She would have kept Shade.

It was Deh-Keya who wouldn't hear of it.

Two days after birth, Shade was passed to strangers.

Visible Moon, the natural daughter of Prairie Aspen and Deh-Keya, was Shade's half-sister.

Almost no one off the reservation knew anything about their relationship, including the CIA. Even Shade didn't know about it until five years ago when a stranger named Visible Moon walked out of the shadows one night and told her a story.

She pushed off the mattress and headed back into the main room.

A spider crawling up the wall came to a standstill.

So simple, to be a spider.

Such an easy life.

She got up close to the spider and studied it for a few heartbeats then slumped to the floor and leaned against the wall. When she closed her eyes, Visible Moon's spirit slowly emerged.

Shade could feel her moving around behind the bar.

She could hear her asking a customer if he wanted another one.

She could feel her yearning for a man in her life.

She could feel the air passing in and out of her lungs.

She opened her eyes.

Visible Moon was still alive.

There was no question.

She stood up, grabbed a warm beer from under the bar and took a long swallow. It tasted like mud. She finished it as she walked to the car and then threw it to the side of the building.

A pickup truck was heading her way.

She recognized it as Tehya's.

Behind the wheel was Mojag.

The asshole himself.

She leaned against her car and waited.

He skidded to a stop, kicking up a cloud of dust that floated directly at her. She didn't move. She was too busy trying to determine how angry she was.

Mojag got out and walked towards her.

He looked exactly like the last time she saw him—six foot, built like thunder, a warrior's face, long black hair braided into a ponytail that hung almost to his waist. He wore tight jeans, cowboy boots and a white V-neck pullover.

When he got close enough, Shade swung a fist at his face. He caught it with an iron grip and squeezed. He kept it locked in, forced her to the ground and then pushed her away.

Shade threw dirt at his face.

He didn't flinch.

"I'm pretty sure I know who did it," he said. "It was a white man at the end of the bar. He was the only one here when I stopped in to check on things an hour before closing."

He extended a hand to pull Shade up.

She hesitated, then grabbed it and got yanked upright.

"Would you recognize him if you saw him again?"

Mojag frowned.

"I think so," he said, "but I only looked at him from the side and that was only for a moment. I'm pretty sure he was from Denver."

"Why?"

"He was wearing a fancy suit. The car in the parking lot was expensive. I never saw him around these parts."

"Do you remember what it was—the car?"

He frowned.

"It was big and black and shiny under the dust," he said. "I'm going to Denver to find him. Then I'm going to bring him back here."

"Are the police doing anything?"

He shook his head.

"It happened on reservation land. No whites got killed. What do you think?"

18

Wilde was halfway out the door, tipping his hat over his left eye, when the phone rang. He hung for a moment, debating, then stepped back and answered.

"This is Earl Johnson," a man said. "I'm the manager of Mercedes Raine. Have you ever heard of her?"

Wilde shook his head.

"No, I can barely hear you."

"I'm calling from New York," Johnson said. "Mercedes has a show in Denver tonight at the Bokaray. We need a drummer. There's a nasty rumor going around that you're the best in the area."

"What happened to your drummer?"

The man grunted.

"He got arrested."

"For what?"

"For being stupid," Johnson said.

"How stupid?"

"Murder stupid."

"He killed someone?"

"That's what the police say," Johnson said. "Anyway, it's not important. What's important is that I need someone with a pair of drumsticks to step in and save my ass tonight. Will you do it?"

Wilde hesitated.

"Where'd you get my name from?"

"Dexter Dex," Johnson said.

A beat.

"Sure, why not? What time?"

"The show starts at nine," Johnson said. "Get there at eight-thirty. Mercedes will go over the play list with you." A pause, then, "When you see her, you're going to fall in love. Resist that urge to the extent possible."

"Why?"

"Because you're saving my life by stepping in. Now I'm returning the favor."

Wilde laughed.

"Now you have my curiosity up."

"Maybe, but don't forget about the cat," Johnson said.

"What cat?"

"The dead one. Thanks again for stepping in. I owe you."

Two minutes later he was walking down Larimer Street to Blondie when someone jumped on his back and wrapped a pair of very nice legs around his waist.

He knew the maneuver all too well.

"Alabama."

She didn't get off.

"Say please."

"Please," he said.

"Put a cherry on top."

"No, no cherries."

"One cherry."

"Okay already, one cherry."

She jumped off, linked her arm through his and fell into step. "I got nothing," she said. "I checked every bar, every restaurant, every nightclub and every hotel in Denver that starts with the letter B. None of them have matchbooks with a red cover."

Wilde shook his head.

This part was supposed to be easy.

"You must have missed one."

"I didn't." She pulled papers from her back pants pocket. "These are the phone book pages. I checked every single B that was listed. Every one. I even marked them in ink—see? I didn't miss any. Wherever those matches came from, it wasn't Denver." They were at Blondie. The top was down. Alabama jumped over the door and landed in the passenger seat. "Where are we heading?"

Wilde frowned.

"You're going to break the springs if you keep doing that," he said.

"No I won't. Where are we heading?"

He fired up the engine and pulled into traffic.

"Back to the scene," he said.

"You mean the dead pinup girl?"

"Right."

"Why?"

"Because that's where we're going."

"Yeah, I know, but why?"

"Because," he said, "that's our destination."

She punched him on the arm.

"Your problem is that you never stop being you," she said.

A half hour later, when they turned off Santa Fe onto the access road for the switching yard, the noise of the tires and the wind softened. The warmth of the sun increased.

Alabama pointed to the boxcar, looming up ahead.

"Is that it?"

Wilde nodded.

"It gives me the creeps," she said. "How does someone even find a place like this?"

Wilde stopped twenty yards short of the rusty bulk and killed the engine. Alabama hopped over the door without opening it and landed in the dirt. She immediately headed for the ladder and started to climb.

"Hold up," Wilde said. "I'm going up first."

"Why?"

"You'll see."

She did as he said.

Wilde watched her face as it came above the top and saw the dead woman. "You had a lot more surprise and shock on your face than Senn-Rae did," he said.

"So I'm the winner?"

Wilde smiled.

Alabama bent down and studied the woman's face.

A distant gaze washed over her face.

"Do you know her?" Wilde asked.

"Know her, no. But she looks familiar. I may have seen her someplace."

"Where?"

"I don't know," she said. "I'm not even sure that I have."

Inside Wilde's pocket was a folded-up page that he tore out of a sleazy men's magazine called Dames in Danger two hours ago. On that page was a dirty little story called Kiss Me to

Death. Half the page was taken up with a painting of a pinup girl in damsel in distress mode.

Wilde unfolded the page and compared it to the body.

It was a perfect match.

The poise was the same, at least the same as it could be given that the woman was dead.

The hair colors matched, the styling was identical.

The makeup was identical.

The clothes were identical.

Everything was identical.

Alabama saw the match and said, "Where'd you get this?"

"I had a feeling there was some kind of inspiration," he said. "That's what I was doing while you were out looking for the matchbook, going through old sleaze magazines. I thought this one looked pretty close. It looks like I was right."

"What magazine did this come from?"

"It's called Dames in Danger," he said. "This particular edition came out in April 1948."

She studied it.

"Maybe the artist killed her."

Wilde chewed on it.

"That would be too easy."

He studied the illustration.

"It's not signed."

"I wouldn't sign it either if I was going to kill her later," Alabama said.

Wilde tilted his head.

"You have a devious mind."

19

The drive north was uneventful all the way to Colorado Springs where the Packard ran out of gas a hundred yards short of a Sunoco. Fallon locked the vehicle, threw the keys in the brush and headed for the station on foot with the gun stuffed in her purse and the briefcase in hand. She bought a pack of Camels, a hotdog and an RC from a coke-bottle glasses kid who'd been busy changing a tire.

He pulled change out of the register, got it greasy and wiped it off before handing it to her.

"Sorry."

She opened the Camels, tapped out two and extended the pack to him.

He pulled one out, lit it immediately, then hers and said, "Thanks."

He had a name on his shirt, Mike.

"No problem, Mike." She blew smoke. "Where's the bus station?"

He wrinkled his forehead.

"It's sort of complicated, how to get there," he said. "I could take you if you want."

She took a bite out of the hotdog.

"Okay."

Two hours later she was in Denver, stepping out of a diesel-sooted Greyhound under a cloudless cerulean sky. She closed her eyes and pointed her face up. The sun bounced off her skin like little gold sparkles.

She was out of Santa Fe.

She was alive.

She had a mysterious briefcase.

She had more money than she would have made working six months as a waitress. She hadn't shot a man even though she should have.

She had a few grease smudges on her left leg, compliments of the coke-bottle guy copping a little feel in exchange for the ride.

Those would wash off.

A REX HOTEL sign two blocks down pulled her in that direction. It turned out to be mid-way between a flophouse and a 5-star, good enough to keep the insects off without breaking the bank.

She took a long shower and combed the tangles out of her hair. The freshness of her skin hi-lighted how grubby her clothes had become. She left them off, sat down naked on the bed and opened the briefcase.

Her hair dripped on the papers.

They were handwritten, unbound, single-sided and consecutively numbered at the bottom. The last one had the number 304.

Some of the writing was narrative but nothing that made sense. The words would mysteriously start, apparently in mid-paragraph, and then cut off several lines later just as mysteriously. Then some type of scientific writing took over, went for several lines, then transformed back into interrupted narrative, which didn't tie in to the previous narrative.

The writing was script.

It was sloppy.

She could only make out an occasional word.

Very strange.

The man who went off the cliff turned out to be a 52-year-old named Richard Zephyr according to the driver's license in his wallet.

Other than the license and the money, the wallet was empty except for one thing, a piece of paper with handwriting on it.

There were several columns of numbers.

39, 2-11

129, 24-37

423, 16-17

3, 32-38

Those were the first four entries in the first column on one side of the paper. There were five columns on that side and four on the other side. Altogether, there were two hundred entries give or take.

Very strange.

She put the wallet and single-sheet of paper in the briefcase and slid it under the bed. Then she got dressed, locked the door, jiggled the handle to be sure the lock had caught, and headed outside.

The buildings were taller to the south.

She walked that way.

Her ass swayed.

The concrete sidewalk felt nice under her feet.

20

Shade and Mojag drove north through a never-ending sea of New Mexico sagebrush, not talking much, with the windows down and the air snapping around like a rabid wolf. Soft white cotton-ball clouds hung low in the horizon. The man had his left arm out the window, his head back and his cowboy hat low. With his right hand he chain-smoked, worked the steering wheel and occasionally took a swallow from a whiskey bottle that he kept in place between his thighs. The vehicle, Tehya's pickup, was all over the road, constantly cutting to the left or right. In fairness to Mojag that was the product of a loose front end.

"I think we should split up when we get to Denver," Shade said.

Mojag grunted.

"You never did like me," he said.

"That's not what I'm talking about," Shade said. "We need to do this smart."

He cast an eye on her.

"What do you mean?"

"If we find him, you're going to kill him, right?"

"That's an understatement."

"Then what?"

He rolled his eyes.

"Then done deal," he said.

"Wrong."

"What are you talking about?"

"Then, you fry in the electric chair."

Mojag wasn't impressed.

"That will never happen."

"Of course it will," Shade said. "Connect the dots. Tehya gets murdered, scalped even. A few days later you head to Denver. You stand out like an Indian in an ocean of white men, which is exactly what you'll be. Then one of their own gets killed. Coincidentally, you disappear right after that. What's your plan, that no one will be smart enough to figure out what happened?"

"You forgot one thing," he said.

A rattlesnake appeared in the road up ahead, slithering across the asphalt. Mojag crossed the centerline and squashed it with the tires.

"I hate those bastards."

"You said I forgot one thing," Shade said.

Right.

He did.

"You forgot that I'm not going to kill him in Denver," he said. "I'm going to bring him back to the reservation and take him to a place where no one can hear him scream. Then I'm going to bury him so deep that a thousand coyotes couldn't dig him up."

Shade shook her head.

"That doesn't change what I'm saying," she said. "All it means is that he disappears instead of gets killed."

"No, it also means they don't have any proof he's dead. They have no body."

"How's he going to disappear? All it takes is one person to see you take him, or even see you in the vicinity anywhere around the time he disappears. You said yourself he's big. He's not going to go quietly."

Mojag took one last drag and threw the butt out the window.

He lit another.

"So what are you getting at, exactly?"

"What I'm getting at is this," Shade said. "When we get to Denver, you and I split up so no one can connect us together. When you spot him, assuming you do, you let me know who he is. Then you head back to the reservation. Go to town, make yourself visible to a hundred white people, be three hundred miles away. Then I'll take care of him."

Mojag gave her a mean look.

"No."

"Why not?"

"He's going to die at my hand, no one else's," he said. "Mine.

Only mine. Do you understand?"

Shade exhaled.

"Okay, fine," she said. "Then what I'll do is bring him to you."

"How?"

"Trust me, it won't be hard."

Mojag slapped the side of the door with his fist.

"If that's the way you want it to play out, then it better play out exactly that way," he said. "If he ends up dead before I get my hands on him, I'm not going to be happy."

Shade reached over, extended her hand and said, "Deal."

Mojag hesitated.

Then he shook.

"Deal."

21

From the top of the boxcar, Wilde looked around and spotted something he didn't expect, namely a magpie perched on the top of Blondie's windshield with the tail end hanging over the interior.

"Don't you dare," he said.

Alabama followed his gaze, saw what he was referring to and said, "Two-bits says he poops."

Wilde hesitated, said "You're on," then shouted, "Hey, get out of there."

The bird cocked a head towards the voice.

It didn't fly away, though.

Wilde pulled a matchbook out of his pocket and threw it at him. It waffled in the air and didn't even make it halfway.

The magpie wiggled its tail.

"He's getting ready," Alabama said.

"No he's not."

Wilde scurried over to the ladder and climbed down with all the speed he had, jumping off halfway and landing with a thud.

The bird looked at him.

Wilde headed for him, waving his arms and shouting. The bird stayed until the last possible second before jumping up and taking off. Wilde checked the interior to find nothing there that shouldn't be.

He smiled.

Alabama was halfway down the ladder.

"You owe me two-bits," he said.

She came over and looked.

The interior was clean.

Suddenly the magpie flew overhead.

Something small and wet tumbled from the bird's tail end and splattered in the middle of the driver's seat. Wilde wiped it off as fast as he could, as if speed could somehow erase what happened. "You still owe me two-bits," he said.

Alabama shook her head.

"No way, cowboy, you're the one who owes me."

"No. He flew off before he did it."

"It doesn't matter," Alabama said. "The bet was, Two-bits says he poops. He pooped. I won."

Wilde almost retorted but realized he'd lose sooner or later. He pulled a quarter out of his pocket and tossed it over.

Alabama stuffed it in her pocket and said, "Now what? Do you want me to find out who painted that pinup picture?"

Wilde re-wiped the seat, hopped in and turned the key. Blondie started. "Good girl," he said, patting the dash. He waited for Alabama to jump over the door and land in the seat, which she did, then he turned around and headed down the road, going slow, not needing any underbody damage.

"That sounds good," he said. "Find out who the artist is. Find out where he lives too, assuming it's not in Denver, which I kind of doubt. Then find out if the red matchbook came from his city."

Alabama nodded, impressed.

"It's times like this that I'm reminded of why I let you work with me," she said.

Wilde wrinkled his forehead.

"I work with you?"

Alabama nodded.

"That reminds me, we need to get the sign on the door changed. Winger & Wilde, Investigators for Hire. How does that sound?"

"It sounds crazy."

She ran her fingers through his hair.

"Don't worry, I'll still let you pretend to be the boss."

22

Whoever killed the pinup girl may have known her, if not personally or socially, maybe by proximity—someone who worked in the same building, rode the same trolley, something like that. She wasn't random. She was too pretty to be random, plus the clothes fit too well. Whoever killed her knew her size, even her shoe size.

Who was she?

What was her name?

Where did she live?

Who did she know?

What were her haunts?

When did she go missing?

Where was the last place she was seen?

Wilde went through old newspapers searching for print about a missing woman. There wasn't any, not in the last few days or even the last few weeks. He went back a full month before giving up.

Strange.

Why no print?

Was she from out of town?

The same town as the red matches?

He lit a Camel, took a long drag and sat in the window with one leg dangling out. Larimer Street below was a mess of activity and noise.

He debated about whether he should do what he was thinking about doing.

Then he did it.

He picked up the phone and dialed Jacqueline White, the Girl Friday at the homicide department.

"Don't hang up," he said.

"Wilde, is that you?"

"Yeah, it's me."

The line went dead.

He smoked another Camel and tried again, dialing from the windowsill.

"This is important," he said.

A beat.

"You got a lot of nerve."

"Look, I'm sorry about all that stuff, but this is important. I need to know something," he said. "I need to know if any women went missing lately that weren't reported in the paper."

"Why?"

"It relates to a case I'm working on," he said. "That's all I'm at liberty to say."

"Why in the name of hell would I even lift a little finger to help you?"

"Because it's not for me," he said. "It's for someone else."

Silence.

"I'm already on thin ice because of you," she said. "If anyone found out—"

Wilde blew smoke.

"You're right, I'm being selfish," he said. "Forget it."

Silence.

Then, "I hate you, you understand that I hope."

"I do."

A pause.

"Give me a little time," she said. "Are you at the office?"

"I am."

The line went dead.

Fifteen minutes later she called back.

"This is the last time," she said. "Tell me you understand that."

"I do."

"I mean it, Bryson."

"Okay."

"You say okay but you don't really mean okay," she said.

"True."

"You're impossible, do you know that?"

"Actually that's not true," he said. "I'm improbable but not impossible."

She laughed.

In a lowered voice she said, "There was a young woman named Natalie Levine who disappeared three months ago, on March 7th."

"Three months ago?"

"Right."

Wilde chewed on it.

Three months.

That was a long time.

"Has there been any news of her since?"

"Nothing," she said. "Not a heartbeat."

"Has her body shown up?"

"Negative. No body, no news, no nothing." A beat, then, "She lives over on Glenarm, 936. The landlord's doing us a favor by letting the unit sit undisturbed for the time being, in case we end up with a homicide and really want to go through it with a fine tooth comb."

"Thanks." He wrote it down. "I'm playing at the Bokaray tonight, nine o'clock. Why don't you stop in?"

He grabbed his hat, locked up and headed down the stairs. Blondie was parked on the street in front of the drugstore. Wilde fired up the engine and was about to pull into traffic when a body suddenly hurled over the passenger door and landed in the seat.

Alabama.

"Where we going?"

"It's possible that the dead pinup girl is someone called Natalie Levine," he said. "We're going to take a look around in her house and see if there's anything there that makes sense." He lit a Camel and said, "Did you get the name of the artist yet?"

She grunted.

"Negative."

He looked over and wrinkled his forehead.

It should be simple.

That's what his expression said.

Alabama held her hands up in self-defense.

"It's the strangest thing," she said. "That magazine is published by a group called Brown & Lancaster. They're out of San Francisco. I called and talked to a receptionist. She had no idea who the artist was and patched me through to one of the uppity-ups, a guy named Martin Brown."

"The first part of the Brown & Lancaster?"

"That's my presumption," Alabama said. "Anyway, he told me that the artist wanted to remain anonymous."

Wilde blew smoke.

"Why?"

"Apparently the guy has a day job he doesn't want to jeopardize."

"What kind of day job?"

"I don't know," she said. "I got the feeling that it was something professional, something that didn't mix with sleaze—a doctor or lawyer or politician or something like that."

Wilde chewed on it.

"Your next assignment is to see if the red matches came from San Francisco."

23

Shade and Mojag arrived in Denver just as the sun dipped over the edge of the earth and the sky softened to a watercolor pink. Neither of them had ever been there before so they drove around for a while to get their bearings. The Rocky Mountains busted up out of the flatlands twenty miles to the west and provided a navigational anchor.

A flophouse.

That's what they were looking for as a base for Mojag, a flophouse.

It would be better than sleeping in the alley, albeit not by much. More importantly, it would be filled with transients, who generally didn't have much love loss for the cops to begin with, and probably wouldn't be around in six weeks to answer questions even if they did.

Colfax was one of the nicer stretches of town.

So was Broadway.

The edgier section turned out to be Larimer Street. And even edgier than that was Market Street, home to a fleabag hotel to end all fleabag hotels, called the Metropolitan. They drove by it twice and decided it would do.

They swung back around and stopped a block short.

"Okay, see that mailbox over there?"

Mojag followed Shade's finger.

"Yeah, I see it."

"Okay," Shade said, "here's how we communicate. If you spot the guy or get some information on him, get a piece of chalk or masking tape or something like that and mark the back of that mailbox with an X. I'll come by every day and check it. If I see it marked, I'll meet you at the pickup at ten o'clock that night."

"How will you know where the truck is?"

"Just be sure it's parked within a couple of blocks of here. I'll find it."

"Okay. Where are you going to stay?"

"I don't know yet," she said. "Somewhere."

She got out, shut the door and leaned in the window.

"Happy hunting."

Then she walked away.

24

With a newly-bought short skirt around her waist and 2" open-toed heels under her feet, Fallon strutted her bouncy little body down 16th Street through the heart of Denver. It was that magical time when the twilight began to morph into the night and the streetlights began to kick on. Cars cruised down both sides of the street, lots of cars, filled with people seeing and being seen.

The temperature was perfect.

The heat of the day had dissipated into the thin Rocky Mountain air.

She tossed her hair.

Eyes were on her.

She could feel them.

There was tension in the air. Santa Fe had it on occasion, but not this big and not outside the weekend. She'd made a good choice to leave that pathetic cow town.

Cross-streets clicked by as she walked.

Glenarm.

Welton.

Champa.

Stout.

After Lawrence she came to a street with lots of bar lights and an edgy, dangerous patina, a street called Larimer. She headed over, curious. Halfway down she turned her head and saw something she didn't expect. Thirty steps behind her was a man. He was thirty or thereabouts, incredibly good looking, dressed in a gray suit and a red tie.

His strut was strong.

She'd seen him before.

Where?

Santa Fe.

That was it, Santa Fe.

That was some time ago, a year at least.

The last thing she needed was for someone from Santa Fe to know she was in Denver. The police were already on the hunt for whoever took that Packard, no question.

Her heart raced.

She picked up her step.

Her skirt swayed.

His eyes were on her ass.

Disappear.

Now.

Now.

Now.

She crossed the street. Two steps into it a terrible sound erupted behind her, the sound of a car slamming to a stop in a panic mode. She turned just in time to see blinding headlights barreling at her, trying to stop but going too fast.

She was going to be run over.

There was nothing she could do.

It was happening too fast.

Then, wham!

The impact came.

Her body contorted.

The world spun.

Everything turned black.

At some point later, which could have been thirty seconds or a hundred times that, colors began to reappear. She was on her back and the ground was hard.

She was in the street.

A crowd was around her, staring down. The closest face belonged to the man in the gray suit, the one who'd been walking behind her.

"Are you okay?" he asked.

"Yes."

That might be true, it might not. All she wanted was to get up and get out. She muscled up to a sitting position.

Her head spun.

"The driver took off," the man said. "He was driving an old

pickup. He looked like an Indian."

Fallon didn't care.

She felt her face and head for blood or cuts and found none. Then she got to her feet. Nothing felt broken. Her legs worked. Her arms worked. Her neck had a pain when she turned her head to the left but it wasn't anything that would kill her.

"Do you want me to call the police?"

She shook her head.

"No, it was my fault," she said. "I didn't look."

"Are you sure?"

"Yes."

He helped her out of the street to the sidewalk.

"My name's Jundee," he said. "Technically I have a first name, James, but everyone just calls me Jundee." He shifted his feet. "I'm an attorney."

She studied him.

"Here in Denver?"

"Yes."

Denver.

Denver wasn't Santa Fe.

The corner of her mouth turned up ever so slightly. She held out her hand and said, "Fallon Leigh. Nice to meet you."

25

It turned out that Senn-Rae lived in the sixth-floor loft where she practiced law, in a separate set of rooms behind a closed door—illegal, from a zoning point of view, but economical. Wilde swung by unannounced early evening and rapped on the door with a pair of drumsticks. The door opened a few inches and got snagged by a chain. Senn-Rae's face appeared in the sliver.

"It's me," Wilde said.

The lawyer let him in.

She wore a white T-shirt that ended just short of her ass. Below that were legs, bare; and feet, equally bare. Her hair was down and loose. A half-glass of red wine dangled in her left hand. A 33 spun on a record machine, Lady Day, set to a low volume. She had a book in her hand.

"This is unexpected," she said.

"For me too," Wilde said. "I have a gig tonight playing drums."

"You play drums?"

"Actually play is probably too strong a word," he said. "Beat on 'em is more accurate. Anyway, I thought you might want to come." Wilde saw hesitation and added, "If you come, I promise to get drunk and make inappropriate advances towards you every chance I get."

She smiled.

"Such a deal."

"I have plans for you afterwards, too."

"Oh really?"

He nodded.

"Do you want to know what those plans are?"

"I think I already know."

"Actually, you don't," he said. "Afterwards, you and me are going to break into someone's house."

She wrinkled her forehead.

"Whose?"

"You'll see."

She shook her head.

"You seem to forget that I'm a lawyer," she said. "I don't do things like that. I could get disbarred. That's why I hired you."

Wilde shrugged.

"Okay," he said. "Then afterwards, we'll go to Plan B."

"What's Plan B?"

He looked at his watch.

"You'll see," he said. "Come on, throw a dress on and indulge me."

She stared at him for a heartbeat, deciding.

Then she said, "Give me five minutes."

Wilde watched her as she walked across the loft. Her ass swung seductively, her thighs were firm and muscular, the bottoms of her feet were dirty.

She turned when she got to the end.

He didn't divert his gaze.

He was a predator.

She was prey.

He wanted her to know it.

She closed the door after she entered but not all the way. It hung open a foot. A shower turned on.

Fifteen minutes later she emerged wearing the sexiest black dress in the world, short and tight, the kind that breaks hearts and makes men act stupid. She rolled soft rouge lipstick over her mouth as she walked across the loft. Her hair was washed but not dry, hanging wet, even letting loose with an occasional drip. Wilde took in her every move.

"I'm ready," she said.

"That's an understatement."

The Bokaray was an up-scale club with designer carpeting, textured walls, opulent chandeliers, a raised stage, a sea of tables, and two long curved bars, all set in a smoky air charged with tension, high-fashion and perfume.

A sexy vixen.

That was the best way to describe Mercedes Raine.

A sexy vixen with a honey voice and a dangerous sway.

She had her eyes on Wilde.

Ordinarily he would have been looking right back.

Not tonight, though.

When the evening was over Senn-Rae locked her arm through Wilde's and said, "I want to come with you."

"Where?"

"To break into that house."

Wilde shook his head.

"You're drunk."

She shrugged.

"It relates to my case, right?"

He nodded.

"The house belongs to the dead pinup girl on the boxcar."

"In that case, I'm definitely going."

"What about that lawyer thing?"

"I'll be a lawyer in the morning. Right now I'm just your co-conspirator."

They were at Blondie.

"Hop in," Wilde said.

He headed downtown and parked in the alley behind Senn-Rea's building.

She wrinkled her brow.

"What are you doing?"

"You're drunk," he said. "I'm not going to let you put yourself in jeopardy."

"That's my choice, not yours."

Wilde stepped out.

Senn-Rae stayed put.

"Come on," he said.

"No."

He opened the door, pulled her out and threw her over his shoulder. Then he carried her up the stairs, all the way to the sixth floor.

"Give me your keys."

She handed him her purse.

He fished them out, opened the door, carried her through the darkness and threw her on the bed. Then he pulled her dress up and ripped her panties off.

She pressed her lips to his.

Hard.

Wild.

Then she stuck her tongue in his mouth.

So wet.

So perfect.

26

Shade got a room at the Albany Hotel on Curtis Street, registering under the name Mandy Pandora, just in case everything that went wrong in Havana found a way here.

Havana.

She'd wait a week or two, then sneak back in and figure out how much of her network was left, if any. Right now she couldn't even think about it.

Right now Visible Moon filled her head.

Well, that wasn't totally true.

Part of her head rang with the fact that she'd disregarded Kent Harvin's direct order to report for the three o'clock debriefing. He wouldn't fire her, that wasn't the issue. The issue was that he deserved the information.

She checked her watch.

It was late and DC was even later.

Harvin would be sleeping.

He'd be angry beyond belief if she woke him up.

He'd be even angrier if she didn't.

Okay.

Do it.

She headed outside, found a public phone a block down the street and called collect. The rasp in Harvin's voice confirmed that he'd been dead to the world. Shade pictured him wrinkling every crease in his 51-year-old face and squinting at the clock.

"It's me," she said.

"Shade?"

"I'm sorry to wake you."

"Where are you?" She was about to tell him when he blurted-ed, "No, don't tell me."

Something was wrong.

"What's going on?"

Harvin exhaled.

"I'm going to go to hell for what I'm about to do, but screw it. Do you know a Cuban named Gurrero?"

"No."

"Well he knows you," Harvin said.

"What does that mean?"

"It means he's been in contact," Harvin said. "He wants out of Cuba, he wants sanctuary in the United States. In return, he's prepared to give up what he has on you."

Shade paced.

"On me?"

"Right."

"Which is what, exactly? What does he say he has on me?"

"He says you're a double spy. He says you're feeding information to the Russians through your Cuban contacts."

"That's bullshit."

"He says he has proof."

Silence.

"I don't even have any information to feed him. You know that."

"He says you have sources that feed you information."

"That's crazy."

"So what's going on then?"

"I don't know," she said. "All I can think is that someone's trying to set me up."

"Who?"

"I don't know."

"Why?"

"I don't know."

"Look," Harvin said, "I'm being deliberately kept out of the investigation because of my relationship with you. All I'm getting is bits and pieces, and I have to call in markers to even get those. My official orders are to direct you to come back to D.C. and not say anything else."

"Thanks for not following orders."

He chuckled.

"I guess I'm a little like you."

"I guess so."

"One more thing," he said. "They were going to search your apartment this evening." A pause. "Are they going to find anything?"

"No. There's nothing to find."

"Are you sure?"

"Trust me, I'm sure."

A beat.

"Okay, call me tomorrow," he said. "In the meantime, watch your back. If someone's going to this much trouble to set you up they might be going to an equal amount of trouble to kill you. If I were you, I'd get out of wherever you are right now. I'd get a thousand miles away, somewhere deep."

27

Senn-Rae knew how to use her body, her incredible body, so taut, so perfect, so unashamed, so willing, so everything. She knew how to build a storm inside a man and make it rage; and not just for a few minutes, for a time that got lost in time. Wilde somehow survived the whole thing, rolled over on his back and said, "Damn."

Senn-Rae laid her head on his chest.

"Double damn."

Five minutes later they were dressed and headed out into the black Denver nightscape. Wilde learned something this afternoon, namely that Natalie Levine's house was adrift in a sea of nosy neighbors. The time to do what needed to be done was now, in the netherworld that followed the stroke of twelve.

The house was dark and sealed tight.

Wilde worked the backdoor lock until it made that little click he was waiting for.

The knob turned.

They entered.

They were in the kitchen, a place of unimportance. Wilde wasted no time there and headed for the living room. He closed all the window coverings then fired up a small flashlight.

"What are we looking for exactly?" Senn-Rae asked.

The sexy little dress was gone, traded for stalking clothes—pants, shirt and shoes, all black. Wilde wore his suit. It smelled like a cigar-infested forest fire that someone tried to put out with wine and sweat, thanks to the club.

What were they looking for?

"We'll know it when we see it," Wilde said.

Then he saw something that got his attention.

It was a photograph of two women with their arms around each other, friends to the end, one blond and one raven. Both were drop-dead stunning.

"One of these must be Natalie," Wilde said.

"Right."

"That's not good."

"Why?"

"Because neither of these two girls are the dead pinup girl."

There were other photos.

The common denominator was the blond.

The blond was Natalie Levine.

The others were friends.

"She's definitely not the girl from the boxcar," Wilde said.

"Let's get out of here then," Senn-Rae said.

Something made Wilde pause, he wasn't sure what, but something. It also made him pull out the Camels and light up.

"What are you doing?" Senn-Rae said.

Wilde sat down on the couch and leaned back.

"Smoking."

Then he realized what made him pause.

"This girl's not the one from the boxcar, but she's just as pretty," he said. "She's pinup quality."

Senn-Rae wrinkled her forehead.

"So?"

"So, I think that means something."

"Like what?"

"I don't know," he said. "Let's keep looking around."

DAY FOUR

June 12
Thursday

28

A knock on the hotel door Thursday morning pulled Fallon out of a deep sleep. She concentrated to make sure she wasn't dreaming then felt her chest tighten. The police? Who else knew she was here?—nobody, that's who. She swung a naked body out of bed, said "Hold on," and slipped into pants and a blouse. On the other side of the door was the last person she expected—James Jundee, the lawyer, dressed in a charcoal suit with an expensive hang. He held two cups of coffee in his hand and handed her one.

"Ready?"

Ready?

Ready for what?

Then she remembered.

"Yes," she said. "I've been waiting for you. You're late."

He smiled.

"If you say so."

"Can you give me thirty more seconds?"

"Sure."

She headed for the bathroom, took a speed shower and emerged five minutes later her hair hanging heavy and wet. "Voila."

"Indeed."

They headed over to 16th Street and hit the department stores, buying an expensive gray pantsuit, a fluffy white blouse, a blue scarf, and black leather shoes—all conservative, all classy. By the time they were done, Fallon's hair was dry and combed and soft rouge lipstick moistened her lips.

Jundee eyed her up and down.

"Perfect."

"You think?"

"I know."

"Are you sure you want to do this?"

"Positive."

"Yeah?"

"Yeah."

Ten minutes later they were in an elevator ascending to the tenth floor of the Daniels & Fisher Tower, which housed Denver's second-largest law firm, Connors & Trench, LLC.

Jundee's office was a small interior one without a window.

"This is what the closet of a first-year associate looks like," he said.

A black metal filing cabinet, a marked wooden desk and a swivel chair, that's all there was and that's all that would fit. Papers and files were everywhere, stacked on one another to the point of teetering.

"You actually bring clients in here?"

"Are you kidding? It would scare them to death. That's what the conference rooms are for."

Okay.

Understood.

They took the stairs up to the eleventh floor and walked down a spacious corridor lined with western landscape oil paintings.

Captivating stuff.

At the end of the hall was a door, a stately door built of oak, with a window. The glass was stenciled with PARKER TRENCH. Jundee rapped lightly then headed in. The office was everything his wasn't.

Spacious.

Views.

Ornate.

A man looked up from behind a car-sized desk in the middle of the room. He focused on Jundee for a heartbeat, said "James," then turned his attention on Fallon. His face was rough and manly, his chest was big and his forearms were muscular. He was about thirty-seven, with thick brown hair, slightly disheveled, and eyes that looked like they could be the meanest in the world or the kindest. Right now they were the latter.

"Parker," Jundee said. "I'd like you to meet Fallon Leigh. I think she's the person you've been looking for. She's from New Mexico and grew up speaking Spanish as much as English."

"Is that true?"

Fallon nodded.

"It's no big deal," she said. "Everyone down there's bilingual."

"Can you write Spanish too?"

"Yes."

He nodded, impressed, and shook her hand.

"I'm Parker Trench," he said. "The firm's going to open a branch in Mexico City. Have you ever been there?"

"I have," she said. "Twice."

Trench looked at Jundee and said, "Where'd you find her?"

"In the street."

Trench wrinkled his brow.

"I don't understand."

"Someone hit her with a car last night," Jundee said.

"Who?"

"Some Indian."

"An Indian?"

"Right. He took off."

Trench shook his head.

"That's wrong."

Fallon jumped in. "It was my fault, I walked out in front of him."

Trench frowned.

"Still, he didn't know if you were okay or not. He shouldn't have left the scene." A beat, then, "Okay, clearly it's fate that you didn't get hurt and fate that you're here. I've argued with fate before and it didn't end up pretty. I'm not going to do it again."

"Does that mean I'm hired?"

He nodded.

"It does."

"Really?"

"Really."

"Just like that?"

"Just like that."

"Wow."

"How do you say that in Spanish?"

"Jcaray."

29

If Visible Moon was alive it wasn't by much. Whoever had her would kill her sooner or later if he hadn't done so already. The chance of Mojag actually bumping into the guy on the streets was infinitesimal. Theoretically it could happen but the likelihood was the size of a pinhead.

Visible Moon deserved more than a pinhead.

Shade wasn't a hunter.

She was a good CIA agent but not a hunter.

Worse, she had nothing to go on even if she was a hunter. She knew a few things, but not many.

The guy was a white man.

He was in his late 20's.

He had a gray suit.

He was attractive.

He was strong.

He drank Coors.

He had a big black car, shiny under the dust.

Other than that, Shade had nothing.

She could pass the guy a thousand times on the street, or sit next to him a thousand times in a bar, and not know it was him.

She needed help.

It would be risky to get someone else involved but there was no alternative.

She didn't have time to be risk-free.

She took a shower, headed down to registration and hung back until the man behind the counter was alone. He was bald and chubby but had a smile that took up half his face.

Shade leaned in.

"I'm looking for a private investigator. Do you know any good ones?"

He did.

He did indeed.

"Bryson Wilde," the man said. "He's got a seedy office down on Larimer but don't let it fool you."

"Do you know him? Personally?"

"No but he's got a reputation. You want a number?"

She tilted her head.

"No but I'll take an address."

The man wrote it down.

"Just head down 17th until you get to Larimer. Take a left and go for one-and-a half blocks, just past 16th."

"Thanks," she said. "This conversation is just between us."

"Absolutely."

She gave him her best smile and patted his hand.

"Thanks again."

She walked across the lobby towards the revolving doors.

His eyes were on her ass.

She could feel the burn.

Outside, the city was buzzing even now at only eight-fifteen in the morning. She stopped at a crowded place called the Down Towner for coffee, orange juice and toast, then called Kent Harvin from a payphone to see if things had gotten themselves sorted out.

"What the hell's going on?" he said.

"What do you mean?"

"What I mean is, I don't know exactly what you had in your apartment, but they found it last night."

"There was nothing there."

Silence.

"If they found something, then someone planted it there," she added. "Someone's setting me up."

"Who?"

She didn't know.

Harvin exhaled.

"I don't know where you are, but they think you're in Denver," he said. "They're sending someone there to hunt you down." A pause. "Shade, I love you like a daughter, you know that. If you got yourself in over your head, I can forgive you. But they can't. They won't. My advice to you, both as your boss and your friend, is to go deep right now, this second. If you're in Denver, get the hell out of there. If you're somewhere else, get out of there too. Go somewhere where you're not and don't leave a trail. Just disappear."

She retreated in thought.

"Kent, I need you to believe me. I didn't do anything wrong. Can you do me a favor?"

"Like what?"

"Find out who's setting me up," she said.

30

Wilde unlocked his office Thursday morning and tossed his hat towards the rack as he stepped through the door. It was off by a mile, heading for a window which should have been closed but wasn't. A woman sitting behind his desk caught it in midair just before it flew out.

She tossed it back to him.

"Try again."

He did.

It was low, hit the pole and dropped to the floor.

The woman was a bombshell with raven hair.

"Two questions," Wilde said. "Who are you? And how'd you get in?"

She studied him.

"You don't look like what I pictured."

"Is that good or bad?"

"Good."

He headed for the coffee maker and found that it was already fired up, with a half-pot gone and an equal amount left. He filled a cup and took a noisy slurp.

"It looks like you've been here a while."

She nodded.

"I hope you don't mind. I behaved myself. I didn't snoop around or anything."

"I did leave the door locked, didn't I?"

"You did. I didn't want to wait on the street. Are you mad?"

He shook his head.

"You made me coffee," he said.

The woman got a serious look on her face.

"You're not the first PI I visited this morning. I stopped by the office of a guy named Peter Willoughby first. He didn't work out."

"Why not?"

"He didn't have what it takes." A pause, then, "You do."

"How can you tell?"

"I just can."

"It's in the way I toss my hat, isn't it?"

She smiled.

"That's it."

Then she got serious.

"There's a Navajo woman named Tehya who got murdered and scalped at a desert bar down in New Mexico. It happened Monday night. The bar was on reservation land, meaning the local police aren't doing any kind of investigation."

Wilde made a face.

"Scalped?"

"Right."

"As in someone cut the top of her head off?"

"Right."

"Damn, that's sick," he said. "I've never even heard of such a thing happening except for in the old days."

The woman went to the window, looked down and then turned. "The bar was being worked solo that night by another Navajo woman named Visible Moon, age twenty-two. She hasn't been seen or heard from since that night."

"What are you saying, that she did it and ran off?"

"No, not in a million years. I'm saying she got taken."

"By who?"

"By the same man who scalped Tehya," the woman said. "Visible Moon is still alive."

"How do you know?"

"Because I can feel her," the woman said. "She's my half-sister. We have the same mother but different fathers."

Wilde tapped two Camels out of a pack, handed one to the woman and lit them up.

He blew smoke.

"You still haven't told me your name."

"Sorry, it's Shade. Shade de Laurent." She walked over, took his hand and squeezed. "Please say you'll help me find her."

He chewed on it.

He was already consumed with Senn-Rae's case, not to mention Senn-Rae herself. This new woman was too attractive. She had the potential to confuse him.

"Please," she said.

He hesitated.

"New Mexico's a long way off."

"This isn't a New Mexico case," Shade said. "The man was from Denver. Visible Moon's being kept somewhere in this area."

"How do you know?"

She exhaled.

Then she took an envelope out of her purse and put it in his hand.

"That's five hundred dollars to get you started. Money isn't the issue. If you run out there's more. Can I start at the beginning and tell you everything I know."

Wilde fiddled with the envelope.

Then he topped his coffee cup off and said, "If I take the case and actually find this guy, what are you going to do?"

"You mean, am I going to kill him?"

Wilde took a slurp and nodded.

"My main goal is to get Visible Moon back home alive."

"Then what? Kill who took her?"

"We'll see."

"I would," he said. "I'd kill him deader than dead if he

really did what you say he did. But first I'd be damn sure I had the right man."

"That will be your job."

He sat on the edge of his desk.

"That's a lot of pressure."

"Not really," Shade said. "He'll have two things that will give him away. One is Visible Moon. The other is the scalp. He took it with him. It's his little souvenir."

Wilde grabbed a pen and paper.

Then a tangent thought struck him.

"Is Visible Moon a beautiful woman?"

Shade pulled a picture out of her purse and handed it to him.

"This is her."

She wasn't beautiful.

She was average.

"Why?"

"Nothing," Wilde said. "Another case I have involves women who are pinup quality. I was wondering if there was a connection."

"Visible Moon was average."

"Got it," Wilde said. "Okay, let's start at the beginning." Before the woman could speak, Wilde had another thought. "What about Tehya?"

"What do you mean?"

"Was she average too?"

"No, she was way above average," Shade said.

"Way above?"

"Right, she was attractive, very attractive. I can get you a picture if you want."

Wilde shrugged.

"Go ahead," he said. "It can't hurt."

31

Fallon got stationed in the office next to Trench and loved every inch of it, especially the window. Fifteen miles to the west, the mountains jutted out of the plains with a jagged edge. Down below, Denver buzzed.

This was her first real job.

It was her first real office.

Yesterday she was a waitress.

Now, this.

She tossed her hair back and got to work.

Trench was in the early stages of looking at potential office space—grade A, strategically positioned in the heart of the matter. He'd flown down to Mexico City two weeks ago, surveyed several potential buildings, and returned with copies of proposed leases.

All of them were in Spanish.

Fallon's job was to translate them into English, typewritten. Later, after the firm chose one, Fallon's job would be to take modifications fed to her by Trench and draft them into Spanish for negotiation.

The going was slow.

She was a two-finger typer.

She was in the thick of it, focused with intensity, when she realized someone was in the doorway.

It was Trench.

"Can I bother you a minute?"

Sure.

Of course.

"I forgot to ask before if you've had any college."

Her heart pounded.

She was a nobody.

A waitress.

He was about to find out.

"No," she said.

"That's fine," he said. "That's not a problem. The only reason I mention it is that after you're around here for a while, you might outgrow what you're doing. You might want to be a lawyer instead of someone on the staff."

"I couldn't even imagine being a lawyer."

"Maybe not now," Trench said. "I have to be honest, though, I see lawyer material in you. I see ambition. If you ever feel you want to go to college and give it a try, let me know. We'll work something out, on the firm."

"Really?"

He nodded.

"Settle in first for the next three or four or five months," he said. "Then if it seems like the right thing to do, we'll put a plan together."

Her head spun.

"Can I do something?"

Trench tilted his head.

"Sure."

She stood up, walked over and gave him a tight hug.

"Thank you."

"No thanks necessary," he said. "Just keep in mind it's not set in stone. You'd have to want it and you'd have to earn it. It's something to think about though."

"I feel like I'm in a dream."

Trench smiled.

"Good. That's the way life is supposed to be."

Jundee swung by at 11:45 and took her to lunch at an upscale place a few blocks down the street called the Paramount Café. They ended up in a nice booth and ordered chicken salads.

She told him about the college conversation with Trench.

"Is he trying to get in my pants?"

Jundee laughed.

"Trench?"

Right.

Trench.

"I don't know, I can only speak for myself," Jundee said.

She took a sip of tea.

"Then do it."

"Do what?"

"Speak for yourself."

He smiled.

"As for me the answer is, of course. The question though is whether it's working or not."

She ran a finger across his hand.

"It might be."

She chewed, debating one last time about whether she should say what she was about to say, then decided to just say it.

"A briefcase full of papers came into my possession," she said. "I don't know what they are but they're valuable. People are killing other people to try to get them. They even tried to kill me."

Jundee halted a fork midway to his mouth.

"Say again?"

32

Wilde was the right man for the job. That should have made Shade feel better but it didn't, primarily because of Wilde's warning—"I don't have much to go on, you appreciate that I hope." She did, she did indeed, but hearing the words out loud from the mouth of another person forced the hopelessness of the situation deeper into her brain.

From Wilde's office, she headed over to Market to see if Mojag marked the mailbox.

He hadn't.

Now what?

She headed back to her hotel, not sure whether to check out or not. Someone on behalf of the CIA would be showing up sometime today, possibly as early as noon. They'd want to take her alive if possible for interrogation.

What information did she give up?

Where did she get that information?

Who did she give it to?

How much was she paid?

How did she keep everything so secret?

Was anyone else in the company working with her?

Getting her alive was more important than revenge.

That didn't mean killing her was out of the equation. It was very much in. If they saw her, say from a distance or in a passing car—in a situation where capture wasn't readily available—they might well take the opportunity to just put her away right then and there, especially if there was any indication that she was going deep.

What to do?

Hotels were too dangerous.

She should find a man.

Stay with him.

Shade called Wilde from a payphone and said, "I've been thinking about what you said ever since you left; namely, the chance of you finding this guy based on the limited information that you know about him is almost negligible."

"That's true."

"There's an option, though."

"As in, what?"

"Okay, here it goes," she said. "It's doubtful that we can find him. It might be possible, though, to have him find us. To be more precise, me."

Wilde heard the words.

He didn't understand them.

"I don't get it."

"It goes like this. I start to get visible, talking to people, frequenting the bars and brothels and things like that, making it clear I'm in town looking for him. I tell people I have information on him—I tell them I saw him from a distance, something like that. He ends up hearing about it and seeing me as a threat. Then he comes to take me out."

"So you turn myself into bait."

Right.

Bait.

Good word for it.

"I'm going to do it," Shade said.

Wilde exhaled. "Bait usually ends up getting eaten; that's why they call it bait."

"Not this time. You'll be there in the shadows when he comes for me."

"I can't guarantee that will happen."

"I'll take that as a yes."

Shade hung up and smiled.

She felt better.

This might actually work.

Then the smile washed off her face. Getting visible to the mystery man meant getting visible to the company.

33

Wilde tossed his hat at the rack and missed. It went to the left, always to the left. He needed to pretend the rack was eight inches to the right—shoot for that, then it should hit. He picked it up, walked back to the door and tossed it again, aiming to the right. It actually hit this time, ricocheting off and falling to the floor.

He smiled.

Closer.

Okay, aim a full foot to the right.

Keep the hat more level, too.

He picked it up, walked back to the door and aimed to the right. Just as he threw, the door opened and knocked into his arm. The hat flew to the right, way to the right, and disappeared out the window.

Alabama came the rest of the way through the door and said, "Did I do that?"

Wilde kissed her on the lips.

"Never come in when I'm shooting."

"How am I supposed to know—"

"I thought we agreed on that."

He bounded down the stairs before some transient ended up having some luck he shouldn't. When he got down, the hat was disappearing up the street on the head of a teenager.

Wilde snatched it off.

The kid turned, startled.

Wilde put it on his head, dipped it over his left eye and said, "Always dip it."

When he got back up to the office, Alabama had moved the rack away from the window.

"There," she said. "Problem solved. Hat safe."

Wilde moved it back.

Alabama put her hands on her hips.

"Why'd you do that?"

"It's more risky that way," Wilde said. "It's a reminder."

"A reminder of what?"

"That things can go wrong," he said. "The more you can remember that, the less likely it is to happen."

Alabama rolled her eyes.

"You're weird sometimes."

"Right, weird like a fox."

"You just proved my point."

"How so?"

"Because foxes aren't weird," she said. "The fact that you inferred that they're weird is in itself weird."

Wilde tried to think of a clever retort, got nothing, then put a serious expression on his face. "We're going to be doing something that's going to take a lot of concentration and coordination to make sure nothing goes wrong."

"Yeah, what?"

Suddenly the door opened and a woman stepped in.

Shade de Laurent.

Wilde introduced the two women to each other and said, "Okay, here's the plan."

The plan was simple.

The Kenmark Hotel had an exterior fire escape on the backside where the alley was. It was designed with a central stairway that went from the ground up to the roof. At each floor, the escape branched out horizontal down a walkway that ran in both directions. The walkway was accessible by climbing out the windows of the rooms.

"What you two do is find two rooms at the end of a floor that are currently available for rent," Wilde said. "You, Shade, rent the room at the very end. Do it under a fake name. In fact, choose one now."

She retreated in thought.

"Marilyn Striker."

"Fine, Marilyn Striker."

To Alabama, "You rent the room next to Shade's. You'll use a fake name too."

"Brenda Belle," she said.

"Fine, Brenda Belle." To Shade, "You know the guy's a white man, right?"

She nodded.

"Correct."

Wilde frowned.

"If I say right, and it is right, your answer should be right, not correct," he said. "Correct upsets the balance of the universe."

She smiled.

"Right," she said.

Wilde nodded.

"You're going to go visit a friend of mine named Michael Baxter," Wilde said. "He's a sax player but dabbles a little in drawing. He's actually pretty good. He's going to draw you a sketch of a white man."

Shade frowned.

"Remember," she said, "I don't really know what the guy

looks like. A sketch won't do any good."

"I doesn't matter if it looks like the guy or not," Wilde said. "What you're going to do is start taking that sketch all over town—bars, restaurants, flophouses, clubs, you name it. You tell people you're looking for the guy in the sketch. You tell them he killed a woman named Tehya and abducted another one named Visible Moon. You tell them you're looking for him. They'll say they've never seen him. Now, here's the important part. You tell them you're staying at the Kenmark in room 418 or whatever it turns out to be. You tell them that if they see the guy, they should contact you there."

Shade nodded.

"Okay."

"If things go as planned," Wilde said, "our friend will get a whiff of the fact that someone's in Denver looking for him. He'll get the word that you've actually seen him somehow and even have a composite drawing of him. He'll get the word that you're staying in the Kenmark. Sooner or later he'll show up there to take you out."

"Brilliant."

Wilde lit two Camels and handed one to Shade.

He took a long drag and held it in.

"Here's the important thing," he said. "You never, ever go to that room unless I'm with you." To Alabama, "What you're going to do, Alabama, is stay in your room and keep an eye on that fire escape because that's how our friend will come to get Shade. Get a look at him but don't be a hero."

"Should I follow him?"

Wilde hesitated.

Alabama added, "It won't do much good for me to only get a look at him. We need to get his license plate number or find out where he goes or something like that."

Wilde blew smoke.

"Okay, you can follow him but only if you can do it safely."

"That won't be a problem."

"We don't know that," Wilde said. "It might be a problem and it might not. If it's a problem or has any potential to become a problem, you abort. If he ever looks at you even once, you drop off and disappear. It ends right there and then, that second. Deal?"

"Sure."

"I'm serious, Alabama. Deal?"

"Okay."

"I mean it," Wilde said. "No hero stuff."

"I heard you."

Wilde set a book of matches on fire and watched the flames as he tried to decide whether there was anything else to discuss. Then he said to Shade, "I'm going way out on a limb here, potentially putting Alabama in harm's way. I've never done that before. Be sure you don't do anything to increase the risk to her."

"Like what?"

"I don't know," he said. "Whatever."

She hugged him.

"If Visible Moon ends up living, it will be because of you."

He grunted.

"You and Alabama are going to be the ones in the crosshairs," he said. "I'm just the guy putting you there."

34

Jundee was intrigued by the mysterious briefcase, so much so that he wanted to see it right now during the lunch hour before they went back to the firm. At the hotel Tom Fallon dragged it out from under the bed and tossed it on the sheets.

Jundee made a face.

"What happened to it?"

"I had to shoot it open."

"All I can say is, I hope you never have to shoot me open."

He studied the papers, keeping them in order, particularly the one on top, which was the folded paper Fallon found in the man's wallet, the one with the numbers on it.

"They're some combination of math, physics, mechanics and engineering," he said. "None of it makes any sense, though. It's almost as if someone copied five or six lines from a source document, then did the same from a second source document, etc. It's all scrambled. None of it flows."

Fallon frowned.

"Weird."

"Very."

Suddenly Jundee put a grin on his face.

"This first page," he said, "the one on top, the one you found in the man's wallet."

"What about it?"

"I'll bet it's a key."

"A key to what?"

"A key to unscrambling the mess."

He studied the document closer, turned two or three pages and flipped onto his back.

"What's going on?"

He sat up and tapped the document. "This first number is the page number," he said. "The numbers right behind it refer to the lines on that page. When you put them all together, you get an unscrambled document."

Fallon checked the first few lines.

It made sense.

When she kept going, however, it didn't. She must have had confusion on her face because Jundee said, "What's wrong?"

"This entry right here is for 412," she said.

Jundee wrinkled his forehead.

"So?"

"So, we only have 300 pages. There is no page 412."

Jundee checked.

She was right.

In fact, there were a lot of entries higher than 300. On close examination, half of them, maybe more, were between 300 and 600.

He paced.

"My theory's right," he said. "This key refers to the page numbers followed by the line items on that page. What's wrong though is that we don't have all the pages. We only have half of them."

"So where are the other half?"

"This briefcase is full," Jundee said. "Only half the papers could fit in here. My guess is that there's a second briefcase. The rest of the documents are there."

"A second briefcase?"

"Yes. Did you see another one in the car?"

"No."

"Are you sure?"

"I would have grabbed it if I saw it."

Jundee chewed on it.

"Were the car windows open when you got down to the scene?"

Fallon reflected back.

"I think so."

"I'll bet the other briefcase flew out of the car." He locked eyes with her. "Is that possible?"

She shrugged.

"I didn't really search around or anything like that. I had no reason to."

Jundee went to the window and looked out silently.

Then he turned and said, "We need to go back to the crash site."

"It's a long way. Five hours."

Jundee looked at his watch.

"We'll take off work early, say three o'clock," he said. "That will get us down there by eight. It'll still be light enough to get down the cliff and look around." A beat, then, "Grab some comfortable clothes now so we don't have to swing by here later."

Black shorts.

A pink T.

White cotton panties.

Tennis shoes.

All that got stuffed into her purse, barely.

"There."

The briefcase went back under the bed.

They hung a *Do Not Disturb* sign on the doorknob, mad sure the lock was engaged, and headed back to the firm.

"What about Trench?" Fallon asked on the way back. "I'm supposed to work until five, right?"

"Trench won't be a problem."

"Are you going to tell him what we're doing?"

"No. Neither of us can tell anyone anything," he said. "We need to figure out what's going on first."

35

Shade wasted no time putting the bait in the trap—flashing a picture of Visible Moon and a sketch of a man all over town, telling people that Visible Moon was either killed or abducted by the man in the sketch, telling them to please, please, please contact her, Marilyn Striker, at Room 318 of the Kenmark if they ended up seeing either person.

Most were cooperative.

Most wrote down the information.

A few looked at the photo of Visible Moon and said, "She's an Indian?"

"Yes."

"Oh."

Oh.

As if the issue was a lost dog.

Shade bit her tongue, forced a smile and told them one more time where to contact her.

Midway through the afternoon, in a rundown bar called the Rainbow Tavern, something unexpected happened. The bartender—a bulky guy with a flattop and a veined nose—took the picture of Visible Moon out of Shade's hand and studied it closer.

"She's an Indian, right?"

"Right."

He tilted his head.

"I saw an Indian woman a couple of days ago, Tuesday evening to be precise," he said. "I don't know if it was her or not."

Shade's blood sang.

"Where?"

"She was in a car," the man said.

"A car?"

"Right. She was in the passenger seat. The car went past me. I just happened to be looking. The whole thing took a second."

"Who was driving?"

"I have no idea."

"You didn't see the driver?"

"No, I only saw the woman."

"What color was the car?"

He retreated in thought.

"Dark," he said.

"Black?"

"Maybe," he said. "Black, dark blue, dark green, something dark. I'm not getting a clear picture. I remember though that it was fairly new. That's what sort of struck me. You don't see that many Indian women in Denver and when you do, it's usually not in a fancy car." He handed the photo back to her. "No offense."

"I understand."

"I'm just saying—"

Shade nodded.

No problem.

"Where was this car when you saw it?"

He wrinkled his forehead, lost, then brightened and said, "It was on Broadway, that's it, yeah, on Broadway, way down on the south edge of town, almost out of the city. That's where a friend of mine lives, a female friend if you catch my drift. The more I think about it, nine o'clock. That's about when I saw her."

Nine o'clock.

South Broadway.

Dark car.

"What's your name?"

"Jim," he said. "Jim Poindexter."

Shade shook his hand.

"It's nice to meet you, Jim Poindexter."

"Likewise."

Shade was almost out the door when she had one more thought and turned. "When you saw the woman, was the car window up or down?"

"Up."

He scratched his head.

Then he added, "Maybe that's why I sort of remember this. It was still warm enough out that people were driving with their windows open."

"Maybe the window was up so she couldn't yell for help," Shade said.

The man shrugged.

"I wouldn't know."

"Maybe she was being held at gunpoint."

"Maybe," he said. "On the other hand, maybe it wasn't even her."

36

Wilde drove down Natalie Levine's street, not sure exactly why. The search of her house last night revealed nothing other than she wasn't the pinup woman from the boxcar. That was all he needed to know.

Still, she was blond.

Young.

Stunning.

Pinup quality.

Missing.

Was her body staged somewhere, waiting to be found?

Was she connected to the boxcar victim?

There was one neighbor mowing the grass across the street. Traffic was thin. Wilde swung around the block, parked and headed back on foot, cutting up the drive of the next-door neighbor and then swinging across the backyard to his destination.

Then he was in.

His heart pounded.

Everything was going exactly as he wanted, but still his heart pounded.

It always pounded.

Every time.

The place looked different by the light of day. Okay, now what? Where could he possibly look that he hadn't already?

He opened drawers and went through them, all the way to the bottom, all the way to the back.

Kitchen drawers.

Bedroom drawers.

Underwear drawers.

Cabinets.

Nothing new, that's what he found, just the same old stuff.

He tugged at the carpet where it met the floorboards, looking for a weakness that might lead to a concealed compartment.

He found nothing.

Upstairs in the bedroom, he pulled the sheets off and looked for holes in the mattress or box springs. They were in good condition. The room had a small closet accessed with folding doors. Lots of clothes hung on hangers. An equal number were piled on the floor. Nothing was in that pile or under it, only clothes. He shut the folding doors and sat down on the bed.

Now what?

He went downstairs, looked in the refrigerator, the oven, the breadbox and the toaster.

He found nothing.

Okay, done.

There was nothing here.

He had his hand on the backdoor knob when a final thought came to him. He went back upstairs, opened the closet and went through the pockets of the clothes on the hangers.

He found nothing.

Then he went through the pockets of the dirty clothes on the floor. Inside the pocket of a pair of white shorts, he found a book of matches, half empty.

The cover was red and had a gold B on it.

It was identical to the boxcar matches.

There was writing on it.

604.

The writing was the same size and style as the boxcar matches.

What had been on those?

He retreated in thought.

Then he remembered.

616.

This one was 604 and the other one was 616.

37

Driving south with Jundee behind the wheel, Fallon lit a cigarette and took a deep drag as the Packard came into view, still sitting where she'd abandoned it. She must have had a look on her face as they passed it because Jundee said, "Are you okay?"

For a heartbeat she considered telling him.

Telling him about the Packard.

Telling him about her past.

Telling him the truth.

Instead she said, "I'm fine."

"You left me there for a second," he said.

She blew smoke.

Suddenly she said, "Pull over."

"Why?"

"Please, fast," she said.

He did.

She hopped out, closed the door then leaned in the window. "I'll be right back."

"Where you going?"

"Ten seconds."

She headed back towards the Packard on foot. When she got close enough to read the license plate number, she memorized it and then trotted back to Jundee, throwing the butt on the ground as she pulled the door open.

Jundee wrinkled his forehead in confusion.

"What was that about?"

"I thought I saw a wallet by the side of the road," she said.

"Sorry."

"A wallet?"

She nodded.

"And?"

"And it wasn't a wallet."

"What was it?"

She racked her brain for something that looked like a wallet and got nothing.

"I don't know. Some kind of junk."

Jundee checked for traffic and took off.

"You don't need stranger's wallets," he said. "I have money."

She gave him a sideways glance and lit another cigarette.

No man was going to own her.

Never again.

When Colorado Springs disappeared in the rearview mirror, the topography heading south suddenly changed, getting more arid and desert-like. The dirt got a redder hue, the horizon line stretched wider and the clouds in the distance took on more of a cotton-ball shape.

"Someone did something nice for me," she said. "I want to send him a thank-you card but I only have his license plate number. Is there a way to find out who he is from that? You know, get his name and address."

"Sure, I suppose. What'd he do for you?"

"He let me use his car."

"And he didn't even know you?"

"No."

"Were you wearing those legs when he let you?"

She laughed.

"Maybe."

"Then that explains it."

"I have a transistor radio at home," Jundee said. "I should have brought it." A beat then, "I guess it's just the same. There's probably no reception out here anyway."

"I like the quiet," Fallon said.

"Really?"

She nodded.

"You can see things better when it's quiet."

"Like what?"

"See that black bird way over there?" she said, pointing. "Like that."

"You don't think you'd see it if a radio was on?"

"I'm not saying necessarily that you wouldn't see it," she said. "Obviously your eyes still work the same. What I'm saying is that you generally see more when your brain isn't worrying about something else. The opposite is true too, you hear more if your eyes aren't working so hard." She stuck the cigarette out the window and flicked ashes. "What are we going to do if we find the other briefcase?"

Jundee grunted.

"That's not the question," he said. "The question is, what are we going to do if we don't find it."

38

Shade left the Rainbow Tavern with the corner of her mouth turned up ever so slightly. The woman Jim Poindexter saw Tuesday night was Visible Moon; it had to be. She was being held at gunpoint or knifepoint, that's why the car window was up. More importantly, she was being taken somewhere.

Where?

Somewhere close?

An abandoned building?

A basement?

A wood shed in the back forty?

Shade needed to rent a car, get out there and drive around, right now, this second. A taxi came down the street from the opposite direction. She ran across, got in front of it and waved her arms.

The vehicle skidded to a stop.

The driver swung the door open and shouted, "Are you crazy lady?"

"I need you to take me where I can rent a car," she said.

"I have a fare."

He pointed.

Shade looked.

Two people were in the back seat, a man and a woman, watching intently.

"Sorry."

"You're going to get yourself killed."

"I'm sorry."

"I almost didn't get stopped."

"I know, I'm sorry, I really am."

Suddenly something caught her eye—a woman on the sidewalk, thirty steps away, stopped in her tracks and watching he with intensity.

She was about thirty and on the short side, five-two or thereabouts, but with an athletic build. Up top was a red baseball hat. A blond ponytail wagged out of it in the back. Down below were black tennis shoes. In her left hand was an oversized purse, yellow.

Their eyes locked for the briefest of moments.

The woman was pretty.

Shade turned and walked away.

She didn't look back.

At the first street she took a right, then a left at the next, then another left at the one after that. She stopped in front of a restaurant and pretended to read the menu as she used the window as a mirror. If the woman was behind her, Shade couldn't tell. She headed inside the restaurant, took a seat at the counter where she could see out the front and ordered a cherry-coke.

The woman never walked past.

Shade put a nickel tip on the table and left.

Outside, she looked in both directions as if deciding which way to go.

The woman was nowhere to be seen.

She headed north and flagged down the first taxi she saw. It actually turned out to be the same one, this time without the startled man and woman in the back.

"That's better," the driver said. "Doing it from the curb, that's better."

"Sorry about before."

"It's okay, it gives me a story."

"Glad I could help."

"I'm going to embellish it though," he said. "It's not quite good enough to be a story just on its own. It's close but it's not quite there. I'm going to have to add to it."

"Like what? What are you going to add?"

"I don't know," he said. "Maybe I'll say your hair was on fire. What do you think?"

She smiled.

"That gives it a little more oomph."

"Yes it does."

"I'd add that," she said, "and something else too. I mean, if you're going to build it up, you might as well really go for it."

The man chewed on it.

"I'll say you actually flagged me down a second time, which is true," he said, "and when you got in, a giant snake stuck its head out from inside your purse."

"I like that."

He got serious.

"That's not going to actually happen though, right?"

"No, I left all my snakes at home."

"Good."

Thirty minutes later she was behind the wheel of a rental—a 1952 Studebaker Starliner—driving south on Broadway, getting closer and closer with each passing street to the edge of the city.

39

The phone rang just as Wilde walked into the office. He tossed his hat at the rack, remembering at the last second to aim to the right, and got a ringer. He shook his head in disbelief and picked up the receiver.

"You're there," a voice said.

It was soft but stressed.

It belonged to Senn-Rae.

"Just got here," Wilde said.

"Don't go anywhere, I'm coming over."

"I just got a ringer."

"Huh?"

"My hat, I just got a ringer."

"Good for you. Don't go anywhere."

"Aim to the right," he said. "That's the secret. It took me five years to figure it out."

The line died.

He picked his hat off the rack, went back to the door and tossed it again, aiming to the right. It curved to the right and missed by two feet.

He picked it up and got positioned again.

"Come on, two out of three."

He tossed it and watched it hook by no more than half an inch.

Good enough.

"Got you."

Fifteen minutes later Senn-Rae busted through the door with a serious expression on her face. "It's official," she said. "My client is being blackmailed. He got the call just a little while ago. The guy wants $10,000."

Wilde winced.

"Who the hell has that kind of money?"

"No one."

"What's the deadline?"

"Monday."

Wilde lit a book of matches on fire and let it burn. Then he stepped to the window, made sure no one was directly below, and tossed it down.

"We'll never find him in time," he said.

"So what do we do?"

"I don't know."

"Well think."

"I am," he said. "We can pretend we have the money and try to catch him at the exchange but I've got a gut feeling he's going to be too smart for that."

He hung his suit jacket on the rack, reached into the left pocket, pulled out the red book of matches and handed them to Senn-Rae.

She wasn't impressed.

She'd seen them before.

"No," Wilde said. "These aren't the ones from the boxcar. These are from Natalie Levine's house."

"From last night?"

"No, I went back again today," he said. "These were in the pocket of a pair of shorts." He opened his desk drawer and pulled out the original book of red matches. "These are the ones from the boxcar. Compare the handwriting."

She did.

It was the same.

Same style.

Same red pen.

"Compare the numbers," Wilde said.

She did.

"616 and 604," she said. "What do they mean?"

Wilde shrugged.

"I don't know, but I'll bet dollars to donuts that Natalie Levine's dead somewhere. Our friend has at least two notches on his belt. Probably more. Your client is the best link we have to this guy. I need to talk to him."

Senn-Rae shook her head.

"That's impossible."

"Why?"

"He doesn't know about you," she said.

"Fine, tell him."

"I can't."

"Why not?"

"He told me not to tell anyone about what's going on, remember?"

Yeah.

He remembered.

"That reminds me of something I've been meaning to ask you," he said. "How well do you know this guy, your client?"

"Not well."

"What's he look like?"

"I wouldn't tell you even if I could," she said. "He's confidential."

"What do you mean, even if you could?"

"It means—"

"You've met him, right?"

"Only by phone."

"You've only talked to him on the phone? You've never seen him face to face?"

"Correct."

"Well that's strange."

Senn-Rae wasn't impressed.

"Not really,' she said. "He killed someone, remember? He's trying to insulate himself, even from me."

Wilde lit a Camel and blew a smoke ring.

"Maybe, maybe not."

"What are you saying?"

"What I'm saying is that you're pretty enough to be a pinup. Maybe his interest in you isn't as a lawyer at all. Maybe it's as a victim." A beat then, "I'm starting to wonder if he's the pinup killer."

Senn-Ray wrinkled her forehead.

"I don't get it."

"What I'm saying is, it's possible that he's actually the person who killed the woman on the boxcar," he said. "He's actually hired you to find himself."

"Why? That's crazy . . ."

"It's a way to get close to you before he kills you."

Wilde turned on the fan and stood in front of it. "I'll admit it's a little farfetched," he said, "but that doesn't necessarily mean I'm wrong. I'm going to find out who he is, just for grins."

"No, it's too dangerous."

He sat down, patted his lap and said, "Sit."

She did.

He put his arm around her waist.

"Look," he said, "if he's not the killer then it's not dangerous, he's just a guy being blackmailed. If he is the killer, though, we need to wonder if this is how he got close to his victims, by entering their worlds under some type of pretext."

She chuckled nervously.

"I don't think I qualify as pinup material."

Wilde smiled.

"You're trying to get a compliment out of me. Compliments are like fishing. Don't try too hard to land them. They taste better if you just wait until they jump out of the water and land in the boat."

40

When Fallon and Jundee got to the cliff, the desert shadows had gotten too long to even be shadows anymore and the sky was gray with twilight. In another half hour, climbing would be dangerous.

They headed down anyway.

"Watch your step," Fallon said. "These rocks are slippery."

"You too."

They made it down with a few missteps but nothing that sent them into a death spiral.

The car was still there.

That was expected.

What wasn't expected is that the body would still be behind the wheel. Two ravens were on the window ledge picking at the face. They didn't stop until Fallon and Jundee got too close for comfort. Then they hopped off and took a perch on the wall of the cliff.

Most of the man's face was gone.

"Nice," Jundee said.

They slowed as they approached, fighting the stench, then forced themselves all the way to the vehicle and looked in the passenger window.

"I don't see anything," Jundee said.

Fallon didn't either.

Jundee opened the door.

No briefcase was anywhere in the front, that was clear. He pushed the seat forward and looked in the back. "Nothing back there," he said.

"Are you sure?"

"Take a look."

Fallon did. She saw nothing.

Then she climbed all the way inside and looked under the seats.

No briefcase was there.

Nothing was there.

A book of red matches, that's all she saw.

She shoved them in her pocket.

No use letting them go to waste.

When she got out, Jundee was at the back of the car. He pulled on the trunk lid, which opened without resistance. The latch was destroyed.

Inside they found a spare tire, a jack, a blanket and several cans of spray paint.

"No briefcase," Fallon said.

Right, no briefcase.

Jundee looked at the vehicle.

"The windows are down like you thought," he said. "Maybe the briefcase flew out on the way down."

They checked.

They checked all around, behind every rock and bush for a good distance in every direction.

No briefcase.

Fallon picked up a rock and threw it.

"The light's going," she said. "We better head up."

Jundee stood there.

"Wait a minute," he said. Then he bent down and looked under the car, from all four sides.

No briefcase.

"Damn," he said. "I had my hopes up for a second."

"Come on, let's go."

They headed off.

Ten steps later Jundee stopped and turned.

He stared at the cliff.

"What's wrong?"

He pointed.

"There's a ledge right there," he said. "See it? It's about halfway down."

Fallon saw it.

"Maybe the briefcase landed there," Jundee said.

Fallon wasn't impressed.

"That would be almost impossible."

"Almost but not totally."

Jundee ran his eyes up above the ledge.

"We won't be able to see it from above," he said. "I'm going to have to climb up."

"No."

"Why not?"

"It's almost straight up."

Jundee swallowed.

"I can do it."

"We're almost out of light," Fallon said.

Suddenly a movement on the ground a step away attracted her peripheral vision.

She looked down.

A rattlesnake was coiled up.

It was huge.

Thick.

It shook its tail for a split-second and then lashed out with a lightning speed. White-hot fangs sunk deep into Fallon's leg, so fast that she didn't even have time to scream.

41

Civilization disappeared as Shade drove farther and farther south. This would be a good place to keep a woman captive, somewhere around here, where the screams could only carry so far. The perfect place hadn't shown up yet but it would. Put yourself in his shoes. You scalped someone. You're holding another woman—a witness no less—captive. The place had to be absolutely foolproof.

It had to be in your control.

So rule out squatting or trespassing, unless you were nuts.

Rule out abandoned buildings where anyone and everyone could stumble in to get out of a storm or see if a still-useable sink or toilet had been abandoned in place.

The best hideaway would be one you owned.

The second best place would be one you rented.

Okay.

Good.

Look for a house or cabin or shed, something off the beaten path, something that was private. While good in theory, the thought wasn't helpful. Every quarter-mile there was another dirt road, a private road, heading off into the terrain. Sometimes the reason was obvious but more often the road just disappeared into the brush. It would take weeks to drive down every one.

She passed a dozen of them.

Then an equal number again.

It was useless.

She turned around.

A mile later she noticed something she didn't before, namely a post sticking out of the ground where a dirt road led to the west. On the ground, lying next to it in the weeds, was a plywood sign with words handwritten in red paint, *For Rent*.

Why was the sign down?

Was it because someone rented the place?

Rented it recently, in fact?

Shade drove another two hundred yards and parked in a small turnoff by a bridge. She headed west on foot into the rolling Colorado prairie until she was invisible from passing cars and then paralleled the road back towards the turnoff.

She didn't have a gun.

She didn't have a knife.

That wouldn't happen again.

When she got back to town, she'd take care of that little omission.

A jackrabbit took off from the dirt ahead where it had been standing still. Now it was too dangerous to play the camouflage game.

Now it was time to run.

"I'm not going to hurt you," Shade said.

She wore shorts and the longer prairie grasses rubbed abrasively against her legs with an irritating itch. The rental theory made more and more sense with each passing step. According to Mojag, the man had worn a gray suit on the night in question. Suits weren't exactly the clothes of choice out here in the north forty. The man probably worked in the downtown area. It was too far to commute from here to there. If he had something out here, it probably wouldn't be something he owned.

A rental would be more likely.

Suddenly the dirt road appeared in front of Shade.

Nothing was visible in either direction.

No cars.

No humans.

No animals.

No nothing.

She turned left and headed deeper into the topography. The walking was easier now. The scratching against her legs was gone.

She picked up the pace.

42

Wilde was about to leave the office when the door opened and Alabama tossed a white cat inside. "Watch him for a second, will you? I'll be back in ten minutes."

"Alabama!"

Too late, she was already gone.

He headed for the window and shouted down, "I don't have time to babysit a cat."

"Just leave him alone," she said. "He won't hurt anything." She took two steps then looked back up, "His name's Tail."

"Whose is he?"

"Yours," Alabama said.

"No he's not."

"Okay, ours then," she said.

"Alabama!"

She blew him a kiss and disappeared behind a beer truck.

Wilde turned to find the animal on his desk.

Tail.

Tail the cat.

Great.

He hesitated, not sure that he was actually going to do what he was thinking about doing, then said, "What the hell?" and picked it up.

"Where did Alabama get you? Did she find you in an alley? You have enough dirt on you, that's for sure." The cat said nothing. It was pure white except for the tail which was pure black. The eyes were green, just like Wilde's.

He set it on the desk.

It walked over to the coffee cup, stuck its head in and took a few careful laps with a sandy pink tongue. It worked the liquid around in its mouth, as if deciding, then stuck its head back in and didn't stop lapping until there were only a few sporadic drops left.

Suddenly the door opened and Alabama walked in.

"Have you two bonded yet?"

"That will never happen. This thing has to go."

Alabama picked it up, then hugged Wilde.

"He's part of us now," she said. "We're a threesome."

"This is not happening."

"It already has, cowboy, so just get used to it. You can change the name if you want. That's just the first thing that came to me."

Wilde shrugged.

"Actually I sort of like it," he said. "Not the cat, the name. What I'm saying is that if a cat has to have a name, that's a good one for this one." Then he noticed something he didn't before.

The cat had a limp.

"Something's wrong with his front leg," he said.

Alabama nodded.

"I'm guessing he only has eight lives left," she said. "So we need to keep that in mind."

Wilde put a serious expression on his face.

Then he told Alabama about finding a book of red matches at Nicole Levine's house earlier this afternoon.

She studied them, especially the handwriting, and said, "they both start with a six—604 and 616."

Wilde nodded.

Right.

He knew that.

"The sixth month of the year is June," Alabama said.

Wilde tilted his head.

"What are you saying, that these are dates?"

"Could be. June 4th and June 16th."

Wilde scratched his head.

"June 16th hasn't come yet," he said. "It wouldn't make sense."

"It would if that's when he's going to strike next," Alabama said.

Wilde lit a pack of matches on fire.

Tail scrambled off the desk so fast that he lost traction and landed on his side. Then he ran to the other side of the room and cowered in the corner.

"Sorry about that, but get used to it," Wilde said. Then to Alabama, "So what you're saying, if I'm following you correctly, is that he leaves a clue with the last victim as to when the next victim will be."

She nodded.

"It makes as much sense as anything."

Today was June 12th.

Thursday.

June 16th was in four days.

Monday.

43

The rattlesnake fangs sunk so deep and so white-hot into Fallon's flesh that she dropped to the ground. The reptile was right next to her face, recoiled and ready to strike again.

Then a large rock hit it with a frantic force.

It uncoiled and tried to get away.

It was injured.

Most of it worked but part of it didn't.

Part of it was flat.

It was cut.

Guts were hanging out.

Fallon didn't care.

It was leaving, that's all that mattered.

Then another rock crashed down, thrown by Jundee with every ounce of strength he had. It ricocheted off the dirt next to the snake's head.

A miss.

Jundee tripped and landed spine first on a rock the size of a breadbox. A noise came from his mouth, partly a scream, partly pain, partly surprise. It was strange enough to force Fallon's eyes off the snake and onto him. Even in that split-second, she could tell he was hurt to the point where he didn't move, other than to roll onto his side and curl his legs.

The snake dragged its broken body behind a man-sized boulder and didn't reappear.

Fallon focused on her leg.

The fang marks were red and obvious but weren't bleeding. The swelling hadn't started yet. She could wiggle her toes. The poison hadn't taken effect yet. She got to her feet and went to Jundee who was still on his side. His face was etched with pain. Suddenly the snake reappeared and headed directly at them.

It seemed disoriented, crazy, unsure of where it was or what it was doing.

It was four steps away, now three.

Fallon grabbed a rock the size of a baseball, waited until the snake was a step away and then threw it directly at the head.

Bones crashed.

The head flattened.

The back end of the snake wiggled furiously for second after second after second, then all movement stopped.

Jundee stared in disbelief then focused on the pain in his back.

"I can't climb," he said.

"I'll help you."

"I'm not talking about getting out of here, I'm talking about getting up to that ledge and getting the briefcase."

"Are you nuts?"

"You're going to have to do it," he said. "My back's hurt too bad."

"No."

"Yes. This is our only chance. We need to do it and we need to do it right now."

Fallon looked at the ledge.

It was high, sixty feet minimum.

The wall was almost straight up.

There were a thousand ways to fall off it and die, even if her body wasn't full of poison.

44

Half a mile up the road Shade spotted a crude wooden house. No vehicles were parked by it. No signs of life came from it—the doors were shut, the windows were shut, the blinds were shut, the whole damn thing was shut as tight as a cage.

Visible Moon was in there.

Shade could feel it, even from a distance.

She quickened the pace, slowing only to pick up a rock the size of a grapefruit, more than adequate to smash a skull to oblivion.

Her blood was on fire.

It pumped through her veins with a force she hadn't felt for a long, long time.

This was it.

Everything had come down to this moment.

Be in there.

Be alive.

That's all I'm asking.

She watched the blinds for signs of movement as she approached. They hung as still and lifeless as death itself.

That was good.

Up close, the structure was even cruder than she thought, as if built without any knowledge or regard for codes. The front door was shut tight. She quietly put her hand on the knob and turned it ever so gently.

It was locked.

She walked around the circumference.

All the windows were shut.

The blinds were closed tight.

She walked around again, this time testing the windows to see if any were unlocked.

Negative.

They were all latched from the inside.

Now what?

Break a window and go in?

She walked to the front door and wondered one last time if what she was about to do was the best course of action. Then she took a deep breath and knocked.

A second passed.

Then another.

Then another.

No one came.

No vibrations came from inside.

Everything remained coffin-quiet.

She knocked again, louder, and shouted, "Anyone home?"

Nothing happened.

"Visible Moon. Are you in there!"

More nothing.

Nothing but nothing.

She could be passed out from drugs. She could be hogtied and gagged.

Shade had to go in.

There was no getting around it.

She headed around to the back and punched a window with the base of her palm. The glass shattered into sharp dangerous pieces. Most fell inside but some landed at her feet. Jagged edges still hung in the frame. She carefully reached through and felt around for a latch.

She couldn't find it.

It wasn't on the top.

It wasn't on the bottom.

It wasn't on the side.

Damn it.

It must be a fixed window.

She'd have to slither in.

She stuck her head close to the opening and shouted, "Visible Moon, are you in there?" She heard nothing. "If you can hear me, kick or something. Make a noise."

No noises came.

She found a good-sized rock and began to knock the jagged pieces of glass off the bottom. Suddenly a noise appeared, barely audible but audible nonetheless. It didn't come from inside the house.

It came from the road.

She concentrated on it.

It was a car.

Someone was coming.

45

Alabama wasn't a fan of Wilde's theory that the pinup killer was actually Senn-Rae's own client, even given the fact that the guy had somehow managed to never meet Senn-Rae face to face. "If someone was a killer, why would they hire someone to find out who they are? It doesn't make sense."

"Yes it does."

"How?"

"Simple."

He let it hang.

"Simple how? Tell me."

"Simple as in easy."

She punched his arm.

"Stop being you for a minute and tell me."

He smiled.

"Simple because it's a game he plays with his upcoming victims. He gets close to them. Every interaction is another kiss on the lips. He knows what's going to happen in the end. She doesn't. He lays in bed at night and jacks off to it."

Alabama rolled her eyes.

"Thanks for the visual," she said. "So is it your theory that the guy got close to the boxcar girl too, before he killed her?"

Wilde nodded.

"That's my theory," he said. "Same thing with Natalie Levine. We need to dig into her past, meaning the week or two prior to when she disappeared, and find out who was in her life."

Alabama picked up Tail and paced by the windows.

"Let's suppose you're right," she said. "Let's suppose I'm right too about the numbers on the matches being dates. When you put the two together, than means that the guy is going to kill Senn-Rae on the 16th which is Monday."

"Either kill her or abduct her on that date," Wilde said. "We don't know which one the date refers to."

"True. Either way, she's safe until then."

Wilde considered it.

"Probably."

"So all we have to do is wait until Monday, guard her like a hawk on that day and catch him in the act."

Wilde chewed on it.

Then he frowned.

"The more I think about it, suppose the date refers to the kill date," he said. "He might do the actual abduction days before that."

"So she's in danger right now, even as we speak."

"Potentially," Wilde said.

He walked to the rack, pulled his wallet out of his suit jacket and counted what was inside—$120.

He gave half to Alabama.

"There's a sporting goods store on 16th near California," he said. "Go down there and buy two Colt 45s and two boxes of bullets."

"What for?"

"One's for Senn-Rae," he said. "The other's for Shade."

"What about me?"

"What about you?"

"I should have one too."

"A gun?"

Wilde grunted and said, "You have Tail."

"*We* have Tail," she said. "Remember, he's half yours."

Alabama stuffed the money in her bra and headed for the door.

"Keep an open mind," she said.

"About what? Tail?"

"No, Tail's already a done deal," she said. "I'm talking about your theory that Senn-Rae's client is the killer. You might be totally wrong. It might be someone else altogether." She smiled and added, "No wrestling with Tail while I'm gone."

Wilde smiled.

"Talk to Jimmy at the store," he said. "Tell him the guns are for me. He'll give you a deal."

"A deal up or a deal down?"

"Not funny."

"A little funny," Alabama said.

"Okay, a little."

46

Fallon cast a nervous glance at the rattlesnake to be sure it wasn't creeping at her with a last breath of hateful life. It wasn't. It was lying right where it should be. Its head was still smashed beyond belief and tilted the exact same way as before, except now three or four flies were crawling on it.

Flies were good.

Flies meant death.

Then she noticed something she didn't expect, not at the fangs end but at the other one.

The rattle wasn't there.

She bent down for a closer look. Sure enough, the end of the reptile slimmed to a point. The end was brown, like a rattle, but it wasn't a rattle. The rattlesnake wasn't a rattlesnake.

"It's a bull snake," she shouted to Jundee.

"Is that good or bad?"

"Good," she said. "Beyond good, way beyond good. Bull snakes look exactly like rattlers but they're not. That's their defense mechanism. The important thing is that they're not poisonous."

"They're not?"

"No."

"So you're okay?"

"I'm beyond okay."

"Good," he said. "You can climb up to the ledge."

"No."

"But—"

"It's too steep plus we're losing light. We need to get the hell out of here."

The place they came down turned out to be too steep for Jundee to negotiate with his back the way it was, but they found a calmer incline a quarter mile farther down the valley that worked.

When they got back to the car, there was a sliver of light left, a window of ten or fifteen minutes where they'd be able to see a short distance.

Jundee grabbed Fallon's arm and squeezed.

"I have a plan."

He pulled the car over to where it was just above the ledge, killed the engine, left the gearshift in first and set the emergency brake.

Then he got a length of rope from the trunk, tied it around the back bumper and tossed the loose end over the side of the cliff.

The plan was for Fallon to walk down the side of the cliff until she was able to see over the outcropping and down onto the ledge. Then they could find out once and for all if the briefcase was there.

Fallon wasn't afraid.

That wasn't the issue.

Her concern is that the rope wasn't long enough.

"Just try and see how far you get," Jundee said.

She hesitated.

"We're almost out of light," Jundee added. "Five minutes, then we're history."

Fallon took a deep breath, tugged on the rope to be sure it was snug, then headed down.

She got to the very end of the rope.

Bad news.

"I need five more feet."

"We don't have five more feet."

"I'm coming up then."

"Hold it."

She stayed where she was.

"What?"

"Let me see if I can back the car up a little," Jundee said.

"Okay but hurry," she said. "My hands are getting tired."

Jundee got behind the wheel, fired up the engine and put the clutch in neutral. With his foot on the brake, he released the emergency brake. Then he lifted his foot slightly off the pedal to see if Fallon's weight was enough to pull the car back.

It wasn't.

He shifted into reverse and let the clutch out as easily as he could.

The car moved backward.

The speed was perfect.

He was moving but barely.

It was hard to tell how far he was going.

Just a little more, then he'd stop.

He went a foot, maybe two, then put his foot on the brake and rolled down the window.

"How's that?" he shouted.

"One more foot."

He exhaled.

He eased the clutch up.

The car moved backwards ever so slowly.

Perfect.

"Six more inches," he told himself.

Six more inches.

The car rolled back ever so slightly, five or six inches, maximum. Jundee was just about to put the full weight of his leg into the brake when the car suddenly jerked backwards and tumbled off the edge.

47

The car coming towards the house was a problem, a big problem, potentially fatal. Shade had busted a window. That would lead to a search, an immediate search. She needed to get out of there.

The topography was wrong.

It was mostly flat and treeless. The best cover would be behind a clumping of rabbit bush.

She ran into the prairie, keeping the house between her and the car. Fifty yards, that's how far she got before the sound of the vehicle got to the house and quit.

She took another twenty steps.

The driver would be at the front door now.

Five more steps; he'd be inside.

Ten more steps; he'd see the broken window and look out.

She dove behind a three-foot-high rabbit bush and laid flat.

It was barely big enough.

Her heart pounded.

She'd be okay unless the guy walked out into the field.

Stay calm.

She remained perfectly still. Her head was too close to the ground to see if anyone was coming. That was dangerous but so was the opposite.

A minute passed.

If the person was going to come into the field, it would be happening by now.

She pictured a man.

A big man; a big man with a gun.

What was that?

A vibration?

Was it feet walking on the ground?

It disappeared.

She felt nothing.

She heard nothing.

She detected nothing.

Had it just been her imagination or had someone merely stopped en route to scout around?

No.

It wasn't her imagination.

There it was again, a distinct vibration.

Someone was out there.

A voice shouted, "Come out now and there won't be a problem." It was twenty or thirty steps away, a man's voice.

Shade's heart raced.

She started to get up when the voice came again, "If you make me hunt you down you're going to regret it. I swear on your grave you'll regret it."

She flattened.

"Okay, have it your way," the man shouted.

Then a gunshot exploded.

48

Late thursday afternoon, Wilde arranged a meeting with Senn-Rae at his office, then hid in the alley behind her building and watched as she left. He sprinted up the stairs two at a time, worked the lock carefully so as to leave no marks, and slipped inside.

His blood raced.

This was wrong.

He had no choice but still it was wrong.

Back at his office, Alabama would tell Senn-Rae that Wilde just called in to say he was running a little late.

She'd keep the woman there.

That didn't give him much time.

The goal was simple, namely find out who Senn-Rae's mystery client was.

Get his name.

The desk was cluttered with papers. He shuffled through them, looking for something that indicated it belonged to the case he was looking for. Senn-Rae's handwriting was Greek, barely readable.

Come on.

Come on.

Come on.

He found something of interest on the corner, a yellow legal-sized notepad with the top ten or twenty sheets that didn't lie flat, as if they had been used for notes. Halfway through was a page of interest.

6/12
TELEPHONE FROM MR. SMITH.
DEMAND IS $10K, DUE MONDAY.
9

There was no phone number or first name.

Wilde flipped to the following pages, which were also dated 6/12 at the top but related to other cases. Was Smith the client's real name or was she keeping the file in code at his request?

What did the 9 stand for?

Did it mean 9 p.m.?

Was something going to happen tonight at nine, a meeting perhaps?

Or did the 9 mean the guy had $9,000 to give but that was it?

He put the pad exactly where he found it.

If Senn-Rae took notes regarding that conversation, she must have done the same with the earlier ones.

Where were they?

On the corner of the desk was a stack of yellow notepads that looked totally spent. Wilde flipped through, going by the dates in the upper left corners.

When did Senn-Rae first talk to Mr. Smith?

Think.

Think.

Think.

Okay, she came to see Wilde yesterday, Wednesday, and said she'd been retained the day before. That would be Tuesday, June 10th.

Wilde was in the wrong legal pad.

He picked up the next one.

It was wrong.

Wronger, even.

Then he found the one he needed and flipped through it.

There it was.

Bingo.

6/10
NEW CLIENT – MR. SMITH – NOT REAL NAME
HIGHLY CONFIDENTIAL
$2,000 CASH RETAINER BY MESSENGER, 1 HOUR.
HE'LL CALL BACK AFTERWARDS AND EXPLAIN CASE
KEEP NO NOTES

Wilde flipped through the following pages to see if any more notes existed on the case.

He found none.

He continued searching all the way through Wednesday, yesterday, just in case there was a phone call he wasn't aware of.

He found none.

Damn it.

Damn it to hell.

49

Shade got as still as death behind the rabbit bush, not moving, not breathing, not looking, not giving the man a reason to get excited. He passed within ten steps, judging by his shouting and swearing, before firing the gun in rapid succession three times and heading back for the house.

Even then Shade didn't move.

Three minutes passed before she raised her head enough to look around the immediate area, not all the way to the house, just close by.

She saw nothing.

She got her eyes up higher and still saw nothing.

Now what?

Slither away deeper into the terrain?

Stay put just in case the guy was up on the roof scouting around with binoculars?

The ground was hard.

Her body was tight from forcing motionless on it so long. If the man returned, she wouldn't be able to stay that still for that long again. It would be better to get out of there.

The topography to the south was flat.

The north had a few more curvatures, not a lot, but a few.

She stayed low and headed north.

Ten steps passed.

Then twenty.

Then fifty.

The roof of the house disappeared entirely over a curvature. Shade got into a full upright position and ran. No shouting came behind her.

No gunfire erupted.

Five minutes went by.

She slowed to a trot.

Ten minutes went by.

She slowed to a walk.

She was safe now.

The danger was gone.

Some type of structure loomed up ahead, something in the nature of a storage shed, made of dark, blotchy wood long past its prime.

She headed for it.

It was about the size of a small garage, maybe used for remote storage of farm equipment or tools at one point. It sat at the end of a long narrow dirt road that was overgrown with weeds and vegetation. That would take her back to the main road. It would be easier walking than through the bare field.

A weather-beaten red cloth of some sort dangled off the roof and down the side for a foot or so.

Strange.

What was up there?

She couldn't tell.

It was too high.

She jumped up and grabbed it but it didn't pull loose of

whatever it was attached to.

It was snug.

She pulled harder.

It came farther down but was definitely attached to something.

She tugged.

Something dangled over the edge of the structure.

It was an arm.

A human arm.

She pulled again with a solid yank.

A head came over the edge and hung limp.

Matted, clumped blond hair draped down from it and swayed for a few heartbeats.

The head belonged to a woman.

She'd been dead for some time.

Shade stepped back and thought about whether she should actually do what she was thinking about doing. Then she decided to just go ahead and do it.

The red cloth was a scarf.

It was wrapped around the neck.

Shade got a double-hand hold on it and tugged, not sure whether it would cut through the neck or pull the body off.

The body was snagged on something.

Shade pulled harder.

Suddenly it shot forward and tumbled down.

It landed in a clump.

What Shade saw she could hardly believe.

The woman was scantily clad in a short white skirt.

Under that were red panties.

On her feet were red high-heels.

On her legs were nylons with a line down the back, held up by a garter belt. Her top was a white blouse with the bottom buttons undone. The ends were tied in a knot above her bellybutton.

She looked like a pinup girl.

50

The more Wilde thought about the mysterious "9" in Senn-Rae's notes, the more he began to believe it referred to nine o'clock. Maybe it meant that Mr. Smith would call Senn-Rae tomorrow morning at nine.

On the other hand, maybe it meant nine tonight.

Maybe they planned to meet.

Maybe Mr. Smith was taking a cat-and-mouse game to the next level.

Wilde would hang in the shadows outside tonight and see.

Starved.

That's what he was right now, starved.

"I'm getting hungry," he said. "It's time to cook the cat."

Alabama punched him on the arm.

"Don't even talk like that." Then to Tail, "He's just joking."

Wilde grabbed his hat and dipped it over his left eye.

"Let's go to the Down Towner. My treat."

"Bryson, are you okay?"

"Yeah, why?"

"You just said, My Treat."

"I did?"

"Yes."

He put a surprised look on his face and shook his head in confusion. "That just goes to show what hunger can do to the brain."

They were halfway out the door when the phone rang.

Wilde gave it an evil look.

This would delay food by seconds.

The voice of Shade came through, excited, urgent, fast. "I think I know where Visible Moon is being kept," she said. "I need your help to get her. The guy has a gun."

Wilde took his hat off.

"Keep talking."

She did.

The more she said, the less Wilde got convinced. When she was done he said, "You got nothing, other than the place is remote. You admit yourself that you shouted in and didn't get any response."

"She's drugged."

Wilde frowned.

"He came after me with a gun," Shade added.

"Every yoyo out in the sticks has a gun," he said. "More like ten. If I was him and came home to find someone tried to break in, I'd take a few minutes to flush the field too."

"The blinds were all closed," Shade said. "That's because he didn't want anyone snooping around."

"Or maybe it's because he didn't want the sun turning the place into an oven while he was gone," Wilde said. "I'll bet if we looked around we could find twenty other places just like that one. From where I sit, you want Visible Moon to be there and you're letting your brain convince you it's true."

Silence.

"Just help me check it out," she said.

Wilde exhaled.

"I'm up to my ass in alligators," he said. "You know that. Let's just stick with our bait plan. Tonight, you'll come back to the hotel room and we'll see if anyone shows up."

"Bryson—"

"I can't go on wild goose chases," he said.

"Fine, I'll do it myself."

Wilde almost relented.

He almost said he'd join her but he didn't.

Time was too valuable.

"Come on, Wilde," Shade said. "This guy's a killer. I can feel Visible Moon inside that house. I know this sounds a little extreme but I know in my heart I'm right."

"What do you mean, he's a killer?"

"I found a body," she said.

Wilde froze.

"You did?"

"Yes."

"Where?"

She told him about finding a woman on top of a shed a half-mile from the man's house. The woman was dressed like a pinup girl.

"He killed her," Shade said.

"How to you know?"

'He's the only one around."

A beat.

"Swing by my office," Wilde said. "We're going out there."

"We are?"

"We are."

He hung up, gave Alabama a five from his wallet and said, "Run down to the Mill and get some grub to go. We're going to eat in the car."

She almost asked for an explanation but headed for the door instead.

"What do you want?" she asked.

Wilde thought about it.

"Cat if they have it," he said. "Otherwise a turkey sandwich. Make it two, plus an RC and chips."

She threw him an evil look, said *Cat if they have it,* then left.

Wilde pulled his gun out of the drawer, checked the chambers and found everything ready to go.

He picked up Tail.

"Just kidding."

51

At the dead body out in the sticks, too much of the face had been eaten away by birds, bugs, sun and wind for Wilde to tell if it belonged to Natalie Levine. He looked around for a way to get on top of the shed and found nothing readily obvious. No ladders were lying in the dirt. The structure had no windows or ledges.

He pulled one of the hinged doors open.

The floor inside was dirt.

A few rusty remnants of machinery were abandoned in place.

Spider webs choked everything.

"She wasn't held captive in here before she was murdered," Wilde said. "No one's been here for years."

Shade agreed.

"I wonder how he got her up there," Wilde added. "It's too high to throw her. He must have brought a ladder."

Shade shrugged.

"He could have backed a pickup in and stood on the side."

Yeah.

Right.

"I want to get up there," Wilde said. "You didn't bring a ladder or a pickup with you, did you?"

Shade smiled.

"Tell Alabama I feel sorry for her," she said.

"You mean for having to spend time with me?"

"Exactly."

"I'll tell her."

He gauged the distance to the roof, jumped up and caught the edge with his hands. He hung for a heartbeat, trying to figure out if splinters were poised to dig into his flesh. He didn't detect any and muscled up.

"He could have done what I just did and then pulled her up with a rope," he said.

"Maybe."

Wilde looked around.

He found no red matchbook.

That pointed towards the victim being Natalie Levine, since a matchbook had been left behind in her clothes. One wouldn't be here too unless the guy placed two of 'em. Then again, maybe he did. Maybe he put one at the victim's house to show he'd been there and a second at the body to tie up the fact that he was the one who did it.

Wilde needed to find out who the prior woman was, the one on the boxcar.

He needed to get inside her house.

He needed to see if there was a second matchbook there, in addition to the one he found at the murder scene.

There were no cigarette butts on top of the shed. That wasn't surprising. They would have blown away by now.

"Nothing up here," he said.

He was just about to lower himself down when something in his peripheral vision grabbed his attention. It was something on the smaller side, mostly buried by dirt.

He picked it up and scraped it off.

It was a money clip.

A number of bills were still inside.

Two fives and fourteen ones.

He shook the dust off each bill one at a time, then folded them up and stuck them in his pocket. A closer examination of the clip itself showed no markings or engravings.

Too bad.

Wilde shoved it in his pocket and made his way back to the ground.

He and Shade spent the next half hour examining the ground around the shed, fanning out in an ever-widening circle.

They found nothing.

No cigarette butts.

No red matchbooks.

No nothing.

"I wonder how she was posed up there," Wilde said.

Shade exhaled.

"We're wasting time," she said. "We need to go get Visible Moon."

52

From the body, Shade and Wilde crept through the field towards the house. A vision shot into Shade's brain, a vision where Visible Moon was drugged and unconscious on a ratty mattress; one ankle was chained to the wall; a few remnants of clothes were all she had left.

Her legs were spread.

A man was between them.

His pants were pulled down to his knees.

He was thrusting into her.

The fat in his ass jiggled.

Over in the corner, Tehya's scalp hung from a string.

"What's wrong?" Wilde asked.

The words snapped her back to reality.

"Nothing."

Wilde had a gun in his right hand.

"Let me carry that," Shade said.

Wilde shook his head.

"We don't know that she's in there," he said. "We don't know anything yet other than we have a body back there. For all we know, this guy's totally innocent."

"He's not," Shade said. "I just had a vision. He's in there raping her even as we speak."

"Yeah, well, I don't believe in visions."

"You will in five minutes. Then you can apologize."

When they got close enough to see the front of the house, there was no car there.

"No one's home," Wilde said.

Shade hesitated.

"He's in there," she said. "It's a trap. He left his car up the road and doubled-back on foot."

"Why would he do that?"

"Because he hasn't caught me yet."

They got up to the house and listened.

No sounds came from within.

The window coverings were drawn.

The front door was locked.

The back window was boarded with plywood.

All the windows were shut tight.

Shade picked up a solid rock and threw it at the closest window. The shattering of glass split the silence like an axe.

She looked at Wilde and took a deep breath.

"If he kills me, kill him back."

She started to crawl through.

Wilde pulled her back.

"Wait here."

53

Inside the structure with the gun in hand, Wilde went from room to room and found no one there, not in the way of a man or in the way of a Visible Moon. He opened the front door and let Shade in. She immediately headed for the back bedroom.

A ratty mattress was on the floor.

Shade squatted down and ran her hand over it.

"This is the exact mattress from my vision."

Wilde studied her to see if she really believed what she was saying.

She did.

"There's food in the kitchen," he said, "but the house is pretty much empty except for the mattress. So someone was holed up here."

Shade paid him no attention.

Her attention was on the mattress.

She was looking for something.

Then she picked something up and held it in front of Wilde's face. At first he didn't see anything but then realized she had a hair.

Shade stretched it out.

"See how long this is?"

It was three feet.

"See what color it is?"

It was pitch-black.

"This belongs to Visible Moon," Shade said. "Hardly anyone has hair this long unless they're Indian."

Wilde nodded.

"There's no ropes or anything like that," he said.

"He took everything," Shade said. "After he saw the window broke this afternoon, he didn't know if someone had come in and seen her or not. He had to assume they did. So he abandoned ship. He got out while the getting was good." She sat down on the mattress and bowed her head. "While he was taking her, I was busy going the other way through the field, saving my own ass."

Wilde sat next to her and put his arm around her shoulders.

"He had a gun," he said. "You didn't know for sure she was in here. You did the right thing."

"No."

"Yes."

"No," she said. "Out in the field, he shot five or six times. He was probably out of bullets. I should have confronted him. If I'd done that, we wouldn't be here right now."

"Not true," Wilde said. "For all you know he had a knife too. Remember, he scalped Tehya. He would have done the same to you. If you had confronted him, the only thing different is that you'd be dead right now and no one, including me, would know about this place. At least now we know he was here. We have a starting point to track him."

Shade shook her head.

"I never even raised my head up to see what he looked like," she said. "The only thing I cared about was saving my own ass."

"If you'd looked up, he would have seen you," Wilde said. "The bottom line is that we need to find something here to use. Let's look around."

They found three more strands of hair on the bed, plus two in the bathtub drain. "He let her wash up at least," Wilde noted.

"Probably to make it nicer when he screwed her."

"Well, you're in a good mood."

"You think he did it just because he was being nice?"

A beat.

"Actually, no," he said. "I think you're probably right. The interesting thing is that if he let her take a bath that means she wasn't unconscious all the time. At least part of the time, maybe even all the time, she wasn't drugged up."

Shade tilted her head.

"You're right."

Wilde smiled.

"Don't act so surprised. I'm like a monkey at a typewriter pounding on the keys. Sooner or later you have to expect me to make a word."

Shade didn't smile.

Instead she headed for the room with the mattress and said, "Come on."

He followed.

"What's going on?"

Shade pulled the mattress to the side. Something was scratched into the wood underneath it.

"This is Navajo writing," Shade said.

"What's it say?"

"I don't know, I never learned," she said. "It's Navajo though. That much I'm positive of."

They looked around for paper and pencil to copy the marks onto. There was none to be had so Wilde ripped a door off the kitchen cabinets and scratched the best replica he could with a key.

Shade wasn't impressed but satisfied.

"Close enough."

The kitchen had no refrigerator and all the food was non-perishable. Most was canned—beans, tuna fish, corn, chili. Some of it was in boxes—crackers, cereal, tortilla chips. Based on the trash, she'd been kept here since the abduction. None of the food items had any markings to indicate that they'd been bought at a certain grocery store as opposed to another.

There was also an ashtray.

It was filled with butts.

Camels.

"Did Visible Moon smoke?"

"No."

Suddenly Shade stood perfectly still and concentrated.

"What's going on?" Wilde said.

"Wait a minute."

Wilde waited.

Then Shade said, "He's out in the field watching us."

"How do you know?"

"I can feel him."

Wilde checked his gun, headed for the door and said over his shoulder, "Stay here."

Shade stayed still for a few heartbeats then checked the kitchen drawer for knives.

She found none.

Damn it.

She ripped off her blouse, wrapped it around the end of a ten-inch piece of broken glass like a handle and headed outside.

54

Fallon woke not knowing where she was or how she got there. The world was mostly dark with night, except for some kind of a mysterious light. Her brain was foggy.

The ground was hard and jagged. A stiff breeze blew.
 The howl of a coyote sounded in the distance.
 She rolled onto her back.
 Her arm fell down, no longer supported by the ground.
 She felt around.
 To one side was a cliff that went up.
 To the other was a precipice that dropped off.
 She was on a ledge, no more than two or three feet wide.
 "Jundee." No answer. "Jundee are you there?"
 Silence.
 She looked down. The mysterious light turned out to be a headlight shining almost straight up, not two headlights, just one. It was yellow and dim as if coming from a weak battery.
 "Jundee!"
 No answer.
 "Don't be dead! Don't leave me here!"

55

Wilde slipped into the shadows down the alley from Senn-Rae's loft as twilight choked the Denver skyline. With any luck, the mysterious "9" from Senn-Rae's notes meant a nine o'clock meeting tonight with her client, Mr. Smith, who may or may not be the pinup killer.
 The lights were on inside Senn-Rae's place.
 The shades were down.
 An occasional shadow floated past one of those shades.
 She was home.
 Good.
 If the meeting was someplace else, she hadn't left yet.
 Wilde checked his watch—8:37 p.m.

He'd cut it closer than he should have.

Right now, Shade-the-bait was parked in her hotel room after rattling Denver cages good and hard earlier today. Alabama was in the adjacent room with the lights out, waiting for a killer to come down the fire escape. Both women had guns, the ones purchased by Alabama this afternoon. That didn't mean they were safe. In a perfect world, Wilde would be there. If anything went wrong he had only himself to blame.

"I need two of myself," he told Alabama earlier.

She rolled her eyes.

"As if the world would allow that."

He hadn't had much luck discovering anything new after leaving the house this afternoon with Shade. A *For Rent* sign was in the weeds at the base of the road, which is why Shade checked the house in the first place. After they left this afternoon, they called the number on that sign a hundred times, hoping to find out who was renting the place.

The phone always rang.

That's all it did, though.

No one answered.

As to the Navajo writing scribed on the floor under the mattress, Shade said there was someone in town who could translate it.

"Who?"

"It's better that you don't know."

"I'll be the one to decide that."

"I don't mean better for you, I mean better for him."

She disappeared to find him.

She couldn't.

Suddenly the lights began to click off one by one until the loft was dark.

Senn-Rae was leaving.

The meeting was off-site.

That complicated things.

Wilde dipped his hat a little farther over his left eye and waited. When the woman appeared, she was wearing a sexy black dress, nylons with a line up the back and tall high-heels. Her hair was down.

That wasn't attorney attire.

What the hell?

She headed around the back corner of the building towards 16th Street. There, she stood for a few moments, checking her watch.

A black car pulled to the curb.

The back door swung open.

Senn-Rae hopped in.

The vehicle took off.

Wilde ran to the street and looked for a cab.

There was none.

Suddenly one came down the street from the opposite direction. Wilde ran across and jumped in front of it, waving his arms. The vehicle screeched to a stop. Wilde jumped in the back and said, "Do a one-eighty."

The driver looked at him, confused.

"Now!"

56

Jundee didn't respond to Fallon's calls, not once. He was dead or unconscious. Daybreak might come in an hour or it might not come for seven; Fallon had no idea what time it was. What she did know is that it was critical to not fall asleep. Sleep might make her roll off the ledge.

Tomorrow would be tough.

How would she get down?

She might have no choice except to jump.

There was nothing but rocks below, rocks and the hard, crooked metal of Jundee's car.

Something would break her leg or ankle or back or skull.

That was almost certain.

Then what?

She wouldn't be able to climb out.

There was nothing left up on the road to indicate someone was down here.

She'd rot to death.

She needed water.

Her throat was sandpaper.

Her eyes were dry.

Her brain was dry.

Her thoughts were dry.

If things were this bad already, how would they be tomorrow?

Wait, there were two cans of Coke in the car.

Right.

Good.

There was a bag of chips in there too.

No, wait.

There was only one can of Coke.

Jundee drank the other one.

Up above were a million stars. Under different circumstances they would have been beautiful. She looked for a constellation or a picture but found none.

Dots.

That's all they were, just a jumble of dry dots.

The briefcase was cursed.
> Everyone who touched it died.
> She wished she'd never seen the stupid thing.

DAY FIVE

June 13
Friday

57

Wilde woke Friday morning in a strange bed in a strange hotel room with a woman's arm draped over his waist and her head buried in his neck. He rolled onto his back and checked the woman's face.

It was Alabama.

The bottom half of her body was under a sheet.

The top half stuck out.

The half that stuck out had no clothes.

Her breathing was deep and heavy.

Dawn crept around the edges of the shade and softened the room with a golden patina. Wilde wasn't under the sheet. He was fully dressed in his shirt, pants, socks and shoes. He swung his legs over the edge of the bed as gently as he could and stood up. The motion must have set off Alabama's sensors because she rolled onto her back and opened her eyes.

"Morning, cowboy."

Then she yawned and stretched her arms above her head.

Her breasts were perfect.

Her arms were perfect.

Her neck was perfect.

If Senn-Rae hadn't come into his life, Wilde might well have bent over and tweaked Alabama's nipples. He might have run an index finger around her bellybutton. He might have given her what she wanted, every single bit of it.

Wilde picked the wrong cab last night. He picked someone who was more interested in obeying traffic laws than catching a black car. After Senn-Rae got away, Wilde went back to the alley behind her loft and waited. If the woman had gone on a business meeting, it shouldn't last more than an hour or so. She was gone for forty-five minutes then got dropped off alone. If Wilde had been smart, he would have hung out on 16th Street instead of the alley. If he'd done that, he'd have a license place number right now.

Oh well.

From there he went over to the hotel to help Alabama guard Shade.

One watched the fire escape while the other slept.

Nothing happened.

No one came.

Wilde had the last shift.

He must have laid down in bed for a minute to rest.

That was last night.

Now it was morning.

Alabama finished her stretch and cupped her hands behind her head.

"You were good last night," she said.

"We didn't do anything."

She frowned.

"You don't remember?"

"Yeah, I remember," he said. "I remember doing nothing."

She smiled.

"Almost had you," she said.

"No you didn't."

"Yes I did."

It was true.

She did.

"Do me a favor," he said. "Go check on Shade and be sure she's okay."

Alabama swung the covers off.

The bottom part of her body was as naked as the top.

"Yes, sir."

58

Fallon woke on the ledge and gasped at the brutal reality that she had fallen asleep. She could have rolled off a thousand times. She was still alive but only by luck. The sky was softer now. The thousands of stars were gone, reduced to all but a handful. The pitch-blackness of the sky had muted to a not-so-pitch blackness.

She could make out shapes.

She could see the ground under her body.

She could see the cliff.

She could see the car down below. It was farther than she thought. Yesterday when she'd looked up at the ledge, it had seemed far but not insanely high. Now, looking down, the distance took on a much deadlier edge.

"Jundee!"

He didn't answer.

She sat up and stretched her body as much as she dared. She rubbed the circulation back into her legs and arms and shoulders.

Her mouth was worse than sandpaper.

She couldn't even spit.

The sky lightened even more.

Daylight was coming.

The sun wouldn't break the horizon for some time but was throwing more than enough light to see close things. She needed to get down and she needed to do it now. If she thought too much about it she'd chicken out. She'd dwell on the fall. She'd dream up too many ways it could kill her.

She got down on her belly and swung her legs over the edge. She edged out even farther, letting her feet sink. Then she felt around for a foothold. She couldn't find one with her right foot but did get one with her left.

It wasn't much.

It was a couple of inches of rock at best.

She couldn't tell if the rock was loose or would hold her.

She put more weight on it.

It seemed stable.

"Okay, do it!"

She put her full weight on it and bent her leg to lower her torso down. Her hands came to the edge of the ledge. The next move would take her completely off the ledge and onto the cliff.

She made the move.

The wall was so vertical that she couldn't see beneath her feet. All she could do was get one loose, lower it and feel around for another hold.

She did it.

She actually got down another foot.

Then she did it again.

And again.

And again.

She might actually be able to do this.

Then something happened that made her heart pound. She couldn't get a lower foothold. She felt everywhere her foot could possibly reach and couldn't detect even an inch of jag to balance on.

She looked down as good as she could.

The car was below her.

It was a two to three story drop.

If she dropped straight down, she'd land on the bumper

and grill. If she kicked off a little bit, she'd land on the windshield. If she kicked off with all her might, maybe she'd clear the car entirely. Maybe she wouldn't. Maybe her head would snap into it.

What to do?

She held on.

Her breathing got more and more frantic.

The time was coming.

Think!

Okay, just drop straight down. That would be the shortest distance. Try not to let your ankle or shin wedge into anything. If that happens, you'll snap your bone right out of your leg.

Okay.

On three.

One.

Two.

Three!

59

The most important thing in the universe was to find Mojag and get him to translate the message Visible Moon scribbled on the flooring under the bed. To that end, Shade went to the fleabag Metro last night only to learn that no Indians were checked in or had been checked in at anytime during the last year, for that matter.

His pickup wasn't parked anywhere within a five block radius.

Nor had any of the neighboring hotels heard of him.

He hadn't marked the mailbox.

What the hell?

Where'd he go?

Did something happen back at the reservation?

Or, even more likely, did he actually spot the guy and take him? Did he do it that way to keep Shade out of it? Was he busy killing him off in some remote corner even as she thought about it?

No, he wouldn't do that.

He'd get information about Visible Moon first.

Shade searched until late, then gave up and headed for the hotel.

That was last night.

Now the first rays of daybreak were sneaking in the window.

She showered and headed for the financial district, which was the most likely place for Mojag to be if in fact he was still in town searching.

Something happened she didn't expect.

She actually spotted him in a coffee shop.

He was at a window table watching the crowd pass.

She headed in and sat down across the table.

"Surprise," she said.

The look on his face was just that, surprise.

"Where have you been?" she asked.

He explained.

The first night in town, he accidentally hit a young woman with his pickup truck down on Market Street. It wasn't his fault—she darted out right in front of him—but he fled the scene.

"Was she hurt?"

He shrugged.

"I don't know."

He got a hotel out of the area, north on Broadway.

The pickup was parked behind the hotel.

He hadn't been using it.

He'd been taking the bus.

"No sign of our man yet," he said. "I'm going to find him though. Today's the day. I can feel it."

Shade pulled a piece of paper out of her back pocket, unfolded it and pushed it across the table.

"What's this say?"

He wrinkled his brow.

"Where'd you get this?"

She explained.

Someone spotted an Indian woman in a car south of the city. Shade drove around looking for a potential hideaway in that area. She found a house that was empty except for a mattress and some food. Under the mattress, scratched in the wood, she found this message.

"It's Navajo," she said. "It's from Visible Moon."

"It's Navajo alright."

"So what's it say?"

Mojag shook his head.

"What did you do, try to make a copy of what was in the wood on this paper?"

"There was actually a step before that," she said. "We didn't have any paper with us so we scratched a duplicate of the floor onto a wooden cabinet door. Then I made this paper from that."

"That explains it," Mojag said. "What's here doesn't make sense. Little changes throw it off. I need to see the original. I need to see the floor itself."

"Okay, let's go."

60

Wilde didn't know what pose the woman on the shed had been left in but did know what she was wearing. His first job this morning was to go through the old editions of Dames in Danger to find the inspiration. It didn't take him long. There it was on page 23 of the March 1950 edition. The painting was unsigned but based on the brushstrokes and style it was done by the same nameless person who painted the boxcar pinup.

Same artist.

Same magazine.

Two pinup paintings.

Two pinup murders.

Both bodies had been staged on top of a structure in a remote area.

Who was doing it?

The artist?

Someone trying to frame the artist?

The publisher?

Some crazed reader?

Yesterday he dialed the number of the For Rent sign a hundred times and got nothing but ringing. He dialed again expecting more of the same and stood up when a woman's voice came through, "Hello?"

"Hello?"

"Yes, hello."

"Hey, I'm really sorry to bother you," Wilde said. "I was driving out in the country and noticed a For Rent sign. It had your number on it. I was wondering if it's for rent or what's going on."

"No, sorry."

"It's not?"

"No." A beat, "I thought we took that sign down."

"You did," Wilde said. "It was in the weeds. I thought it might have blown down. Is it already rented?"

"No, it's not for rent. We were going to rent it but no one called and then we changed our mind."

"Okay."

"Sorry."

"I understand."

Wilde almost hung up but searched for any lingering questions.

He found none.

Okay.

Good enough.

Dead end.

"Goodbye."

His focus turned back to the stack of Dames in Danger on the desk. What he needed to do was go through all of them and find all the paintings by the same artist.

Why?

He wasn't sure.

Maybe he'd see something he wasn't already seeing.

He sat down in his chair and spun around.

Then he took out a book of matches and set it on fire. The sweet smell of sulfur filled the air. The flames got higher and more intense. Wilde held them in his left hand, took the receiver off the phone with his right and dialed.

The same woman answered again.

"It's me again," Wilde said. "This is a weird question but I was wondering if anyone else called recently wanting to rent that place."

"Someone did, why?"

"When?"

Silence, she was thinking.

"I don't know, two weeks ago, maybe. Something like that."

"Two weeks ago?"

"Yes, give or take. Why? What's going on?"

"Did he say who he was?"

"He said his name was Mr. Smith."

Mr. Smith.

Mr. Smith.

Mr. Smith.

"Did he say why he wanted to rent it?"

"No, he just asked if it was for rent," she said. "I told him the same thing I told you, namely that it had been for rent but we changed our minds. We're going to fix it up this fall and make it into a weekend place."

"I didn't know you were going to fix it up this fall."

"Well, we are."

"Did he ever call back?"

"No."

"When was the last time you were out there?"

"God, I can't even remember," she said. "It's not furnished or anything. You can't live in it. I keep asking what's going on and you keep not answering."

He hesitated.

"I'm a private investigator," he said. "My name's Bryson Wilde. I'm trying to find a guy who might be interested in renting a place out in the country." He gave her his number. "Can you tell me anything else about Mr. Smith?"

No.

She couldn't.

"We only talked for a few seconds," she said.

Okay.

Good enough.

"Oh wait," the woman said. "I do remember one more thing. Just before he hung up, someone in the background—a woman—said something like, *You got a cigarette I can borrow?* Something like that. Something about a cigarette."

61

On three.
One.
Two.
Three!

Fallon released her grip on the cliff and pushed off slightly with her feet so she wouldn't rip her flesh on the jags. The freefall immediately shot her stomach into her mouth, a warning that something was dreadfully wrong, something that could kill her. She focused as specifically as she could on the car below.

It was coming too fast.

She couldn't pick a spot.

She couldn't adjust her body.

She couldn't do anything.

Wham!

Her body crunched and contorted with the impact. The first hit was onto the front end of the car and the second hit was onto the ground, flat on her back The air shot out of her lungs.

She was hurt.

How bad?

She immediately tried to get to her feet, desperate to know if the parts of her body worked. There wasn't enough air in her lungs to support the motion.

Lie here. Just lie here. Calm down for a second.

She stared up at the cliff.

She wasn't dead.

That was the main thing.

She was off the cliff and still alive.

Something tickled her upper thigh.

It was blood, lots of blood, flowing steadily out of a wide gash.

Her whole leg was covered.

Something on the car must have snagged her.

She got to her feet.

Her head spun but she forced herself to not fall.

She pulled her T-shirt over her head, ripped it and wrapped the pieces around the gash, then applied pressure with her hand.

Her thoughts were getting more and more unfocused.

She sat on the ground and leaned back against the car.

Just rest.

Just stay still until the bleeding stops.

Suddenly she had a terrible image.

Jundee was in the car.

He was right behind her.

Dead or unconscious.

"Jundee!"

Silence.

She got to her feet and braced herself to witness whatever carnage was waiting for her.

She looked in the window.

What she saw she could hardly believe.

62

Shade parked at the same place as before, by the bridge, to avoid getting blocked in. The guy was probably gone forever but there was no sense in taking a chance, even with Mojag at her side. They hoofed it through the prairie under a bright blue Colorado sky.

"I have someone after me," Shade said.

Mojag wasn't impressed but turned his head in her direction for a moment.

"Who?"

"Someone from the CIA."

"The CIA?"

"Yes."

"Why?"

"I'm with them," she said. "I'm an agent."

"I didn't know that."

"No reason you would," she said. "Anyway, someone's framing me. They're planting evidence to make it look like I'm a double spy."

"Why?"

"I don't know," she said. "It makes no sense. Here's the important thing as far as you're concerned. If I disappear, that's why. They got me. What I need from you is a promise that you'll keep looking for Visible Moon."

"That won't be necessary."

"Why not?"

"Because I'm not going to let anything happen to you. We'll stick together from now on."

She stopped and grabbed his arm.

"Listen," she said, "nothing you're doing has anything to do with me. I'm only telling you what I am so you'll understand what happened. If I disappear, just let it go. Concentrate on Visible Moon."

He grunted.

"Promise me," she said.

"I'll concentrate on Visible Moon, but first," he said. "If someone hurts you, they're not going to keep walking this planet as if nothing happened. We'll stick together."

"That's not wise."

"Why not?"

"We'll make more distance if I keep running down my end and you spend your time keeping your eyes peeled for the white man."

The structure appeared up ahead in the distance.

"That's it," Shade said.

Mojag picked up the pace.

No car was around and no signs of life came from inside the house. They entered through the back window, which was just as broken as before.

"It doesn't look like he's been back," Shade said.

Inside, Shade pulled the mattress to the side.

The scratches in the floor came into view.

"That's them," she said.

Mojag kneeled down and studied them.

He shook his head.

"This isn't good," he said.

63

Wilde walked to Senn-Rae's place, knocked on the door and entered without waiting for an answer. She looked up from her desk, startled. "You call your client Mr. Smith," Wilde said. "Is that a name he told you or one you came up with?"

"He used the name. Why?"

"Because another Mr. Smith has entered the picture," he said. Then he told her about the man who inquired about renting the house. "Two Mr. Smiths are one too many. They're one and the same. Your client is the pinup killer, no question."

Senn-Rae saw the logic.

She wasn't impressed.

"He doesn't strike me that way."

"Based on what?"

"Based on the way he talks," Senn-Rae said.

Wilde sat on the edge of her desk and leaned over.

"You went out last night a little before nine," he said. "What was that about? Did you have a meeting with Mr. Smith?"

The woman leaned back.

"You were spying on me?"

"No, I was protecting you."

She gave him a cold look.

"Someone was in my office yesterday," she said. "Was that you?"

Wilde's first instinct was to lie.

He went with it and said, "No."

"No?"

"No."

"You weren't in my office? That's what you're telling me?"

He shuffled his feet.

The lie didn't fit.

He didn't like telling it.

"Okay, I was," he said.

"So you were in my office."

"Right."

"And right now, when you said you weren't, you were lying."

"Technically that's correct," he said, "but only for a few seconds."

She stood up, walked to the door and held it open.

"Get out," she said.

"You're kidding, right?"

No, she wasn't.

"I brought you a simple case," she said, "a simple case to find out who's blackmailing my client. Instead of figuring that out, you spend all your time trying to figure out who my client is. Now you're spying on me, lying to me and doing whatever else you're doing that I don't even know about. Enough's enough, you're done."

"What are you saying, that you're taking me off the case?"

"You took yourself off the case," she said. "You had your chance, your chance is over. In hindsight I made a mistake."

"Look, I'm sorry if—"

She rattled the door.

"Keep the retainer."

"I don't want the retainer."

"Then send it back, I don't care," she said. "Use a messenger. I don't want to see you again."

64

Jundee wasn't in the front of the car, the back, hanging through a window, on the ground or anywhere else. He wasn't anywhere. There was dried blood on the front seat indicating he'd been in the car when it went over the cliff.

"Jundee!"

No response.

Everything inside the car was bunched up at the lowest point—the rear window. Fallon climbed inside and sifted through until she found what she was looking for, a can of Coke and bag of chips. She consumed them outside, leaning against the car.

The T-shirt wrapped around her leg was thick with blood.

She put a hand on the wound and pressed.

It was too big to close on its own, at least not for a long, long time—hours.

She didn't have hours.

The Coke did a little to take the sandpaper off her tongue but not much. What it did do was punctuate how seriously she had dehydrated.

Her skin was dry.

Her eyes were turning to dust.

She was on her way to dying.

She needed to get up to the road where someone would find her. She needed to do it now, this minute, before she lost even more of the little strength she had.

This was it.

It was now or never.

She muscled to her feet, got her balance and took one step after another, keeping pressure on the wound.

She could walk, that should have given her comfort, but it didn't. The effort was too great. It made her realize she couldn't climb.

Up ahead, a far distance, she saw something lying motionless on the ground.

As she approached, it took shape.

It was Jundee.

65

Mojag punched the wall. The plaster cracked. He punched it again. This time his fist went through. He pulled it out and paced.

"What's it say?" Shade asked.

Mojag shook his head with disgust.

"I will die tonight. I am ready. Do not cry for me."

Shade repeated it in her mind, then leaned against the wall and slumped to the floor. She buried her head in her hands and rocked. "Tonight" was last night, at the latest. It might have even been written days ago.

Do not cry for me.

It was so like Visible Moon to say something like that.

Mojag pulled a book of matches out of his jeans pocket, struck one and held the flame under the broken wall plaster until it caught.

Shade didn't understand.

"What are you doing?"

"Sending the guy a message," Mojag said.

The flames grew longer and spread up the wall.

Smoke collected at the ceiling.

Mojag took one last look at the writing on the floor, grabbed Shade's arm and pulled her to her feet.

"Time to go," he said.

66

Wilde left Senn-Rae's, fired from a case for the first time in his life. He headed down the stairs as the door slammed behind him. In the alley he leaned against the building and lit a cigarette.

Damn it.

Damn it to hell.

He headed back to his office.

Senn-Rae was a bitch.

Screw her.

He was almost at the corner of Larimer Street when he suddenly turned and went back. He threw the butt on the ground, ran up the stairs two at a time and pounded on the door.

Senn-Rae answered.

The look on her face hadn't changed.

It was as hard and cold as before.

Wilde picked her up, threw her over his shoulder and kicked the door closed with his foot. He carried her to the bedroom and threw her on the bed.

Her head bounced.

Blood came from her lower lip.

It must have cut on a tooth.

She wiped the back of her hand across it.

Wilde ripped his shirt off and threw it across the room.

"If you want me to stop, say so now."

She stared at him with defiance but said nothing.

Wilde straddled her and pinned her arms above her head. Then he licked the blood off her mouth.

"I hate you," she said.

"Join the club."

He ripped her clothes off and took her.

He took her hard.

He took her rough.

He took her with every ounce of power he had.

It's always strange when you end up in public immediately after having sex. You can picture yourself with strangers doing the same thing you just did no more than a few minutes ago. That's how the walk back to his office was after Wilde left Senn-Rae's place.

They didn't say anything after the fact.

Wilde simply got up and left.

He didn't mumble a word.

Neither did Senn-Rae.

Wilde didn't want to dilute what just happened, that's why he said nothing. Maybe it was the same for Senn-Rae, or maybe it was because she hated him, or maybe it was because she loved him.

He didn't know.

When he got back to the office, Alabama was hanging up the phone. She studied his face and said, "What happened to you?"

He tossed his hat at the rack.

He did it so quick he forgot to aim to the right.

The hat flew past the rack on the left, hit the wall and fell to the floor.

Alabama picked it up and tossed it back.

He tried again aiming to the right this time. It flew through the air on the exact path as before and ended up on the floor.

"I'm never going to get it."

"No you're not," Alabama said. "So answer my question. What happened to you?"

"Nothing."

"Nothing?"

"No, nothing," he said. "I just stopped over at Senn-Rae's to say hello."

Alabama rolled her eyes.

"What part of your body did you do the talking with?"

He wrinkled his forehead, then put a serious expression on his face and said, "Senn-Rae's client Mr. Smith is the pinup killer."

"How do you know?"

He lit a book of matches on fire and looked at her through the flames as he told her about the Mr. Smith, the second Mr. Smith, the one who inquired about the rental property.

Alabama was impressed.

"So our work's done," she said.

"Not quite," Wilde said. "She doesn't know who he is, remember?"

"She doesn't need to," Alabama said. "All she needs to know is that she has a problem. Just tell her to make up a story about why she has to drop out of the case."

"That won't get her off the guy's radar screen."

67

Fallon shook Jundee's limp body and got no response. The left side of his head was matted with blood but it was dry. The bleeding had stopped. His face was still warm and breath came from his lips. A faint pulse thumped in his neck.

He wasn't dead.

He might be in a coma but he wasn't dead.

She gauged the climb up and decided she couldn't do it; maybe later but not now. The struggle of staying awake all night on the ledge was assaulting her strength. She laid down next to Jundee with her face pointed towards the sky. The dirt was gritty on her back. The valley was still thick with shadows and would be for a long time. She put pressure on her leg.

Sleep.

She needed sleep.

There might be rattlesnakes.

Too much blood might seep out of her leg.

She didn't care.

The only thing she cared about was closing her eyes.

She needed everything to turn black.

Nothing else mattered.

If she died, she died.

Her life had been good, relatively speaking.

She had no regrets.

She closed her eyes.

The darkness felt like cool, clean water.

Then everything went black.

The next few hours were surreal. Jundee regained consciousness. They made it out of the valley and hitched a ride into Santa Fe with a cancer-nosed farmer who had a pronounced spit-gap between his front teeth. Fallon got her leg stitched up, Jundee got diagnosed with a mild concussion, then they hopped on the first Greyhound pointed towards Denver and claimed the back seat. The New Mexico desert rolled along at 65 outside their window.

"All that for no briefcase," Jundee said.

Fallon patted his knee

"Well, at least we had fun."

A smile crept onto his face.

Then he got serious.

"That was the worst feeling of my life, when I got out of the car after the crash and couldn't find you anywhere," he said. "Blood was dripping into my eyes, my head was spinning and I thought for sure you were squashed under the back of the car. That was the worst moment of my life, realizing that I'd killed you."

"Next time bring longer rope," Fallon said.

He shook his head.

"You're too much."

"The briefcase is cursed."

"There's no such thing as cursed," he said. "There's such a thing as stupidity and I had more than enough of that to go around last night. But cursed, no."

"There's nothing good about any of this," Fallon said.

"We can't turn back now."

Fallon pulled back and focused on his face.

"You're not serious," she said.

"I am. We need to find that second briefcase."

"Why? Who cares?"

He frowned.

"I think the two briefcases together are the plans for a bomb."

"An atomic bomb? Like Hiroshima?"

He shook his head.

"No, something bigger."

"What's bigger than Hiroshima?"

"That's what we're going to find out. We need to find out more about the guy who was transporting the briefcases, too. I'm pretty sure he's a spy of some sort."

"That's crazy."

"Is it? He had the documents sorted into two briefcases that couldn't be put together without a code," he said. "He was also carrying a gun and lots of cash. Don't forget about the two guys in the car who chased you, too. My money says they were CIA or FBI; either that or they were other spies who knew the guy was en route and were out to steal everything from him. Whatever's going on, it's huge."

"Cursed."

They rode in silence.

Immediately behind their seats, the diesel engine rumbled and spit fumes into the air. The deadly New Mexico sun beat down on the roof of the Greyhound and baked the insides.

Every window was open.

It did no good.

"I just thought of something," Fallon said. "When I came out of the valley that first day, I had the one briefcase in my hand. There was a woman up on the road. She took a real interest in me. It was so weird that I wrote down her license plate number. Maybe she went down to the wreck after I left. Maybe the other briefcase was in the trunk—where I never looked—or on the ground, somewhere where I didn't see it. Maybe she took it."

Jundee's face lit up

He kissed her.

"Bingo."

68

Thick black smoke spiraled into the sky as Shade and Mojag walked away from the burning structure. Mojag stepped around a Yucca plant and said, "I have to be honest with you. Last night, I stopped feeling Visible Moon's presence in the world."

"Bullshit."

"I'm just saying—"

"She's not dead," Shade said.

Mojag gave her a sideways glance and said nothing.

The sky was warm and blue.

The air was alive with scents.

A bee sucked on an orange wildflower, paying them no mind as they walked past.

"She's not dead," Shade repeated. The words were defiant, daring Mojag to disagree.

"Okay."

"She's not dead."

"Okay, I said."

That was the end of the talking until they got to the car. Mojag slipped behind the wheel, fired up the engine and said, "So what's the plan?"

"Your half of the plan is the same," Shade said. "Get back down to the financial district and look at faces."

Back in Denver, Shade checked her hotel room and found it the same as she left it. No predators had come around sniffing for bait.

The plan wasn't working.

She needed to talk to Wilde.

They needed to come up with new sticks to beat the bushes with. They needed to figure out where the guy would hole up with Visible Moon now that his first choice was a pile of ashes. In hindsight, Shade shouldn't have let Mojag burn the place. Before, there was at least a chance the guy would return, possibly on an emergency basis. Now there was no chance at all.

She splashed water on her face, dabbed on rouge and lipstick and headed down to street level, making sure the door was locked behind her.

She hadn't gone thirty steps when something happened.

A person appeared next to her and fell into step.

It was the blond with the red baseball cap, the one who was there when Shade almost got hit by the taxi, the one who Shade thought might be following her. She was about thirty. Her body had a power to it. Shade wasn't sure if she could take her in a fair fight.

The woman smiled at her.

To a stranger, they were old friends.

"I have a gun," she said. "If you run, I'm going to shoot you. It doesn't matter that we're in public. If you run, you die. Do you understand?"

The woman would do it.

Shade could see it in her eyes.

"What do you want?"

"I want you to follow directions," the woman said. "If you do that, everything's going to be just ducky."

"Someone's setting me up."

"That's between you and them. My job is to bring you in if I can or kill you if I can't. Your choice."

Shade looked at her watch.

It was 11:48.

"I'm starved," she said. "Let's get some lunch. My treat."

"Funny."

"I'm serious," Shade said. "There are a few things you should know before you take me in—or kill me, my choice."

69

The questions were piling up so thick and deep that Wilde could hardly see over the top. Who was Senn-Rae's client? That was the big one. He lit a Camel, took a long drag and blew a smoke ring at Tail, who was sitting on the edge of the desk. The cat swiped a nervous paw at it and then jumped down.

The toilet in the adjacent room flushed.

Two heartbeats later, Alabama came out, in the process of pulling her zipper up.

She caught Wilde looking at her and said, "You want this up or down."

He blew smoke.

"Up."

"You're going to say down sooner or later."

He shrugged.

"I probably am." He flicked ashes into the tray and said, "I'm going to make an appointment with Senn-Rae for some time later today. While I'm keeping her busy I want you to get into her office and find out who her client is."

Alabama picked up Tail and sat on the edge of the desk.

"I thought you liked her."

"I do."

"You're going to drive her away," she said. "A girl needs her privacy."

Wilde wasn't impressed.

"Not this kind. This kind will kill her."

"I'm just saying," Alabama said. "The path you're on, you may end up saving her and loosing her in one simultaneous motion."

"Then that's the way it will be," he said. He told her about the notebooks on Senn-Rae's desk. If there was information as to where she went last night or something new about who the client was, that's where it would probably be. "The important thing is to put everything back exactly as you found it. Don't move anything until you study it first to see how it's laying. I still don't know how she knew I was in there."

"I'll be careful."

She held Tail in front of her face, rubbed noses and said, "Do you want to come with me? Yes? Was that a yes?"

The phone rang.

Alabama picked it up and said, "Wilde man's office." Then she handed it to Wilde.

"Some lady, not your squeeze."

He took one last drag and mashed the butt in the ashtray.

It turned out to be Jacqueline White from the homicide department.

"This call never happened," she said.

"It absolutely never happened."

"There's a rumor floating around about another missing woman," she said. "She's someone named Jennifer Pazour."

"You got an address?"

"No, it's not even anything official," she said. "It's just something I heard on the street. I don't know if it's true or not."

"Thanks, I owe you one."

"I've already been thinking about how you can repay me."

"Yeah? How?"

"Take me out some night and get me drunk."

"Done."

"You're messing with me."

"No, I'm serious."

"In that case there's a second part too," she said. "Afterwards, I want you to take me behind the bleachers, like before."

Wilde pulled up an image from high school, out back behind the bleachers, when they used to wrestle on the grass and pin each other down.

"You're a bad girl."

"Apparently so."

He hung up, pulled the phonebook out of the drawer and flipped to the P's.

Pazour, Jennifer.

There she was.

He grabbed his hat, dipped it over his left eye and told Alabama, "Come on. We're taking a field trip."

70

During a ten-minute stop in Colorado Springs, Jundee made two phone calls from the bus station. One was to the law firm to let them know that neither he nor Fallon would be able to make it in today because they got in a traffic accident down in New Mexico while on a case. The other was to a Denver PI named Jacob Whitecliff, with directions to find out who belonged to a certain license plate number, together with as much information as Whitecliff could dig up on that person in the next couple of hours.

Whitecliff had a report waiting when Jundee got to Denver.

"The plate belongs to a woman named Rebecca Vampire," he said.

Jundee raised an eyebrow.

"Vampire?"

"Right."

"You're messing with me. Just go on and get to the punch line."

"Ain't one," Whitecliff said. "She's an honest-to-God real life Vampire, at least in name. Rebecca Vampire, I kid you not. That's not the strange part, though. The strange part is that she lives in a fancy mansion up on Capitol Hill."

Jundee waited for the punch line.

"And?"

"And, there's no explanation for how she affords it," Whitecliff said. "She doesn't work. She's not married."

"Must have a sugar-daddy," Jundee said.

Whitecliff nodded.

"That's my guess. Either that, or she's up to her ass in illegal alligators."

"Is she a looker?"

Whitecliff shrugged.

"I drove by but she wasn't outside."

Jundee asked what the damage was and paid in cash, plus a $20.00 bonus.

"This is confidential," he said. "Don't get drunk and let your lips wag."

"Never," Whitecliff said. "Does this have something to do with one of your cases?"

Jundee nodded.

"Right."

"You smell like diesel."

"Thanks for noticing."

From Whitecliff's office, they picked up sandwiches from a deli and ate them as they walked to Fallon's hotel. The briefcase was still safe and sound under the bed.

Fallon headed for the bathroom and closed the door.

She got the shower going, stripped and stepped in as soon as the temperature got up.

The soap was heaven.

The diesel fumes were no match.

Jundee paced for two minutes, wondering if he dared to actually do what he was about to do.

Screw it.

Just go for it.

It's now or never.

He took off his clothes, every last stitch, and walked into the bathroom.

Then he pulled the curtain back.

Fallon's body was more perfect than he envisioned.

Her face was washed of all makeup.

Her hair was soaked and flat to her head.

Water ran down her forehead and cascaded off her nose.

She was too good for him.

He stepped back.

Suddenly she grabbed his hand and pulled him in.

"It took you long enough," she said.

"Yeah?"

"Yeah."

71

Shade and her captor ended up in a dark booth next to a jukebox in a place that served as a café in the day and a bar at night. The speakers were spilling out scratchy hillbilly music through a worn needle. The place smelled like a forest fire that someone tried to put out with beer. They ordered cherry cokes and burgers without the cockroaches.

"Nice place," Shade said. "What's your name?"

The woman took her baseball cap off and ruffled long blond locks with her fingers.

She was pretty.

A fly landed on her arm.

She shooed it off.

"London," she said. "My last name's *you can't talk your way out of this.*"

Shade tilted her head.

"Are you CIA, FBI or independent?"

"Indy, fully sanctioned."

Shade understood the term. It meant that the woman could kill her during capture if necessary and the CIA would ensure there would be no local charges or complications. She was as empowered as a cop bringing a scumbag into the station. She had full, unbridled immunity.

"Sanctioned," Shade said. "At least, so they say."

"So they say and so they do," London said. "They've already proven themselves twice."

"You've killed two people bringing them in?"

The woman nodded.

"Possibly three," she said. "That will depend on you."

Shade shrugged.

"Two's enough."

"I hope so."

"How much do you know of what's going on?"

"I know you're a double spy," London said.

"Alleged double spy."

"It makes no difference. My job's the same either way."

The food arrived.

The burger was hot.

The coke was cold.

Shade took a bite, chewed and said, "Not bad."

"I'm surprised."

"There's a mole in the company," Shade said.

London nodded.

"Right, you."

"No, not me," Shade said. "It's been going on for some time. Mole hunts are always done internally by the company. What that means is that the people in the top 10 percent are never under scrutiny because they're running the show. The mole in this case is someone in or very near that group. The white house has hired me directly to find out who the mole is. It's the mole who's setting me up. He or she found out I was snooping around. That's what this whole thing is about."

London wasn't impressed.

"Easy to claim," she said. "What proof do you have?"

"When you got the assignment, they told you to err on the side of killing me. They told you that bringing me in alive wasn't a top priority," Shade said. "Tell me I'm wrong."

Silence.

London took a bite of burger and washed it down with a slurp through the straw.

"I'm part Navajo," Shade added. "I have a half-sister named

Visible Moon. Monday night she was abducted out of a bar she worked at on a reservation in New Mexico. A friend of hers, also Navajo, got brutally murdered at the bar that same night. She was actually scalped."

"Scalped?"

"Right. The man who did all of this is from Denver," Shade said. "That's why I'm here. I'm trying to find Visible Moon. I can't do that if you get in my way." She sipped coke through the straw and said, "Who in the company hired you? Was it Penelope Tap?"

72

The woman who may or may not be missing, Jennifer Pazour, lived in a small brick bungalow on the far east side of the city, almost all the way to Colorado Boulevard. The front door was closed, so were the blinds. Wilde found a spot for Blondie three doors down and headed back on foot.

"I have a bad feeling about this," he said.

Alabama gave him a sideways glance.

"You always jump to the worst."

"Saves time."

He rapped on the front door.

No one answered.

He tried the doorknob and it actually turned.

"Unlocked," he said. "That's not good."

He opened the door, stuck his head in and said, "Anyone home?"

No one answered.

They entered and shut the door behind them.

"Shit."

The word came from Alabama.

She was looking at a photograph frame propped up diagonally against a lamp on an end table. Inside that frame was a picture of two women in their early twenties with their arms around each other, sticking their tongues out at whoever it was that was working the camera. The woman on the left was the pinup girl from the top of the shed.

"Goddamn it," Wilde said.

He didn't know whether to punch the wall, slump down on the couch or storm out the front door. Then his fist decided for him. It swung with all its might into the wall, hitting drywall instead of a stud.

Wilde shook plaster off.

They spent the next hour going through every crack and crevice in the house, assembling anything and everything that had any possible lead as to who the people were in the victim's life or what she'd been doing over the last month. What they didn't find was a red book of matches with a gold B.

"We're screwing up a crime scene," Alabama said.

Wilde frowned.

That was true.

Hearing the words made it even truer.

It was very possible—even probable—that the woman was abducted from this very place. That would explain why the door wasn't locked. The guy didn't bother with it. He got his pretty little pinup fun into the trunk of a car and then got the hell out of there.

"What we're doing is probably a felony or something," Alabama nodded.

"Add it to the list of reasons I'm going to end up in hell."

She smiled.

"How long is that list?"

"Ballpark?"

"Yeah."

He shrugged. "I don't know, two or three miles."

"No way," she said. "You've put two or three miles on just since I've known you."

"Thanks for noticing."

"You're welcome."

They dumped all their goodies into a pillowcase and left. On the walk back to Blondie, Alabama said, "Now what?"

"Now I make an excuse to see Senn-Rae and get her out of the office so you can have a look around."

"That'll be two break-ins in one day for me," she said. "That's not a personal best, in case you're wondering. Not even half a personal best."

Wilde knew he should smile.

He didn't though.

He was too preoccupied thinking about something they found in the house.

73

Early evening in a rented Ford Customline, Jundee and Fallon swung by Rebecca Vampire's stoic Capitol Hill residence, which turned out to be just three doors down from the governor's mansion. It looked like a castle dropped into a park and then surrounded by a six-foot stone wall with spikes on the top.

"I've seen smaller countries," Jundee said.

"Like Transylvania for instance."

He smiled.

"Like all the 'Vanias put together. Whatever she's doing,

she's doing it right." A beat then, "If we get busted in there, we're in some serious trouble. She's got to have connections to beat the band. She'll make sure we fry."

"Then let's forget it," Fallon said. "This whole briefcase thing is cursed. We ought to just take the one we have, burn it at the stake and call it a day."

"Can't."

"Why not?"

"We need to figure out if it's a bomb."

"You already said it is."

"True, it is, we do know that, at least I'm pretty sure we do. But we also need to know who had it, how they got it and where it was going. I don't know if it was our bomb being smuggled to the Russians, or theirs being smuggled to us, or what."

"Why do we care?"

"Because we need to know who the players are before we jump into the game."

"What game?"

"Whatever game is going on," he said. "The only thing I know for sure is that the stakes are high. That means there's money to be had. I'm not talking about wallets full of money. I'm talking about wheelbarrows full of it. Big, overflowing wheelbarrows."

"I still say forget it."

"Look, you can live twenty lifetimes and not get lucky enough to get even one chance like this," he said. "We got that chance right out of the box. Do you really want to walk away from it?"

She retreated in thought.

"Yes."

"Where's your sense of adventure?"

Fallon grabbed his forearm and squeezed.

"This isn't a game, Jundee."

He frowned.

"Look, we're either in this together or we're not," he said. "We need to get that decided and we need to do it right now." He paused. "So what's it going to be? Are we going to be partners and do what it takes to see this thing through or did we topple over the cliff back there for nothing?"

She exhaled.

"We're going to rot in hell."

"Does that mean you're in?"

"I think it does."

"No thinking."

"Okay, it does."

Jundee swung around the block and drove past the place one more time. The driveway gate was open. The woman's car was parked on the cobblestone next to a fountain up near the house.

"We'll bide our time until dark," Jundee said. "The briefcase is in there, I can smell it. It will be too big to fit into a safe. She'll have it hidden somewhere but it won't be in a safe."

"Jundee, you're a lawyer."

"And?"

"And if you get caught you'll be disbarred."

"I don't care."

"Yes you do."

"Okay, I care but it's worth the risk."

"I hope you're right."

"I'm always right."

Fallon watched the mansion disappear behind them, then the corner of her mouth turned up ever so slightly.

"Except for when you talk," she said.

Jundee laughed.

Right.

Except for when he talked.

Then he got serious.

"I'm glad that car hit you down on Larimer Street. If I ever find the guy who was driving I'm going to buy him a beer."

74

Shade wiped sweaty palms on her legs, exhaled and locked eyes with her captor. They both knew that the time had come. Shade didn't know how it would end, only that it would. From the expression on London's face, she didn't know either. The next few minutes would tell it all.

Shade drank what was left of the cherry-coke.

An ice cube fell into her mouth.

She chewed.

"That means sexual frustration," she said. "Chewing ice."

"I didn't know that."

"It relieves the tension."

Shade reached across the table and put her hand on London's arm. "Do you know why you were chosen for this job as opposed to every other person in the universe?"

"No. Why don't you tell me?"

"Because you have two priors," Shade said. "They don't want me back alive." A beat then, "I've been in this establishment before. There's a window in the ladies' room. I'm going to go use the facilities. After I do, I'm going to climb out that window. You can shoot me or not but that's what I'm going to do. I'm staying at the Kenmark Hotel, room 318. If you decide not to shoot me, meet me there tonight at eleven."

London frowned.

She pulled her arm back.

Shade's hand came off and dropped to the table.

"I can't let you go."

Shade studied her.

The woman was resolved.

"Do you have any family?" Shade said.

"I have a sister."

Shade said nothing.

She let the words hang.

Then she stood up and said, "I'm going to go now."

She got two steps when the woman said, "Hey."

Shade stopped and turned.

"Just for your information, I hate her."

"Your sister?"

"Right."

"That's too bad," Shade said.

Then she headed for the ladies' room.

75

Wilde dialed Senn-Rae and poured milk in a saucer for Tail while the phone rang. The poor cat must have had sandpaper for a tongue because it couldn't wait for the flow to stop before he stuck his head in. Wilde drenched the poor thing before he realized what he was doing. With the fur matted down, the head shrank to half size. "That's not a good look for you," Wilde said.

Alabama stepped in from the adjacent room, pulling her zipper up.

"What are you doing to Tail?"

"Tail did it to himself."

"God, Wilde, I can't leave you alone for ten seconds."

Suddenly Senn-Rae answered.

"It's me," Wilde said. "I need you to stop over at my office and look at something."

"What?"

"I'll show you when you get here."

"It's not something that lives behind a zipper, is it?" she said.

He laughed.

"No, something else, although you're welcome to—"

"When?"

"Now."

A pause.

"I'll be there in fifteen."

He hung up and told Alabama, "Okay, you're up. She'll be here at least an hour, an hour and one minute if I make love to her."

"You can last a whole minute?"

"It's hard but I have a secret."

"Which is what?"

"I bite my tongue and at the same time think of something unpleasant."

"Like what?"

"Like eating bugs, whatever," he said. "The important thing is that you don't cross paths with Senn-Rae on her way over. Swing around her."

"Aye aye, captain." She headed for the door. "Try not to use up any of Tail's lives while I'm gone."

Fifteen minutes later, Senn-Rae rapped lightly on the door and walked in without waiting for an answer. By the look on her face, she expected just about anything other than for a cat to run over and rub against her shin.

She picked it up.

"What happened to your head? Did that mean man over there do something to it?"

Wilde smiled.

"We were playing a game called Milk Head."

"It looks like the cat lost," she said. "What's his name?"

"Tail."

"Is he yours?"

Wilde shrugged.

"I think so," he said. "You want to buy him? He's on sale today."

"How much?"

"A half-hour of sex."

"In that case, I already own half of him."

Wilde considered it.

"More like two-thirds."

He tapped a Camel out of a pack, dangled it in his lips and struck a match. Tail jumped out of Senn-Rae's arms and scampered into the corner.

"He's getting better," Wilde said. "You should have seen him the first time."

Senn-Rae held her arm in front of Wilde's face.

Blood was dripping out of a scratch mark.

"This is better?"

Wilde shrugged.

"I didn't say perfect."

He wiped her arm with a Kleenex, got serious and said, "I found out who the dead pinup girl is from the shed. Her name's Jennifer Pazour. Me and Alabama snuck into her house this morning and looked around for anything that might identify who was in her life or how she'd been spending her time. It's all over there inside that pillowcase." He nodded towards the desk. "Your job is to go through it and see if any of it relates to your client."

"Relates how?"

"Relates in any way, shape or form at all," he said. "Did

they know each other? That's the thing I'm most interested in figuring out."

Tail came out of the corner.

Slowly.

Timidly.

He jumped up on the desk and sat next to the pillowcase.

"Tail will help you."

Halfway into it, Senn-Rae got a look on her face as she studied a photograph of two women—the victim and another woman, one with a raven-black Bettie Paige haircut and a seriously stunning face.

"Got something?"

Senn-Rae tapped on the stunner.

"I've seen this woman somewhere."

"Where?"

She concentrated.

Her face got soft.

"I don't know."

Wilde took the photo out of her fingers and studied it.

"She's pinup quality," he said. "They both are."

"Would it be hard to track her down and find out who she is?"

Wilde shook his head.

"Should be doable."

76

Blanche Golden's house wasn't anything to brag about. Her job teaching physics at the University of Denver didn't pay as well as people thought. The discretionary money she did manage to set aside got used to support her travel addiction. She was only thirty-eight but had already been to more places than National Geographic. "It's the journey, not the destination." That's what she told people and that's what she wanted carved on her tombstone.

People who knew her thought they knew her.

They were half right.

She had a second half, a carefully hidden half, that almost no one knew about.

Last year, that other half got her into trouble.

She ended up needing a lawyer.

The lawyer she got was a man named Jundee.

She had to tell him secrets.

He got her out of trouble.

More importantly, he did it in a way that her secret life remained secret. She paid him every cent he had coming, but that didn't mean she still didn't owe him, not to mention that he still knew what almost no one else knew.

At 7:47, a rap came on her front door.

Standing there was Jundee and a strikingly beautiful younger woman. In Jundee's hand was a briefcase. It looked like it had been shot to death. He wiggled it and said, "This is it."

She held the door open.

"Come in."

They ended up at the kitchen table where the professor carefully went through the documents, particularly those portions referenced in the key. Jundee and Fallon stayed quiet and let her concentrate.

Ten minutes passed, followed by thirty more.

Then the woman leaned back in her chair and looked at Jundee and said, "How much do you know about fission bombs?"

He tilted his head.

"I know that atomic bombs were dropped on Hiroshima and Nagasaki," he said. "I know we're in an arms race with the Russians. Other than that, not much."

"Hold on."

She pulled a bottle of red wine out of a kitchen cabinet, filled three water glasses half way and handed one to Jundee and Fallon. After taking a long swallow out of hers she said, "Let me give you a little background."

Jundee took a sip.

The wine was cheap and sweet.

"Okay."

"The atomic bombs that we used on Japan in the war were developed under something known as the Manhattan Project, which was basically a joint venture between the United States, Canada and England, led by American physicist Robert Oppenheimer. The scientific knowledge was centralized at a secret laboratory in Los Alamos, New Mexico. The goal was to develop a fission bomb. That goal was met. The end product was the atomic bomb which was eventually dropped on Japan and led to the end of the war."

Jundee nodded.

"Okay."

"Shortly after we bombed Nagasaki, the United States government released an official technical history of the Manhattan Project, mostly to justify the huge expense," she said. "In hindsight that was a mistake. The Russians used that report as a blueprint to develop their own atomic bomb, which they tested on August 29, 1949, latter dubbed Joe-1."

Jundee took a sip of wine.

It dropped into his stomach and tingled his blood.

"I'm with you," he said.

Good.

Very good.

"Anyway," Golden said, "the Russian's bomb totally took us by surprise. We knew they'd eventually develop it but had no idea it would be so far ahead of our projections. Within months of Joe-1—I think it was January 1950—President Truman sent the United States into a crash program to develop a super bomb, which was projected to be a thousand times more powerful than the atomic bomb. It would be based on hydrogen fusion. That was the official start of the nuclear arms race. The best scientific minds were brought back to Los Alamos where the Manhattan Project had been developed." She exhaled. "There's been a rumor floating around the community that they were getting close. The problem, as I understand it, was to separate the fusion and non-fusion components of the weapon and use the radiation produced by the fusion bomb to first compress the fusion fuel before igniting it."

Jundee raised his hands in surrender.

"Hold on," he said. "I was with you until that last part."

"What I'm saying is that these documents—together with the ones that are missing, meaning the ones from the second briefcase—appear to give the blueprint for a hydrogen bomb."

"One that actually works?"

"Unknown," Golden said, "but my suspicion is, yes. A good portion of these documents appear to give the answer to the one remaining technical issue, namely how to use the radiation to compress the fusion fuel before igniting it."

"Wow."

Right.

Wow.

"If you can find the rest of the documents, I'll be able to give you a definitive answer."

77

In the ladies' room, Shade splashed water on her face and looked at herself in the mirror. At any second, London could storm through the door and pull a trigger. Shade didn't want to get the bullet in the back. She wanted it in the heart. She wanted to be facing the woman when it happened. She wanted to see the finger squeeze on the trigger. She wanted to see the bullet as it came out. She wanted to know the exact second she would die. She didn't want to be surprised.

A second passed, then another.

The door didn't open.

Without drying her face, she walked over to the window and pushed it up. It didn't budge, then she saw why—it was screwed shut.

She punched it with the palm of her right hand, making contact just enough to break the glass but not so powerful as to not be able to pull back at the exact right time.

The glass shattered.

There was no blood on her hand or wrist.

Jags stuck out from all four sides.

She pulled her tennis shoe off and knocked them out, then threw the shoe out and climbed into the opening, keeping as much weight as she could on the outside edge of the sill where the jags couldn't shred her. The plan was to twist around and drop to her feet. That wasn't going to work. There wasn't enough room to swing her legs around. She protected herself as much as she could with her arms and dropped down head-first.

Her face hit the ground but not with full impact.

There.

She was out.

She was free, in an alley.

She pulled her shoe on as fast as she could and ran. At the end of the alley, London came around the corner. Her stance was wide. Her gun was out and pointed at Shade's heart. A silencer was screwed into the barrel.

Shade stopped as fast as she could.

Five steps away, that's how far she was.

Too far to charge.

Her instinct was to turn and run but an image of the bullet burying itself into her spine stopped her.

She froze.

She couldn't go forward.

She couldn't go backwards.

All she could do was stare into the woman's eyes.

They were dark.

They were filled with intensity.

The barrel of the weapon rose from the heart to the face.

"You left me no choice," London said. "Number three.'

Then the gun fired.

78

Wilde had a bad feeling about Jennifer Pazour's raven-haired friend in the photograph. Every time he closed his eyes he pictured her dressed up in some pinup outfit and sprawled out on top of a roof. The plan was to call every phone number that they'd found in the victim's apartment and find out who answered.

Wilde picked up the phone.

Before he could dial, Alabama snatched it out of his hand. "I'll do the talking."

"Why?"

"Because I'm the one who knows how to be nice," she said.

"And I don't?"

"You're okay but you're not me."

"You almost shot me once," Wilde said. "Did we forget about that?"

"That was a warning shot and you know it."

She dialed the first number. As it rang she added, "Don't stop arguing just because you always lose. One of these days I'm going to let you win."

"Let me?"

She nodded.

"It might even be this week. You never know."

Over the next hour they got a lot of empty phone rings. The few people who did answer didn't have much to say. None of them were particularly close to Pazour. Then something happened that they didn't expect. A ringing phone was answered with, "Law firm."

"Law firm?"

"Yes, Stuart Black's office. Can I help you?"

"Is Jennifer Pazour there?"

"Nobody by that name works here."

"We're trying to find her and this number was in her notes," Alabama said. "Maybe she's a client."

"Hold on."

A hand went over the phone.

The woman on the other end was shouting something to someone.

Then she was back.

"I just talked to Stuart. He's never heard of anyone named Jennifer Pazour and neither have I. Sorry."

"Why does she have your number?"

"I wouldn't know. Maybe someone referred Stuart to her."

Right.

That made sense.

"Thanks."

"No problem."

79

After dark Friday night Fallon and Jundee drove past Vampire's house. The woman's car was in the driveway, most of the lower level was lit and two upper rooms had lights on. "She's getting ready to go out," Jundee said. "That smaller window on the upper level is probably the bathroom. The one next to it is a bedroom." They pulled to the curb as far down the street as they could while still maintaining surveillance and killed the engine.

"Maybe she's just going to bed," Fallon said.

Jundee tapped two Camels out of a pack, lit them both and handed one to Fallon.

"No," he said. "If she was doing that she would have turned the downstairs lights off first. She's going out. Her wild side's calling her."

"That's right. It's Friday night, isn't it? You know what? After we do this we should go out somewhere and get drunk."

"Deal."

"Yeah?"

"Yeah."

Nothing changed at Vampires while they smoked their cigarettes.

Fallon wore black shorts, white ankle socks, tennis shoes and a dark blue sleeveless blouse. The streetlights were a good distance away.

The interior of the car was dark.

Jundee flicked his butt out the window, still lit, and watched it bounce across the street. Then he squeezed Fallon's knee.

"Take your shorts off."

She hesitated, then pulled her shoes off and wiggled her shorts down.

Jundee twirled them on a finger and tossed them on the dash.

Then he put a hand on each one of her knees and spread her legs.

She let him.

She wore white cotton panties.

"Don't move a muscle."

"Okay."

He got down on the floorboard between her legs and nibbled on her knee.

It tickled.

She wiggled.

"No moving."

"Sorry."

"Stay perfectly still."

"Okay."

He nibbled his way up to her panties but didn't touch them, not with his tongue, not with his chin, not with anything. Then he did the same up her other leg. Her breathing was deep and she started to moan.

He brought his face up and pressured his mouth and chin between her legs.

She spread her knees wider.

He nibbled on the cotton, soaking it.

Then he put a hand on each side of her panties and ripped them off.

He threw them out the window.

Then he ran his tongue up and down between her legs and didn't stop until he owned her.

80

The bullet passed so close to Shade's head that the vacuum actually moved her hair. "If you ever make me pull this trigger again the results won't be as pretty," London said. "Do we have an understanding?"

Shade knew the right answer.

What came out of her mouth was the wrong one.

"No we don't have an understanding. You're either going to have to kill me or let me go."

She turned and walked.

"Stop!"

She didn't.

"Last chance!"

She braced for the bullet but kept walking.

"Damn you're a little bitch."

Shade stopped and turned.

"I'll make you a deal," London said. "We'll stick together until this Visible Moon thing is done. You don't try to shake me and I don't kill you. When the time's right, though, after it's all over, you come back with me with no resistance. You don't try to escape. You don't do anything to force me to kill you."

Shade chewed on it.

"I made a promise to ferret out a mole," she said. "If I let you take me back, the mole wins."

London made a mean face.

She pointed the barrel straight up in the air and pulled the trigger.

"You're not making this easy for me."

"Do this," Shade said. "Help me find Visible Moon. I won't escape or sneak off. We'll work out the rest of it later."

London frowned.

"Like I said, you're a little bitch."

Shade nodded.

"I trust that means we have a deal?"

London unscrewed the silencer and shoved it in her purse, followed by the gun.

"It looks that way," she said.

"Good. You won't be sorry."

They walked down the alley to the main street.

"You were right about what you guessed before," London said. "It was Penelope Tap who hired me. She didn't do it directly, she did it through a chain of command, but she was the one at the top of that chain."

"I'm not surprised."

"Is she the mole?"

"I'm almost positive," Shade said. "Maybe you can help me get the proof."

"You're kidding, right?"

No.

She wasn't.

Not even a little bit.

"You have ties to her," Shade said. "Maybe we can use that somehow. She's playing you for a sucker. Don't let her."

81

Jennifer Pazour was a taxi driver before she disappeared. "I'll bet dollars to donuts the guy who killed her started out as a fare," Wilde said, grabbing his hat. Fifteen minutes later they walked into the main office of the Yellow Cab Company and asked to speak to the main guy in charge.

"That's Gunny Bob. He's out back."

Out back they found a man bent into the open hood of an earwax-yellow vehicle with grease up to his elbows and a cigar dangling from his mouth.

"You Gunny Bob?"

The man looked up, first at Wilde then at Alabama.

"Yeah, maybe."

"Someone said you're in charge of this place."

"I am. You want to shake my hand?"

Wilde fixated on the grease, pictured it migrating to his suit in spite of his best intentions, but extended his hand anyway. Gunny Bob pulled back at the last second and said, "Okay, you passed. What can I do for you?"

"Jennifer Pazour worked here," Wilde said.

The man nodded.

"Worked is the right tense," he said. "She stopped showing up, never called or nothing."

"We know, we're trying to find her," Wilde said.

It was a lie but it made things simple.

"Why, did something happen to her?"

"She disappeared," Wilde said. "I'm a P.I. and this is my assistant."

Alabama grabbed Gunny Joe's hand and shook it.

"Actually I'm his boss," she said. "He just has a hard time admitting it."

The man smiled.

"I'll bet you are."

He handed her a rag.

Alabama took it, wiped her hands and said, "We were wondering if she picked up the wrong fare."

Gunny Bob frowned.

"She was too pretty to be a driver," he said. "I told her that a hundred times. She always dressed down, never wore any makeup or anything like that, and kept her hair tucked under a baseball cap. She tried to look like a guy as much as she could. Even with all that, though, she was still a looker. It always bothered me that she was too pretty for the job, especially driving nights."

"She drove nights?"

He nodded.

"Four nights a week," he said. "She liked to keep her days free."

"For what?"

"Modeling," Gunny Bob said.

"For magazines and stuff like that?"

Right.

That.

"Plus she modeled for art classes," he said.

Wilde spotted a rusty Coke can by his feet and kicked it. "What about her fares? Did anything weird happen before she stopped showing up for work?"

Gunny Bob didn't hesitate.

"One guy, she complained about," he said. "He was paying with a $5.00 bill and it dropped into her lap. He reached down and picked it up before she even knew what was going on. In the process he made contact, if you catch my drift. He didn't grab her or anything, but there was a brushing involved."

"Tell me about him."

"That's it," Gunny Bob said. "I don't know any more than what I just told you."

"Did she describe him or tell you his name?"

"No."

"Where'd she pick him up?"

"I don't know," he said. "She never said."

"When did it happen? How long before she stopped coming to work?"

Gunny Bob wrinkled his forehead and scratched his nose.

When he took his finger away grease marked the spot.

"I'm guessing so don't quote me on this," he said. "It was a week or so ago."

Walking back to Blondie, Alabama said, "Do you think the crotch guy killed her?"

"Maybe but it's more likely he was just a pervert," Wilde said. "I'm a lot more interested in the modeling she did for art students. If the killer is the pinup painter, maybe that's where he meets his victims."

He hopped in, fired up the engine then shut it off.

"Be right back," he said.

He trotted around to the back, pulled Gunny Bob out of the engine compartment and showed him a picture of Jennifer

Pazour and a raven-haired woman.

"Do you know her?"

The man nodded.

"That's Jennifer."

"No, I mean the one with the black hair."

The man studied it.

Then he shook his head.

"No, a face that pretty, I'd remember. I've never seen her before in my life."

"Okay, thanks for everything."

82

When Vampire's upstairs lights went out, Jundee pointed and said, "She's done primping. We're getting close." Five minutes later a black car pulled into the driveway. The headlights stayed on, no one got out. The mansion door opened and the silhouette of a woman appeared, a woman wearing a long tight white dress and a large fluffy hat.

"That's Vampire," Fallon said.

"She's not what I expected."

A red scarf dangled off the woman's right shoulder. She slid into the passenger seat and the car pulled away almost immediately.

Jundee and Fallon ducked down as it drove past.

After the taillights disappeared around the corner, they got out and headed for the house on foot. The lower level was still lit but no shadows or movements played behind the window coverings.

The gate was open.

They walked up the driveway and knocked on the front door.

No one came.

They knocked louder.

Jundee tried the knob and found it locked.

"Come on."

They headed around to the back.

The privacy was absolute.

No one from a street or house could see them.

All the windows at ground level were closed and locked but the upper floors were open. Fallon climbed a trellis, which brought her four feet to the left of a window. She took a deep breath and jumped. One hand bounced off the sill but the other got a grip. She muscled in then came down and unlocked the back door for Jundee.

They were in.

"We're officially insane," Fallon said.

"Shit," Jundee said.

Fallon followed his eyes to her leg.

Blood was tricking out of the bottom stitch, not rampant but already trailing past her knee and halfway down her calf.

She looked around for something to wipe it with.

A washer and dryer were to their left.

In the corner was a large basket of dirty clothes. Fallon grabbed whatever it was on top and wiped her leg. What she used turned out to be a white blouse. They could wash it for two days and still not get the blood out.

"We need to take that with us when we leave," Jundee said.

"In that case—"

She ripped off a strip and tied it around her leg. The rest of the garment got stuffed into her back pocket as far as it would go, with the rest hanging out.

"Let's get this over with."

"Right."

They headed into the guts of the structure, across the first floor, under a crystal chandelier, past a large saltwater aquarium and up a winding oak staircase with a fancy oriental runner.

"It's up here," Jundee said. "I can smell it."

"Something doesn't feel right."

Jundee halted in the middle of a step.

He heard nothing he shouldn't.

"It's okay," he said.

Fallon shook her head.

"No, something's wrong."

"What?"

"I don't know. Something."

Jundee continued up the stairs.

"Your nerves are playing tricks on you."

She didn't follow.

"Let's just forget it and get out of here," she said.

"No, we're already here."

83

Shade told London everything she knew about Visible Moon—how the woman was abducted, how Tehya was scalped, how Mojag was in Denver trying to spot the man he saw in the bar that night, how she hired a PI named Bryson Wilde, how she found the rental house down south where Visible Moon had been held captive and, most importantly, the scribbling on the floor to the effect that Visible Moon would die that night.

"Mojag said he didn't feel Visible Moon's presence in the world any more after last night," she said.

London pulled her baseball cap off.

Her hair was matted and sweaty.

She ruffled it.

"What about you? Have you felt her presence?"

Shade wrinkled her brow.

"In the end, that's all just mind play. It doesn't mean anything."

"I'll take that as a no," London said. "How about before? Did you feel her presence then?"

She nodded.

"I hate to say it, but yes."

London put her hat back on.

"To me, none of that mind stuff is real. It has no basis in reality. What we need to do is focus on why the guy took her in the first place. What's his agenda?"

"Unknown."

"You must have some idea."

"I do, but it's not grounded in any facts," Shade said. "I picture him as a snake. He ate Tehya, which got him full. Then he took the remaining food and is keeping it alive for later, when he gets hungry again."

They were near Market Street and swung by the mailbox to see if Mojag had marked it.

What Shade saw she could hardly believe.

There on the back of the box was a big red X.

It was written in lipstick.

"I can't believe it. He actually spotted the guy."

"You think?"

"It's either that or something's going on that's so important that he wants to meet tonight," Shade said. "I can't imagine that anything happened since this morning other than he spotted the guy."

"So now what?"

"I can't wait that long. Let's head down to the financial district and see if we can find him."

84

Alabama's search for client information at Senn-Rae's loft had come up empty. It was starting to make less and less of a difference given the new information coming in, but it was still the most direct path. Instead of heading over to the art school and running down that lead, Wilde went over to Senn-Rae's and took the stairs up two at a time.

"It's time for you to tell me who your client is," he said.

The woman shook her head in disbelief.

"I told you, I don't know."

Wilde lit a cigarette and paced.

"Here's the thing," he said. "Whoever is doing the killing is the same person who abducted the Indian, Visible Moon. We know that because the house where she was kept was too damn close to the shed where Jennifer Pazour was found."

"And?"

"And, there's someone in town—a Navajo—who can identify the person who took Visible Moon. I want him to have a look at your client. That's all he has to do, just look at the guy. The client will never even know it's happening. He'll never know you told me a word."

He paused, waiting.

Senn-Rae sighed.

"Okay. I'll tell you his name."

"Good. What is it?"

She walked over as if she was going to whisper in his ear. Instead she shoved him on the chest with both hands and infuriated her face.

"Bryson, I told you. I don't know. Get it through your brain. I don't know who he is. I don't know who he is. I don't know who he is. Get it? He's a voice on the phone, that's all he is."

Wilde blew smoke.

"Okay."

"Do you believe me?"

"Yes."

"God, you're impossible."

He smiled.

"Is that a bad thing?"

"Don't press me," she said. "I'm right on the edge."

He wrapped his arms around her and pulled her stomach to his.

"The edge of what? Sex?"

"Don't even think about it," she said. "You're wearing me out."

"Yeah?"

"Yeah. It's bordering on crazy."

He frowned.

"Can't have bordering," he said. "It needs to be on one side or the other."

He walked over and locked the door.

"Bryson, don't even think about it."

"Trust me, I'm not thinking."

He picked her up, flung her over his shoulder and took her to the bedroom. "We're going to find out who he is tonight," he said.

"How?"

"I don't know," he said. "You need to think of something. Will you do that?"

"Okay."

"Promise me."

"I promise."

"Good," he said. "Now where was I?"

She wrapped her arms around his neck and kissed him.

"You were just about to screw me silly," she said.

He stood up.

"Now I remember," he said. "I was going to run down a lead. Got to go."

"Bryson, don't you dare!"

"Got to," he said. "I'll call you in a couple of hours."

"Don't bother, I hate you."

He blew her a kiss.

"I'm going to spend the afternoon thinking of ways to kill you," she said.

He nodded.

"As long as you're thinking of me, that's the main thing."

Then he left.

85

Upstairs in Vampire's bedroom, Fallon came across something she really didn't expect, namely a briefcase under the bed. She pulled it out, shined a flashlight on it and said, "Bingo."

Jundee opened it.

Nothing was inside.

"Where's the stuff?"

"It's the same as mine," Fallon said. "It's identical. Look, even the latches are the same. This has to be from the wreck."

"It's from the wreck alright," Jundee said. "She must have taken the papers out."

"Why?"

Good question.

Very good question.

"If she was going to give them to someone, I don't see why she wouldn't have just left them inside. My gut tells me she took 'em out to put 'em in a safe," he said. "Put this thing back exactly how you found it."

She did.

Then they searched for a safe.

It wasn't in the master closet.

It wasn't behind any of the wall paintings.

It wasn't anywhere.

"She's got it hidden, that's for sure."

"It doesn't matter," Fallon said. "We can't open it anyway."

"We can find out what kind it is," Jundee said. "I have people I can call. They'll be able to tell me if they can break into it or not."

"I didn't know you knew those kinds of people."

"I'm a lawyer," he said. "Remember?"

Suddenly a door slammed downstairs.

Someone was in the house.

They turned their flashlights off.

Now what?

They were in the master bedroom, which was the only major room on that side of the floor. To get to the other side they'd have to pass the staircase.

Voices were coming up.

There was no time to open a window and jump.

"Get under the bed!"

86

Mojag was nowhere to be found in the financial district. Shade crisscrossed again and again to no avail. Maybe he was in a deep shadow, waiting patiently for his mark to end the workday and walk out a front door. Maybe he had already intercepted the man and taken him somewhere for interrogation.

Mojag was hotheaded.

That was the problem.

He might make a move he shouldn't.

He might do it without waiting for Shade.

"What are you going to do when you find him?" London asked.

Shade wiped sweat off her forehead with the back of her hand. The city was hotter than it had a right to be. The sun was beating the life out of everything. "We're going to find out what he did with Visible Moon. After that, let's just say that it's not a healthy situation to scalp Mojag's woman and then let him get his hands on you."

London nodded.

"Where's he going to do it?"

"Back at the reservation."

"Are you going to help him?"

"Yes, but only here in Denver. I'm going to help catch him." A pause then, "You don't want to be around when that happens."

"We'll see."

"For your own good," Shade said.

"Like I said, we'll see. Tell me about Penelope Tap. Why do you think she's the mole?"

"Come on, I'll buy you an RC."

They ducked into a fountain bar and sat at the end of the counter closest to the sidewalk. If Mojag walked past, they'd see him. The air conditioning was an arctic storm. The barstools were a gift. The ice cubes were small and chewable.

"Penelope Tap," London said.

Right.

Penelope Tap.

Shade pulled up the image of a mid-thirties, Harvard-educated, multi-lingual bombshell who had an actual stint in the underbelly of Russia for more than five years. No one knew exactly how many kills she had logged but everyone agreed the number was big. Her smile was sugar, sweet and tempting.

"We have high-level information making its way to the Russians," Shade said. "It mostly involves our current research and development into the hydrogen bomb, but it also involves the foundation of that program, such as policies, decision makers, dates and times of meetings, funding, timetables, and a lot more. We had no idea how big the leak was until two months ago when a Russian woman made contact with the FBI. She wanted passage to the U.S., immunity, plus protection and money. In exchange, she'd help us bring down a mole."

"Who?"

"She wouldn't say," Shade said. "She gave enough specifications about the information that had been passed to demonstrate that a mole really did exist."

London tipped her glass up, got an ice cube in her mouth and crunched down on it.

"So what happened?"

"The fourth contact that was supposed to happen never happened," Shade said.

"She's dead?"

Shade nodded.

"That's the thinking," she said. "Anyway, one thing the FBI was pretty sure about by that point is that the information was being fed through Cuba. Since the mole was high-up in the CIA, the FBI took their information directly to the white house. The white house approached me. I'd been working Cuba for the last four years, getting information from my sources as to what Russia is doing in its weapons development."

London tilted her head.

"Why weren't you a suspect?"

Shade laughed.

"Me? I don't operate at those levels," she said. "I don't have access to the information that was being passed. Only an upper-level CIA agent, or a Senator or Congressman, or someone in the upper levels of the white house would have that kind of information."

"Okay."

"Anyway, I've been working my sources, plying them with large amounts of money in an effort to find out who the Cuban connection is. They must have been getting close because everything suddenly went to hell. Tuesday night I was in Havana. A meeting that should have gone smooth as a summer day ended up with my source getting killed and me having to steal a sailboat to make it out of the country alive. After not getting killed, I'm suddenly framed for being a spy."

"Okay, but why do you think Penelope Tap is behind it?"

"She's the one who hired you," Shade said. "That was the cincher. Before that, though, I already had my suspicions. She has the Russian connection. It would be easy for one of her sources over there to set up a line of communication through Cuba. Plus, I never liked the woman, not from day one. She's too good at what she does. She's too slick. She's gotten too many people in the company to believe she's the most patriotic person that ever existed."

London got the attention of the gal behind the counter and ordered two more RCs.

"She's a dangerous woman," Shade added. "I hope you like bullets in your brain because if she finds out that you're talking to me instead of bringing me in, that's what you're going to get. If I was in your shoes, I'd bring me in. I really would."

87

Wilde swung by the office and honked the horn until Alabama stuck her head out. Ten seconds later she came out of the building, threw Tail in the back seat and hopped over the passenger door without opening it.

"You're going to ruin my springs," Wilde said.

Tail climbed between the seats into Wilde's lap.

He tossed it into Alabama's.

"Where are we going?"

He checked for cars, had to wait for two then pulled out. "Back to Jennifer Pazour's house."

"Why?"

"Because we never found the matches."

"So what? Are you starting a collection?"

"If we didn't find them that means we didn't look deep enough."

Alabama wasn't impressed.

"You know," she said, "sometimes it's downright embarrassing to be your boss."

He smiled.

Fifteen minutes later they were back in the victim's house, hopefully without being spotted by a nosy neighbor. Tail came with them on account of the top being down on Blondie.

"They're somewhere in her dirty clothes," Wilde said. "We didn't check there last time."

They checked.

The matches weren't there.

He did, however, find the woman's checkbook in one of her pants pockets and stuffed it into his jacket. "We're going to tear this place apart until we find them," he said.

"Why?"

"I want to know what date the guy wrote on them."

They tore the place apart, not literally, but in the sense that they looked into every crack, crevice or corner that something as small as a matchbook could be hiding.

If it was there it was being a stubborn little thing.

It never showed its face.

"It must be with the body," Wilde said.

"We already checked."

"Apparently not good enough. Let's go."

"Tell me we aren't going back to the body."

"Can't," Wilde said. "I'd be lying."

He stuffed all the papers from the desk into a large brown bag and headed for the back door.

"What's all that for?"

"You never know," Wilde said.

The ride south into the country was candy to the eyes but the sun turned Wilde into a hot tamale to the point that he had to pull over and put the top up.

They parked at the bridge under a tree and rolled the windows up to where Tail couldn't climb through. Wilde picked the animal up, held it face-to-face and said, "Here's a math lesson for you. If you scratch my seats while I'm gone, that's two lives. Two out of your nine. Get it?"

Tail said nothing.

The air smelled like stale smoke.

They found out why soon enough.

Someone had burnt the house to the ground.

The interesting thing was that no one had shown up to put it out. It died on its own of natural causes.

The shed was exactly as they'd left it.

The body was on the ground next to it.

"Check the body," Wilde said.

"For the matches?"

"Right."

"What are you going to do?"

"I'm going to check the weeds."

"I'll check the weeds," Alabama said. "You check the body."

"Take her shoes off," Wilde said. "See if they're inside. If they're not, check the rest of her clothes. Pull them open to where you can see inside."

"No way."

"Come on."

"Why not you?" Alabama said.

"Because she's a woman, that's why."

"So?"

"So, I'd feel like a pervert."

Alabama shook her head.

"You do the body, I'll do the weeds. After you do it, though, don't tell her you're going to call her if you're really not."

"Not funny. I need you to do it. That's too much for me."

"Hey it was your idea Romeo, not mine." She chuckled and added, "At least check her mouth first. Kiss her before you go all the way."

"Still not funny."

Irrespective, it wasn't a bad idea.

He checked the mouth with a stick.

Inside there was no red book of matches with a gold B.

He looked up to find Alabama staring at him. "Well, are you going to do it cowboy or not?"

He frowned.

"I think I'll help you check the weeds."

He took the back area, walking back and forth and studying the ground with hawk eyes, then widening the circle.

"You're too far," Alabama said

She was at least 90 percent right. Even if the matches had started off on the top of the shed and got sucked off by a hellacious wind, it was still doubtful they'd carry this far.

One more pass, that's all he'd do.

Just one more.

Suddenly he spotted something twenty steps farther out.

He headed over.

"Hey, 'Bama. Come over here and check this out."

She headed towards him.

"Did you find them?"

"No but look at this."

88

Fallon got coffin-quiet under Vampire's bed. Thunder pounded through her veins but she didn't let it press a noise out of her lips. Next to her, Jundee was equally still. The voices were getting closer. One belonged to a man and one to a woman, no doubt Vampire and a lover.

They were coming to the bedroom to get nasty.

Fallon could feel it.

She grabbed Jundee's hand and squeezed.

He squeezed back.

Then something happened she didn't expect. The voices didn't turn right at the top of the staircase, they turned left. She exhaled with relief so loudly that she heard the air pass out of her mouth.

Jundee squeezed her hand.

It was a signal.

Be quiet.

This was more of the curse of the briefcase. If she lived through it, she was through. It was over. She didn't care about any of it any more. She just wanted to be free from it.

Just do what you're going to do, go downstairs and leave.

Do it.

Do it.

Do it.

No lights turned on from the other end of the house.

That was weird.

Suddenly the flicker of a flashlight scrapped across the wall outside the bedroom, there and gone. Then a strange noise came from the other end of the house, almost like tools clanging together. Then a drill turned on and the bit sank into metal.

"They're robbers," Jundee whispered. "The safe must be down there. They're drilling out the tumbler."

"Let's get out of here."

"How?"

"Out the window."

"That's a serious drop," Jundee said.

"The stairs then."

"No," he said. "We might be seen. Just stay here. They have no reason to come in here. They'll never look under the bed."

"How long do you think they'll be there?"

"I don't know. Ten minutes, maybe twenty."

"I can't last that long."

"Yes you can," he said. "They already cased the place. They

knew right where to go. They're going to get what they came for and then get the hell out of here. Just stay calm and wait until it's over."

"I can't breathe."

"Everything will be fine."

Her breath got short.

She gasped.

Her chest ached with pressure.

"I can't breathe!"

"Stop it, they're going to hear you."

"I can't stop it. I can't breathe!"

She scooted out from under the bed and headed for the door.

"Fallon! Come back here!"

She heard him.

She knew he was right.

She couldn't stop though.

Not in a million years.

She needed to get out of there.

She needed to get outside.

She needed to get air before she died.

89

At the Kenmark, Shade spent Friday evening playing the bait while London watched the fire escape through a crack in the curtains from Alabama's room. Outside, the heat of the day still trickled from the asphalt and concrete. That would change in a half hour.

She took a cool shower, as cool as she could stand it.

The spray bounced off her face and hair and head.

Tonight would be pivotal.

Tonight she'd learn if Visible Moon was alive.

Tonight everything would come to a head.

She was ready for it.

The sun sank.

The night came.

She dressed in all things black. In her purse was the Colt 45 Wilde bought for her, together with a folding knife with a six-inch serrated blade. She stepped out of the room, made sure the door was locked and knocked on London's door.

"I'm heading out."

"I'm coming with you."

Shade knew the woman would say that. She had prepared the negative words but suddenly they weren't right. Suddenly things were serious. London would be a good person to have at her side.

"I'll leave it up to you."

"Then let's go."

At street level Shade said, "Thanks for coming."

"Not a problem."

It was 9:20.

The secret was to find Mojag's truck, which was supposed to be parked within a couple of blocks of the Metropolitan. That's where they'd meet at ten o'clock, his truck.

Being Friday night, Denver buzzed.

Cars were cruising.

Drunks were drinking.

Socialites were being seen.

Lovers were groping.

Eaters were eating.

Hustlers were hustling.

Mojag's truck wasn't on Larimer. That wasn't surprising given the fight for parking. The women headed over to Market. There the night was darker. This is the kind of place Mojag would pick.

Lots of people had the idea of parking there and walking over to 16th Street.

There were enough cars for one to block the next.

The women walked farther and farther down the street.

The activity got less and less.

The cars got fewer and fewer.

Then they spotted the silhouette of a pickup truck way down, next to a Volkswagen.

"That's got to be it," Shade said.

"Right."

They picked up the pace.

Headlights approached from behind, moving slowly, not much faster than a walk. It was almost as if someone was studying them—a couple of guys looking for action?

Shade's heart pounded.

She didn't need any extra trouble right now.

The lights didn't speed up or slow down.

Shade pulled the gun out of her purse.

"I don't like this."

"Me either."

Suddenly the car pulled into a parking spot and the lights went out.

A door opened.

Shade turned to make sure nothing was happening that shouldn't be.

The dark silhouette of a man was standing next to the car.

He was facing them but wasn't approaching.

His arm rose up.

Then orange fire exploded from the barrel of a gun.

London screamed, "I'm hit!"

The gun fired again.

90

What got Wilde's attention behind the shed was a mound with all the suspicions of a grave. Three large rocks were on it but they couldn't mask the fact that the vegetation was shorter, much shorter. If something had been buried there, it happened this summer.

Alabama tried to roll one of the rocks off but couldn't.

"Whoever put these here was a gorilla."

Wilde laid his suit coat over a rabbit bush, threw his tie on top, rolled his sleeves up and went to work on the rock. He couldn't stand it up to where he could roll it but was able to pull an edge over three inches, then the other, and work it to the side. The other two were bigger but rounder.

His breathing was heavy.

His body was on fire.

He wiped sweat off his forehead with the back of his hand.

"We need something to dig with."

"Hold on," Alabama said.

She trotted to the shed and came back with a broken two-by-four.

They scrapped the dirt off, taking turns.

The soil was loose.

Something had definitely been buried there.

They got down a foot and still found nothing.

They kept going.

The sun beat down with every ounce of soul-sapping radiation it had.

"Ouch," Wilde said.

"What's wrong?"

He examined his finger.

"Great."

Alabama took a look. It was a splinter under the skin a good half-inch but wasn't totally embedded. The edge stuck out, not far, but enough to grab with her fingernails.

"Hold still," she said.

"Don't break it off."

"I won't," she said. A beat then, "I'm going to push it through so it comes out the other side."

Wilde pulled his hand back, not sure if she was serious.

"Relax," Alabama said. "I only do that with arrows."

"You wouldn't be joking if this was you."

"Stop being a baby and give it up."

He gave it to her and looked away.

She got a fingernail under the edge, then squeezed down with the other one and pulled. Instead of coming out, the edge broke off.

"Oh, oh."

Wilde looked.

"'Bama!"

"Hey, that was an accident," she said. "I didn't do it on purpose."

Wilde gave her a mean look.

"Honest," she said. "It's old wood. It's soft."

He sat down in the shade of a bush and scraped at the open end with a fingernail until enough skin came off to expose the end. Then he kept scraping until the whole thing was exposed and pulled it out with his teeth.

There.

Back to normal.

He stood up.

"That arrow thing," he said. "If I ever get one, I'll get it out myself."

"Fine."

She smiled.

"What about a spear?"

"I'll do that one myself too."

"Okay, but don't come crying to me when it actually happens. You're on your own."

"I'll take my chances. Cannonballs are different," Wilde said. "If I get one stuck halfway in me, you can pull it out."

"I'll see what mood I'm in."

They kept digging—scraping the dirt off, to be more precise. Six inches deeper they hit something.

Fur.

Black fur.

"It's a dog," Alabama said.

Wilde scrapped more dirt away.

There was no question.

It was a dog, nothing more, just a lousy dog.

"This is how my life works," Wilde said. "Get used to it."

91

Fallon bounded down the stairs two at a time, trying to stay quiet but needing to get outside before she ran out of air. She didn't turn around. If someone was behind her she didn't care. At the lower level she headed for the front door. As she reached for the knob the door opened and she came face to face with a woman.

It was the one from the wreck.

Vampire.

"Someone's upstairs robbing your safe," she said.

Then she pushed around and ran into the night.

"Wait a minute!"

She didn't wait.

She kept running.

"Hold on!"

She took a quick glance back as she ran and found Vampire on her tail. The woman had her dress hiked up to her waist and was moving as fast as she could in high-heels, running on the balls of her feet.

Her speed was surprising.

Lose her!

Lose her!

Lose her!

"Stop, I'm not going to hurt you!"

Fallon lifted her knees up higher, sprinter style. The stitches on her leg were tearing apart and shooting hot pain into her brain. She reached down to see if she was bleeding.

She was.

Badly.

"Stop."

The voice was right behind her, dangerously close.

Three more steps, that's how far she got, three more steps, then strong arms wrapped around her from behind and forced her feet out from under her. She fell hard, directly on her chest, with the other woman landing on top.

The wind came out of her lungs.

She couldn't move.

Her strength was gone.

The other woman twisted her over onto her back, straddled her chest, forced her arms over her head and pinned her down.

She struggled with her last ounce of strength.

It was no use.

She was caught.

It was over.

Vampire kept her pinned but said nothing, breathing heavily, catching her breath, sinking her weight down. Suddenly the explosion of a gun rang through the night.

It wasn't at them.

No bullets flew by.

It came from inside the mansion.

Someone inside shot at someone else inside.

Fallon twisted but couldn't get free.

Jundee!

92

London was hit, how badly and how deep Shade didn't know, nor did she have time to think about it. She let her reflexes take over, firing at the silhouette, wanting one thing and one thing only, to get him before he got her. Within seconds one of them would be dead.

Bam!

Bam!

Bam!

The shape slumped to the ground. It wasn't the fast motion of someone avoiding fire, it was the motion of a body that had suddenly lost all strength and was succumbing to gravity. Shade fired again, two more times, into the darkness next to the car, where the body should be. She couldn't tell if she hit him again or not but didn't hear anything ricochet into the distance.

"I'm bleeding like a pig," London said.

"Where?"

"My head."

It had to be a graze, otherwise she'd be dead.

"Let me feel."

The woman was little more than a black shape. Her hand made contact on the top of London's head and she felt nothing. As she brought it down the side, though, the woman's hair was thick with blood. Then she found the wound.

"It's your ear."

"How much?"

"I can't tell," Shade said. "Keep pressure on it and stay here."

"Where are you going?"

"Just stay here."

Gun in hand, she ran over to the shooter, slowing as she got there, keeping her weapon trained. The man was on the ground, not moving, face down. He didn't twitch or make a sound when Shade shook him. She felt a pulse in his neck and wrist, got nothing either place and rolled him over.

His face was destroyed.

At least one bullet got it.

More like two or three.

He was deader than dead.

She went through his suit jacket and found nothing. Then, in the back pocket of his pants, she found a wallet and shoved it in her bra. People were congregating at the end of the block, timid black shadows wondering what the noise was all about.

She ran back to London and pulled her towards the dark end of the block.

"Come on, we got to get out of here."

93

If the matchbook was out there around the shed somewhere, Wilde couldn't find it. They gave up and headed through the prairie for Blondie. A hundred yards into it Wilde stopped, wiped sweat off his brow and turned around.

"What's up?" Alabama said.

"We're going back."

She grabbed his sleeve.

"Bryson, it's not there. Maybe it was once, but now it's not. Just give it up."

"Can't," he said. "Do you remember that picture of Pazour and the other woman, the one with the black hair?"

Yes.

She did.

"What about it?"

"Do you remember what was in the background?"

"No."

"A dog," he said. "A black dog."

"So?"

"Do you remember what we just dug up?"

She tilted her head.

"It's hot. Tail's probably tearing the car apart. Let's just get out of here." Wilde pulled up an image of claw marks up and down the interior. It was strong enough that he actually slowed down for a step or two. Then he came back up to speed.

Back behind the shed, he scraped the dirt off the dog until it was well exposed.

"Okay, pull it out," he said.

"If you think I'm touching that thing—"

"Just grab his front paws and pull him out."

She shook her head.

"What does Senn-Rae see in you? I don't get it."

"It is baffling, isn't it?"

"Baffling isn't a strong enough word."

He grabbed the animal's front legs and dragged it out.

Underneath was dirt.

He scrapped it away with the board, inch after inch after inch, not getting anything other than dirt. Then what he thought might happen actually did.

He got something other than dirt.

He got a body.

"Damn," Alabama said.

Right.

Damn.

He scooped around with his hands, clearing the lifeless form enough to drag it out. It was the raven-haired woman from the photograph, as he thought it would be.

Unlike the pinup girls, she didn't die pretty.

"It looks like someone stabbed her in the side of the head."

Alabama nodded.

True.

She was dressed in ordinary clothes—cotton pants, a long-sleeved shirt, white crew socks and tennis shoes. Her hair was in a ponytail.

"How come she's not a pinup?"

"I don't know," Wilde said. "My guess is that Jennifer Pazour was the plan and she was more in the nature of a surprise, something that happened during the plan."

He went back to the hole and began sifting through the dirt with his fingers.

"What are you looking for?"

"The matchbook."

94

When the shot rang out from inside the mansion, Vampire kept Fallon pinned for a few desperate seconds, then got off and stood up, looking at the structure but not moving towards it or away. Fallon struggled to her feet and broke into a run up the driveway.

Jundee was in trouble.

That's what the shot was about.

One of the robbers must have spotted him.

He didn't have a gun.

The shot couldn't have come from him.

It had to have been at him.

He was hurt or dead and it was Fallon's fault.

She should have stayed under the bed and kept quiet.

She got to the front door and yanked it open. The interior of the structure was eerily quiet. Not a sound came from upstairs.

"Jundee!"

No one answered.

She had no weapon.

She hardly had any strength.

Her leg was bloody and felt like a volcano was erupting inside.

She didn't care.

She'd probably end up dead but she didn't care. She had to do what she was going to do. If she died, she died. That was it.

She bounded up the stairs.

"Jundee!"

No one answered.

She called again.

More silence.

At the top of the stairs she turned right and made her way down the dark hallway, into the master bedroom. Jundee wasn't under the bed. She knew that would be the case but the sight still took the breath out of her lungs. She looked around for a weapon and spotted a poker next to a small fireplace. The steel was cold in her hand but it was the right weight, not too heavy to swing but weighty enough to do damage.

She took a deep breath and headed down the dark hallway towards the other end of the house.

DAY SIX

June 14
Saturday

95

Shade woke up to find herself in a bed sleeping next to London, whose pillow was caked with dried blood. A faint patina of golden light framed the edges of the window covering. It was daylight Saturday morning but barely so, no more than six o'clock or thereabouts.

That was good.

At this point every hour was more precious than it had a right to be.

She bent over and examined the woman's ear.

It bled during the night but the stitches were still in there. They hadn't gone to a doctor to avoid being tied to the scene. They did the dirty work right here in the hotel room and then went to bed.

She got out of bed without waking the woman, then got the shower warmed up and stepped in. She squatted under the spray, took a long heaven-sent piss, and got busy lathering up.

She had killed a man last night; shot him dead.

A man named Jack Mack, according to his wallet.

It was self-defense.

She'd do it again.

She'd do it again a hundred times.

That wasn't the issue.

The issue was, even though it was justified until the end of time, she still couldn't get the picture of his destroyed face out of her brain.

Who was he?

Shade had a pretty good idea what happened. Someone saw

her and London together on the streets. London wasn't bringing her in, she was acting more like a companion or a friend. That couldn't be tolerated. The CIA sent a new person in, Jack Mack.

Unlike London, he was a local.

She got out of the shower to find London sitting up and swinging her legs over the side of the bed. "Get in the shower, then we're heading out."

London stretched.

"To where?"

"To visit the apartment of our new friend, Mr. Jack Mack."

"What for?"

"To find out who hired him."

"I can already tell you. The CIA hired him, same as me."

"I know that," Shade said. "I want a name or phone number or someone specific. I want to see if the words Penelope Tap are written down anywhere."

London shook her head.

"Forget specifics. There's too big a chance the cops will show up."

"They have to figure out who he is first," Shade said. "They don't have his wallet, remember? I do."

London wasn't impressed.

"They have his car. He's a local. That means they might even personally know him."

"True, but they won't be going anywhere until they get a donut or two down the hatch. We're going now."

London headed for the shower.

Over her shoulder she said, "Just for the record, you're no fun to wake up with."

"So I've been told."

It turned out that Jack Mack lived on the third floor of a ratty apartment building sandwiched between two used car dealerships on east Colfax, neither of which could afford an electric sign but could afford tons of wooden ones to shine floodlights on.

The ugliest was a large piece of plywood with red painted letters that said, Big Sale! Today Only! It was faded with years of sun and wind. Pigeons sat on top and dropped their droppings down the face.

"Big sale today," Shade said. "We better hurry up."

London smiled.

No cop cars were sitting outside the apartment building. Everything looked normal. Shade parked on a side street two blocks off Broadway and said, "We're up."

The building had an elevator.

A cardboard sign was taped on the door.

Broke.

They headed up the stairway, not talking.

Just after they passed the second floor, steps came down. Turning around would be suspicious. They held their course and intersected with a muscular man in a white sleeveless undershirt. He took a drag from a cigarette and ran his eyes up and down them as they passed. He was about to say something—Hey, baby, or something equivalent—but didn't.

The encounter was too fast.

The drag on the cigarette ruined his chance.

From below, Shade could feel him looking up, studying her ass.

At the third floor she whispered to London, "Keep going."

They went to the fourth, hung quiet for a minute to see if the man was coming back, then walked down to the third.

Jack Mack's rat hole was at the end the hall.

The door wasn't closed all the way.

It was actually ajar an inch or so.

This wasn't the kind of place where you'd do something like

that. It was more the kind of place that you'd make sure the lock was locked three times before heading out.

They listened and heard nothing.

Shade made her voice as innocent as she could and said, "Anyone home?"

No one answered.

She looked at London, giving her a chance to stop her.

Instead of doing it, the woman simply shrugged.

Okay.

This was it.

They both pulled their guns out of their purses and headed in.

96

Friday evening Wilde showed up at Senn-Rae's with two bottles of wine and enough cigarettes to get him through the night, unsure if she'd slam the door in his face or pull him into the bedroom by his tie.

She did neither.

She let him in, got two glasses out of the cupboard, filled them with ice and said, "Follow me."

She took him to the roof.

There she retrieved two folding chairs from behind a ventilation duct and set them up at the west edge where the parapet was only a foot high.

A seriously stunning sunset unfolded over the mountains, fifteen miles or so to the west. A shorter building blocked most of the direct view of 16th Street but none of the sounds.

The Friday night buzz was palpable.

Electric signs were on, growing more and more prominent

as the night descended.

Wilde sat down, filled their glasses and took a deep sip.

The wine was sweet.

He was more of a beer guy but tonight wasn't about him.

"I don't know what your day was like but it was better than mine," he said.

"Why, what happened?"

"I spent an hour digging a dog and a woman out of a grave," he said.

"The same grave?"

He nodded.

"Why?"

"Well, I didn't know it was a grave when I started digging." With that, he gave her all the details and, at the end added, "I sifted around in the dirt thinking the matchbook would be there. If it was I couldn't find it."

"So what'd you do with the body?"

"Put it back where I got it."

"You reburied it?"

"Right, the dog too," he said.

"Why?"

"In case the guy's monitoring the place," he said. "We're getting closer. I don't want him to know it."

"This is a dangerous game you're playing."

He raked his hair back with his fingers.

"You're the one who got me into it, remember?"

"I know," she said. "That's why I wish you'd let me fire you."

"That isn't going to happen," he said. "If you want to give me a bigger retainer, though, that would be fine."

She frowned.

"I thought you were protecting me because you cared," she said. "Now I see you're just in it for the money."

"Not just the money," Wilde said. "The other thing too."

"Which is what?"

"Sex."

"Sex?"

Right.

Sex.

"If you'd like to make a payment tonight, that would be fine."

"By payment, you don't mean the retainer."

No.

He didn't.

"I mean the other one."

She gave him a kiss.

"How big of a payment are you looking for, exactly?"

He opened his arms wide.

"About this big."

"That's pretty big."

"Yes it is."

Senn-Rae grabbed his hands and pulled them even wider.

"How about something like that?"

"I don't know," he said. "Something like that might kill me."

That was last night.

Now it was morning and he was still alive, he shouldn't be but he was. He crawled out of bed without waking Senn-Rae, lit a cigarette and headed for the shower.

When he got out, the woman was still sleeping.

Her naked body lay on top of the sheets, bathed in a soft morning light.

If there was anything more beautiful in the world, Wilde had never seen it.

He wanted her.

She was the one.

He knew it before but knew it even better now.

He gave her a kiss on the cheek and headed for the office.

97

Fallon woke in a cold sweat. It was the middle of the night—one or two or three in the morning, she didn't know, all she knew is that it was still pitch-black outside. She needed daylight to come. She needed to get this night over with.

Jundee swung his arm around her.

"Are you up again?"

"Sorry."

"It'll all work out, I promise."

"Okay."

He kissed her.

"That's my girl."

He rolled away, curled into a ball and snuggled into the pillow. Almost immediately his breathing got heavy and rhythmic.

He might have killed a man a few hours ago.

They'd find out tomorrow.

Fallon couldn't stop replaying it in her head. After she ran down the stairs, Jundee came after her. The intruder—the male one, the gorilla—heard either one or both of them. Fallon got out of the house okay. Jundee didn't. He got attacked with furious fists.

Then a gun fired.

Jundee looked at the explosion just long enough to see a woman pointing the weapon at him.

"Don't!" the man shouted. "You're going to hit me!"

In that microsecond, Jundee bolted for the back door and made it out. The attacker pursued, with a knife in hand. Jundee stayed ahead for fifty steps then got caught.

The blade swung at his face.

He pulled back.

The knife slashed across his neck.

He'd been cut.

He could already feel the blood.

Then something snapped.

He wrestled the knife out of the man's hand and threw it as far as he could. The man kept coming.

He kept attacking.

He wouldn't give up, ever.

They ended up on the ground wrapped around each other. Jundee got the man's head in his arms and twisted as fast and as hard as he could.

The man's power weakened.

Jundee broke loose and ran.

He didn't know if he'd killed the man or not.

He doubled back and encountered Vampire in the front yard. "She's in the house."

He bolted upstairs.

Fallon was in a room at the end of the hall.

She was alone.

The other intruder, the female, was nowhere to be seen.

The safe was only half drilled, still closed and secure.

"Come on!"

They ducked out the back, made it to Jundee's house and cleaned the wound on his neck. Then they curled up in each other's arms and went to sleep.

That was last night.

Now it was two or three hours later, the middle of the night. Fallon flopped onto her back and wondered if she was crazy enough to actually do what she was thinking about doing.

She was.

Damn it, she was.

She got out of bed without waking Jundee, got dressed and grabbed his car keys.

Then she headed out the front door, closing it gently behind her.

The night was cool and crisp.

A dog somewhere out in the darkness barked twice.

98

Shade took a chance on whether Wilde would be in the office on a Saturday and got lucky, finding him alone except for a cat. "Got some information for you." She pulled two cigarettes out of her purse, lit them and handed one over.

Wilde took a long deep drag and blew a smoke ring.

"Tell."

She informed him about the London encounter yesterday which didn't result in either of them being killed, followed by their attempt to meet up with Mojag last night, which did result in someone being killed.

A man named Jack Mack.

"Jack Mack," Wilde repeated. "Never heard of him."

"He's a local," Shade said. "Me and London paid a visit to his apartment this morning. From what we can tell, he's nothing more than a two-bit punk with a record as long as your dick."

Wilde smiled.

"He must have started in the 1800s."

"I'll take your word for it," she said. "The point is, he's not the kind of guy the CIA usually hires to do jobs. The fact they hired him means they wanted me out of the picture yesterday. They didn't even have time to fly someone into town."

Wilde flicked ashes into a tray.

"So what's the rush?"

"I don't know," she said. "But I do know one thing. They wouldn't sit back and see if he got the job done or not. They'd have someone en route just in case he blew it. That person will get into town today."

"That's not good but it's only half of it," Wilde said. "The other half is that the cops will be looking for you. Did you leave a trail?"

"Not that I know of," she said. "It was pretty dark. The guy was a scumbag. Do you think the cops are really going to be looking that hard?"

Wilde shrugged.

"They might, if they think another scumbag did it and they can get two for the price of one."

Shade tilted her head.

"Well, if they catch me, at least I know a good lawyer."

"Who's that?"

"Someone named Stuart Black," she said. "That's the one my friend Mack used to stay on the streets."

Wilde froze.

"Stuart Black?"

She nodded.

"Yeah, there were papers in his apartment."

"What kind of papers?"

"You know, correspondence, bills, payments, that kind of thing. Why? What are you making that face for?"

He told her.

Stuart Black's phone number was written on a piece of paper he found in the house of Jennifer Pazour, a pinup victim.

Shade mashed what was left of her butt into the ashtray and

lit another, two actually, one for Wilde.

"What's weird," she said. "This guy's name, popping up in two places."

Wilde pulled a book of matches out of his pocket and set it on fire with the cigarette.

Tail scampered into the corner.

"You just took a life out of that cat," Shade said.

"He's still got three or four."

"Well, then, don't worry about it."

The flames caught the flap of the matchbook and rose higher. Wilde watched them burn.

"Earth to Bryson," Shade said. "Are you there?"

He shook the fire out and threw the remains in the ashtray.

"Yeah, I'm here."

Stuart Black may well be the pinup killer.

Wilde could feel it building like a storm in his blood.

"Look," Shade said. "The reason I'm here is because I might end up dead today, or arrested, or who knows what. I want to be sure you find Visible Moon if something happens to me."

Wilde nodded.

"I already promised you that."

She blew smoke.

"I'm going to be looking for Mojag today," she said. "I may or may not end up finding him. If I don't, I want you to help me meet up with him tonight. If I disappear between now and then and don't get back to you by this evening, I want you to do it on your own. Let me tell you how to do it. You'll need to find his truck and meet him there at ten. It'll be parked within a couple of blocks of here."

"What's it look like?"

She told him.

"You'll meet him, if I don't show up?"

Wilde nodded.

"I will."

"You promise?"

"I promise."

"And hope to die?"

"And hope to die twice," he said. "Good enough?"

She nodded.

99

When Shade left, Wilde headed over to Senn-Rae's and told her about his theory that Stuart Black might be the pinup killer.

She wasn't impressed.

"I see the connection to the Pazour woman since his number was written down," she said. "That's the only connection I see though. So what if he did defense work for some two-bit scumbag who took a potshot at this other client of yours. How does that tie him to the pinup murders?"

"I think he has Visible Moon," Wilde said. "She's either a victim or a victim-to-be."

"She's not pretty, right?"

"Right."

"All the pinup victims were beautiful, right?"

"Right."

"Do you see where I'm going with this?"

He did.

He didn't care.

"What I'm going to do is get this Stuart Black guy on the phone," he said. "I want you to listen to his voice and see if he's your mystery client."

She shrugged.

"Okay but don't expect anything. I can already tell you you're off base."

"You'll be honest with me if it is him, right?"

"How can you even ask me something like that?"

"Does that mean, yes?"

She shook her head.

"For a smart guy you sure know how to say a lot of dumb things."

He nodded.

"It doesn't come natural," he said. "I have to work at it. Where's your phone book?"

She pulled it out of a drawer.

Wilde looked up the lawyer's number and dialed.

Ring.

Ring.

Ring.

Ring.

Damn it

No answer.

"It's Saturday," Senn-Rae said.

Right.

That it was.

Saturday.

He checked the phone book again to see if the man's home number was listed.

It wasn't.

He grabbed his hat and dipped it over the left eye.

"Where are you going?"

"To his office."

"He won't be there."

"That's why I'm going."

"What are you going to do, break in?"

"That's exactly what I'm going to do." A beat, then he added, "The things I do for you. You should be impressed."

"Are you doing it for me or the retainer?"

He opened the door, turned and said, "Yes."

Then he bounded down the stairs two at a time.

Halfway down he turned and trotted back up.

Senn-Rae jumped when he opened the door.

"You're impressed, right?"

She smiled.

"Yes."

Then she got serious.

"Be careful, Wilde, just in case you're right."

"Okay."

"What I'm saying is, if you have to get shot be sure it's not between the legs."

He pictured it.

"Trust me, if he's pointing there I'll drop so he gets the heart instead."

100

This was the worst idea Fallon ever had but she couldn't live another minute without knowing if the man Jundee fought with was dead or not. She was the reason that encounter came to be, meaning if Jundee was a killer then it was her fault.

She fired up the engine, shifted into first and pointed the front end towards Vampire's house.

When she swung by, the lights were out and no activity appeared.

Did the woman—Vampire—make a police report?

She'd seen Fallon, not only earlier tonight but also from the wreck. She could describe her with particularity. She'd also seen Jundee, albeit for only a moment, but the moment would be fresh in her mind. If the police were looking for her then they were looking for him. There was nothing she could do about it.

Screw it.

She didn't know exactly where the fight took place but had a pretty good idea from Jundee's description. It wasn't on a sidewalk. It was several steps off in a yard next to some bushes. She drove down the street where it happened according to her best guess and didn't see anything unusual.

She went by Vampire's house again.

It was the same.

Dark.

Inactive.

No other headlights were anywhere in the area. All the sane people of the world were sleeping. She parked two blocks over and headed back on foot, hugging the shadows where she could and trying to not look suspicious.

She realized she was wearing white shorts.

Brilliant.

Underneath she had black panties.

Should she do what she was thinking of doing?

She chewed on it, then slipped the shorts off and tucked them up her T-shirt into her bra.

There.

Better.

She was pretty sure she had the correct street, which was the one behind Vampire's. Starting at the first house, she ducked into the yard fifteen steps and walked parallel to the sidewalk.

She saw no body.

Suddenly headlights came around the corner.

Damn it!

She looked for cover and ended up flat on her belly behind a grouping of junipers in the front yard.

The car motored past without slowing.

She poked her head up just enough to take a quick look after it swept by.

It was a cop car.

Two cops were inside.

Her heart pounded.

Were they trolling the area because of a murder or was it just a normal routine?

She headed for the next yard.

No body was there, at least that she could see. It was too dark, though. She could be almost on it and not even know.

She kept going.

There was no body in the next yard.

Wait.

Bushes were coming up.

A black shape was next to them, not much darker than the ground but discernable nevertheless. Fallon swallowed and headed that way one careful step at a time.

The shape was a body.

She shook it and got no response.

It was hard and muscular, like Jundee described. The head was tilted at a strange angle.

She felt for a pulse and got none.

Then she wiggled the head.

It moved freely as if the skull was no longer connected to a spine.

Suddenly headlights swung onto the street from around the corner several houses down. It came from the same dark area that the cop car disappeared into.

Fallon laid on her stomach next to the body.

A second passed.

Then another.

Her arms shook.

Her instinct was to move.

She couldn't.

Her chest was tight.

She couldn't breathe.

101

Today was the day Shade would die. She could feel it in her blood. It would be violent which wasn't necessarily a bad thing. Violence was quick. The adrenalin would weaken the pain. Wilde would carry on with Visible Moon. He said he would and was telling the truth. What they hadn't discussed, though, is whether Wilde would kill the man if it turned out that Visible Moon was already dead.

He probably wouldn't.

He'd beat the daylight out of him.

He'd turn him over to the police.

He wouldn't kill him though.

Wait, what needed to happen was for Wilde to give the information to Mojag.

She was two blocks away from Wilde's office.

She turned back.

She needed to be absolutely sure that Wilde got the information to Mojag. She needed to get his promise that he'd handle it like that.

She was just rounding the corner onto Larimer Street when a cab pulled next to her and screeched to a stop. London rolled down the window and said, "Get in!"

The woman's stress was palpable.

Something was wrong.

She hopped in.

London hit the driver on the arm and said, "Go!"

The vehicle pulled away with a stiff acceleration that sent Shade falling back into the seat. A car honked, cut off and not happy about it.

"What's going on?"

"Not now," London said.

She turned and looked out the back window.

To the driver she said, "Make a left at the next corner."

"You got it, lady."

102

The lawyer, Stuart Black, practiced out of a pretty nice three-story standalone building on Bannock that looked like it started life as a mid-sized mansion and then got converted. The front door was locked and the lights were out. Wilde knocked, got no response and cupped his hands on the glass to see inside. A receptionist area had a desk cluttered with papers. Gray plastic covered a typewriter. A green banker's lamp was off.

Wilde headed around to the back.

There he found an alley but not anything private by any means. On the other side was the rear end of a four-story hotel. Two weathered oak doors were propped open. Between them was a large dumpster. Someone could come out any second. They'd be steps away.

Speed was important.

The back door was locked, no big surprise, but the mechanism wasn't the old skeleton kind from the earlier days.

It had been updated.

It would be difficult to jimmy.

Wilde punched the glass out with his elbow, reached through and unlocked the latch.

Then he was in.

No one was in the alley.

Someone might have seen him from one of the upper windows of the hotel, but there was nothing he could do about it.

Okay.

Get moving.

Don't dawdle.

The first floor was filled with the reception area, a large conference room that doubled as a library, restroom facilities and a kitchen.

Wilde headed up a wooden staircase with a fancy oak banister to the second level. The front half of that floor was a large office paneled with dark wood. The back was a room with an old desk and scores of boxes stacked on top of each other along three walls. Handwriting on the ends identified the client files that were stored in those boxes.

Wilde ran his eyes from one to the next until he found the one he was looking for—MACK, JACK. Inside he found four separate expandable files pertaining to the man. He pulled them out, set them on the floor at the top of the stairs and then read the outsides of the remaining boxes.

No more were relevant to the Mack.

He headed into the lawyer's primary office.

He didn't like being on the second floor.

There was no way out.

He was vulnerable.

No sirens were headed his way. That was good. If someone from the hotel had seen him, the cops would be on their way by now.

Stop thinking.

Keep moving.

The desk was piled with papers, none of them relevant to anything. Pencils, pens, paperclips, junk—that's what was inside the desk drawers.

In the corner was a gray metal filing cabinet.

He opened the top drawer.

Inside were client files, probably current cases still being worked on. He riffled through them, reading the names on the tabs.

Nothing.

Nothing.

Nothing.

He opened the next drawer.

More nothing.

It wasn't until he got to the bottom drawer that he found something of interest, namely that it was locked. He pried it open with a pair of scissors. Inside were more client files. One of the names jumped out at him, it was so unusual.

Vampire.

Rebecca Vampire.

He kept going. The very last file was an expandable one with several manila folders inside.

The word *Shadow* was written on the outside.

103

The headlights moved eerily slow as they came up the street and punched out images of curbs and sidewalks and manicured grounds.

They dimly sprayed on Fallon.

They sprayed on the dead body next to her.

The spray was indirect, hardly a spray at all.

It was enough though.

It was more than enough.

Keep going.

Keep going.

Keep going.

They did.

They passed.

It was the cop car.

Then they suddenly stopped. Fallon didn't move, not a muscle. The driver had his foot on the brake. The taillights threw an orange mist into the nightscape.

Suddenly one of the doors opened.

Fallon scooted over to the hedges and crawled backwards, keeping her eyes pointed at the street. Suddenly the dark silhouette of a man appeared at the edge of the yard. He walked towards her.

One step.

Two steps.

Three steps.

She got onto her knees, ready to bolt, hoping beyond hope she could outrun him. He'd shoot, no question, but it was almost pitch-black. If she zigged and zagged she might live.

Suddenly the man stopped.

There was a slight motion to his body. What was he doing, pulling out a gun? Then a strange sound came. She'd heard it before but couldn't place it.

"Ahhh."

Pissing.

The guy was pissing.

He was pissing on the bushes.

She breathed in and out through an open mouth, as controlled and quiet as she could. The man sneezed, zipped up and left.

The taillights disappeared into the night.

Five minutes later she was back at the car.

Did she dare do what she was thinking of?

Yes.

She had no option.

She got Jundee into this mess and it was her responsibility to get him out. She fired up the car, left the headlights off and motored back to the body. There she kept the engine running but shifted the clutch into neutral. She dragged the body towards the car along the hedges, got it into the trunk and took off.

No one saw her.

Two blocks away she let her mouth smile.

She did it.

In hindsight it wasn't all that bad.

Not bad at all.

She checked the clock.

It was 2:45 in the morning.

She cut over to Santa Fe and drove south. The plan was to keep going until she got out of the city, way out of the city, then look for a nice quiet place to dump the body.

She wondered if she should tell Jundee that he actually killed a man.

Maybe she should just keep quiet about the whole thing.

There'd be no newspaper article of a dead body found in Capitol Hill.

He'd assume the man had simply regained consciousness and gone back to his little life of crime.

What would she want Jundee to do if the situation was reversed?

Tell her, or not?

She laughed.

What a dumb-ass cop.

He was right there taking a piss not more than ten steps away and never had a clue. Before she died, she needed to find out who he was, call him anonymously and tell him look around better the next time he takes a piss.

The miles clicked by.

Suddenly flashing lights appeared in her rearview mirror.

She was the only vehicle on the road.

They were for her, no question.

She looked at the speedometer—45.

She was almost positive that was the speed limit.

She wasn't speeding.

She wasn't weaving.

What was the issue?

Damn it.

Okay, don't panic.

Just stay calm.

She pulled over.

The flashing lights pulled in behind her.

Almost immediately two cops got out and approached.

104

Shade had serious questions as to what was going on but it was clear London didn't want to talk in front of the cab driver so she kept her mouth shut and stared out the window. One of the questions related to where they were going; London was giving detailed directions, she knew what she was doing. After fifteen minutes of zigs and zags she said, "Stop here."

They were next to railroad tracks on the west edge of the city.

"Here?"

"Yes."

"Are you sure?"

"Yes. What's the fare?"

He checked.

"A buck thirty two."

London dangled a ten-dollar bill in her fingers. "You never had this fare, okay?"

He smiled.

"What fare?"

She gave him the bill followed with a quick kiss on the cheek.

"Have a nice life."

"You too."

They watched until he was completely out of sight, then London said, "Come on," and started walking down the tracks.

Shade fell into step.

"The cops showed up at the hotel while you were out,"

London said.

The cops?

Right.

The cops.

"I got out the fire escape before they busted in. We're going to a safe place. I have a car there."

They walked for a half hour then cut west into an industrial area. The first structure they came to was an abandoned metal building surrounded by weeds. London pulled a key out of her purse and opened a dirty steel door at the backside.

"In case you're wondering, this is where I was going to keep you if the need arose," she said.

Parked inside was a newer model Packard.

"That's how I was going to transport you," she added. "It has a big trunk."

Shade frowned.

"I'm claustrophobic."

"I was going to give you the chance to sit up front handcuffed to the door," she said. "The trunk was only a last resort, if you didn't behave yourself."

"I probably wouldn't have."

"No argument here," London said. "There's food and water in the back seat."

Shade opened the driver's door and slid in.

The seat felt good.

Her feet were tired.

The keys were in the ignition.

The front end of the car faced the street, behind an overhead door.

"Open the door," Shade said. "We're going to take a ride."

London shook her head.

"It's too dangerous. We'll just lay low."

"Visible Moon isn't laying low." Shade fired up the engine.

Carbon monoxide shot out the tailpipe and choked the air. "Open the door or I'll bust through it."

105

Wilde was almost out of Stuart Black's building when he paused to decide whether he really wanted to steal files out of a lawyer's office. That was serious business. Once done, it couldn't be undone.

He was getting too wild.

Sure, his cases justified extreme measures and maybe even demanded them, but at this rate he'd end up in jail.

He needed to be smarter.

He needed to reduce the risk.

He should read the files right here by the back door and then put them back where he found them. If someone came in the front while he was reading he'd be able to slip out the back without being seen.

He set the Jack Mack files to the side and concentrated on the expandable file, the one from the bottom drawer.

The Shadow file.

Natalie Levine.

That was the top folder inside the file and the one he pulled out first. Inside was a single sheet of lined yellow paper with pencil handwriting:

NATALIE LEVINE

MARCH 7

SOUTH PLATTE INDUSTRIAL PARK, ABANDONED GRAY METAL BUILDING, ROOF BEHIND HEATING DUCT.

Dames in Danger, Jan. 1950, page 39.
Very strong.
Put up a sexy little fight.
Got all horny, bought a hooker that night.

A second piece of paper was also in the folder. It was a page torn out of a magazine that had a pinup painting that went along with a story called "A Slut by Night." On closer examination, the page number at the bottom was 39 and the header at the top was Dames in Danger.

He opened the next file.

Lana Corbin.

Inside, as before, was a single sheet of lined yellow paper with pencil handwriting:

Lana Corbin
June 4
Top of boxcar at old abandoned railroad yard south of Denver, off Santa Fe
Dames in Danger, April 1948, page 17
Fun to kill.
Took a long time to die.
Delicious face.

A second piece of paper was also in the folder, namely a page torn out of Dames in Danger. Wilde recognized it as the same one he found in his earlier research.

He opened the next file.

Charlotte Wade.

Inside was a sheet of paper with pencil handwriting:

Charlotte Wade

July 19, 1951
Top of abandoned barn west of Brighton
Dames in Danger, Dec. 1945, page 41.
Bitchy.
Deserved to die.

The corresponding page from Dames in Danger was also in the folder.

There were four more files but they'd have to wait a few seconds. Wilde set them on a table next to the Jack Mack files, headed for the restroom and took a piss that had been too long in the making. He was just about to flush when he heard a key turning in the front door.

Someone was coming in.

He was trapped.

He opened the bathroom window as quietly as he could and found he was on the north side of the house near the back. Across the alley three hotel workers were milling around, smoking and talking animatedly. He recognized one of them as a guy who got drunk at the Larimer bars. They'd seen each other dozens of times. The guy didn't know him by name but could finger him if he wanted to.

Damn it.

The front door slammed shut.

Whoever was coming in was in.

106

The cops shined flashlights into the interior of the vehicle, one from the driver's side and one from the other, lighting up the vinyl seats and Fallon's legs. One of the lights played briefly on her crotch then moved up the front of her body. A rap came on the window.

She rolled it down.

The cop had a square jaw and mean eyes.

"Step out of the car please."

Her heart pounded. For a brief second she considered flooring it. They didn't have guns drawn. She'd at least get a head start.

No.

Don't.

That would be suicide.

She pulled up on the handle and swung the door open.

"Turn the engine off first."

She did.

Then she stepped outside. The cop backed up to give her room, but not much. He stayed closer than he should have.

"What's your name?"

She hesitated.

"Mary Green."

As soon as the words came out of her mouth she wanted to suck them back in and swallow them.

"Mary Green?"

She nodded.

"Yeah."

"Yeah? You don't sound too sure."

"I'm sure."

"Do you have a driver's license, Mary Green?"

She had a license, it was right there in her purse. It didn't belong to Mary Green though.

"Not with me."

"Does that mean you have one?"

"I do but it's not with me."

The cop grabbed her elbow and led her to the back of the car.

"Put you hands on the trunk and spread your feet," he said.

She froze.

"Do it."

She complied.

"Don't move a muscle, do you hear me?"

"Yes."

"Have you been drinking?"

"No."

"Do you know why we pulled you over?"

"No."

"You didn't have your headlights on," he said.

That wasn't true. She knew it because she could read the speedometer.

"Yes I did."

"You had your parking lights on but not your headlights," he said. "Do you know who usually does a little trick like that? Someone who's been drinking."

"I haven't been drinking."

"Search it," the cop told the other one.

The search didn't reveal anything other than her purse. Inside that purse was a driver's license, one belonging to Fallon Leigh.

"She's not Mary Green," the other cop said. "She's really Fallon Leigh."

The cop with the square face wrinkled his brow.

"Is that true?"

She said nothing.

"I said, is that true?"

"I guess so."

"You guess so," he said. "That's a lie to a police officer. Why'd you lie to me?"

"I don't know."

"You don't know," he said. "Do you know why people lie to cops? Because they have something to hide. Do you have something to hide?"

"No."

The man paced back and forth behind her.

"This is bad," he said. "Very bad. Don't move."

He walked over to the other cop and they had a private conversation. Then he came back and got his face close to hers. "There are two ways we can handle this," he said. "We can take you down to the station and book you. Is that what you want?"

"No."

"The other option is this," he said. "Our primary concern is that you were driving drunk. We haven't found any cans or bottles in the car but that doesn't mean you don't have any on your person. If you want, we can search you. If we don't find anything, you're free to go."

She exhaled.

"Well, what's your pleasure?"

"Search me."

"Is that what you want us to do? Search you?"

"Yes."

"Okay, we'll oblige if that's what you want. Don't move while we're doing it. Do you understand?"

Yes.

She did.

He squatted down, put both hands on her left ankle and walked his fingers up and over her calve, up to her knee, giving her leg a good feel.

"Nothing so far," he told the other cop.

He did the same to the right leg.

"Still nothing."

"She's got something, I can tell," the other cop said. "Be thorough."

"Don't worry, I will."

He went back to the first leg, started at the knee and worked his fingers slowly up her thigh, going up higher and higher until he got to the crack of her ass.

"Nice legs," he said.

She said nothing.

He did the same to the other leg.

"She's clean so far," he said.

Then he reached between her legs and rubbed his fingers back and forth on her crotch, over and over and over.

"There's something in there," he told the other cop.

"I thought there would be."

He slapped her on the ass.

"What do you have in there? A flask?"

"No, nothing."

"Don't move," he said.

Then he reached around, unzipped her shorts and pulled them down to her ankles.

He put his hand between her legs.

"Check inside," the other cop said. "She could have stuffed it in there."

The man slid a finger into her.

Then two.

He slipped them in and out, again and again and again.

"Getting anything?" the other cop said.

"No bottles but she's wet," he said. "I think it's beer."

"Check between her tits."

"Good idea." Then to Fallon, "Lift your arms."

She complied.

He pulled her T-shirt up and over her head, then took her bra off.

"Hands back on the trunk."

She did it.

He reached around and cupped his hands on her breasts and tweaked her nipples.

Fallon kept her hands where they were but turned and looked over her shoulder into his eyes.

She memorized them.

She memorized his whole face.

At some point in the future at another time and place, she'd watch the life go out of those eyes.

"That's a promise," she mumbled.

"What'd you say?"

"Nothing."

"Damn right nothing," he said. To the other cop, "Your turn. Be sure I didn't miss anything."

"You bet I will."

Ten minutes later Fallon was back on the road, pulling away naked with her clothes crumpled in a pile on the seat next to her. The cop car did a one-eighty, turning into red taillights that got smaller and dimmer and finally disappeared altogether.

Fallon's instinct was to pull over and get dressed.

She didn't.

She turned on the heater and kept going.

107

From the warehouse, Shade pointed the front end of the Packard towards Wilde's office, swinging around the neighborhood three or four times first to see if she could spot Mojag's truck. She ended up parking on Market Street, exactly where Jack Mack had been when he shot at them last night.

"This is insane," London said as they got out.

"Insaner," Shade said. "Is that a word?"

"If it isn't it should be."

They got to Wilde's office to find the door halfway ajar. "Bryson, you here?"

No answer.

She checked the adjacent room.

He wasn't there.

Then she looked out the window down onto the street. He wasn't there smoking or hanging out or taking a walk.

"Strange," she said.

"For someone who's supposed to maintain confidentiality, I wouldn't give the open door high marks."

Shade sat in the chair behind the desk.

"We'll wait."

The remains of a half-dozen burnt matchbooks littered the ashtray together with a tangle of white butts. None of them were fresh. Shade dumped them in the wastebasket and washed the ashtray in the sink.

"Damn it, I made a clean spot."

She wet a rag and wiped Wilde's desk, the chairs, the windowsills, the door and doorknobs.

London watched without expression.

"You like him," she said.

"Who?"

"Wilde. You like him."

"No, not like that."

"Like what, then?"

"Like nothing," Shade said. "We're from different worlds."

"That's probably why you like him."

She didn't answer.

Something was off.

"What's wrong?" London said.

"I don't know."

"You're really weird today," London said. "When was the last time you got laid?"

Shade smiled.

"I can't remember," she said. "The only thing I remember about it was hearing a T-Rex running by outside the cave."

Ten minutes later the door opened and Alabama walked in as she adjusted her bra, startled to find guests.

"How'd you get in?"

"The door was open."

Alabama pointed, "That door?"

Right.

That door.

"I thought for sure I shut it," she said. "Do me a favor and don't tell Wilde, okay?"

Shade paced by the windows.

"Did Wilde tell you about me shooting a man named Jack Mack last night?"

"You shot someone?"

"In self defense," Shade said. "Wilde knows all about it, I told him this morning. When's he coming back?"

"Unknown."

"Where is he?"

"Same place, unknown."

Shade tapped out a Camel and offered one to Alabama who wasn't interested. She lit up, blew smoke and said, "Give him an update for me. Tell him the cops showed up at my hotel room this morning. London was there, I wasn't, and she ducked out. I don't know exactly why they were there but my suspicion is it's because of Jack Mack. What I need Wilde to do is find out what the police know about London and me. Do they know we did it? Do they have a description of us? That kind of thing."

"I can probably handle that," Alabama said.

Shade tapped ashes into the ashtray.

"Either way," she said. "What I'm really interested in knowing is where they got their lead. Did someone see us? That's the question."

Alabama wrinkled her face.

"A witness," she said. "That's the kind of information they don't just blurt out."

"I think what you're going to find out is that it was an anonymous phone tip," she said. "My guess is that it came from the CIA, who hired the guy in the first place. It's their way of tightening the net around us. In fact, they probably knew he'd get killed from the get-go."

Alabama nodded.

"Understood."

"One more thing," Shade said. "Tell Wilde that if I die and he later finds out who took Visible Moon, tell him to share that information with Mojag."

"Okay."

"Mojag will handle it from there."

"Understood." She looked around and saw no Tail. "Was there a cat here when you came in?"

"No."

108

Wilde climbed out the lawyer's bathroom window with every ounce of self-control he could muster, keeping every movement quieter than death itself. It paid off because he dropped to the ground without anyone running through the door. He knew to keep his face pointed away from the hotel but was so desperate to know if anyone saw him that he threw a quick glance that way.

Bad move.

The three workers were staring directly at him. The face of the one he knew from Larimer Street broke into an expression of recognition.

The man actually waved at him.

Wilde waved back and headed away.

Damn it.

All he had to do was not turn his face.

He headed towards the thick of the city and turned into a suit in a sea of a thousand people. At the first public phone he opened the white pages and flipped to the C's.

Caster.

Cordoza.

Cedarwide.

Corbin.

Corbin, Bob.

Corbin, Lana.

Bingo.

She lived at 1329 Marion.

She was the pinup girl from the boxcar.

He called and let the phone ring ten times before hanging up. No one answering might mean she lived alone, although she might not and the other person might be at work. He'd sneak in later after dark and find what he could.

Right now he was more interested in the crime scene of Natalie Levine, who'd been missing since March 7th. If the lawyer's file was correct, her body was at *South Platte industrial park, abandoned gray metal building, roof behind heating duct.*

He headed for Blondie, who was parked two doors down from his office.

As he passed under his windows he heard, "Hey Wilde," from above.

It was Alabama.

"Where you going?"

"Field trip."

"Hold on, I'll go with you."

He felt his front pocket and found it was empty.

"Bring some matches with you."

"No, you're going to burn the world down."

109

Fallon drove through a black world paying enough attention to the eerie nightscape as the headlights punched through it to stay on the road but using all her energy to build images of herself killing the cops.

She'd do it.

There was no question.

It might take years but she'd do it.

Thirty minutes later even the fringes of civilization were

gone.

She could drive for two more hours and still not be in a place any more remote than where she was right now.

Okay look around.

Find a good spot.

Find a spot where the body won't be seen or smelled or stumbled on for the next ten years.

Find the last corner of the universe.

The night was blacker than black.

There were no other cars.

Low clouds blotted out the stars and the moon.

It was difficult to tell what was out there, other than the immediate road in front of her.

She pulled to a stop, turned off the headlights and put her shorts on.

The blackness was absolute.

She couldn't see her hands.

She couldn't see her legs.

She couldn't see the steering wheel.

She took a deep breath, killed the engine and stepped out. No sounds came from the night, not a coyote or an insect or a twist of wind.

She felt her way along the side of the car to the back.

It took a while for her fingers to locate the trunk latch and a little longer to get the key in the hole.

She got the trunk open and stuck the keys in the front pocket of her shorts.

The body had an odor.

The stench of death was already on it.

She didn't want to touch it.

The sooner she did, though, the sooner it would be over with. She wrestled it over the edge of the trunk and let it dump to the ground. She got the man on his back, grabbed his feet and dragged him into the darkness. She might be leaving a trail but it didn't matter. Anyone driving by out here would be doing fifty and wouldn't see it. The first rain would wash it away.

She kept going, counting her steps.

At fifty she stopped to rest.

The rest wasn't long.

She went to a hundred.

Then two hundred.

Then five hundred.

She was going slightly downhill at that point, on the backside of a hump. No one would be able to see the body from the road. She dragged it behind a rabbit bush and nudged it into the base.

Then she checked the man's pockets.

Strangely, there was nothing to be found—not a wallet or keys or pack of smokes or spare change or anything.

She headed back for the road, pretty sure she was going in the right direction but not positive.

It was too dark to tell.

She concentrated on going in as straight a line as possible. The last thing she needed to do was curve off into nowhere.

In hindsight, she should have left the parking lights on.

A coyote barked.

It wasn't far off, less than a hundred yards.

She stopped and turned towards it.

It howled.

More joined in.

Then even more.

There was a whole pack, a big pack.

They were moving, on a run, coming towards her.

She kept her face pointed towards them as they swept behind her. They were going past, not heading for her at all, when they suddenly stopped.

One of them smelled her.
He barked and headed closer.
The others came with him.
"Go away!"
They suddenly got quiet.
Then they all barked, frantic and rapid.
They weren't leaving.
They weren't scared.

110

Shade and London split up so they'd be harder to spot but kept within sight of one another as they crisscrossed the financial district. The main goal right now was to hook up with Mojag and find out why he'd marked the mailbox yesterday. Hopefully it was because he'd spotted his man.

The only place Shade had bumped into him prior was the coffee shop so she peeked in the window every time she passed.

Early afternoon, what she hoped would happen actually did.

He was in there at the same table as before.

In front of him was a cup of coffee.

She went in and sat down.

Mojag wore a blue bandana that played nice against his tanned face. Strong arms stuck out of a black T-shirt. He was a specimen, a man's man, born to live. He had that raw bad-boy edge that spelled danger.

His brow was wrinkled.

His eyes were stressed.

He reached across the table and squeezed Shade's hand.

"What's wrong?" she said.

He pushed a half-full cup of coffee to the side and said,

"Not here."

They walked to his truck, which was on California, up several blocks, away from the buzz. London shadowed them fifty steps behind, staying in the cool shady parts as much as she could.

The truck wasn't locked.

The windows were down.

Still, the inside baked.

Mojag slipped in behind the wheel and told Shade to get in. When she opened the passenger door and complied he said, "Look in the glove box."

She opened it.

Inside was a scalp.

It was long and black.

"That's from Tehya's head," he said. There was water in his eyes. "Prepare yourself for what I'm about to say because it's not what you want to hear."

"Is it about Visible Moon?"

He nodded.

"Unfortunately it is."

111

The South Platte industrial area was a spiraling mishmash of wooden, cinderblock and metal buildings that buzzed during the war but now sat largely decayed and abandoned. The new manufacturing area was up north, closer to the rails, highways and suppliers.

Here, the asphalt was cracked and potholed.

Weeds choked everything.

Trees were nonexistent.

Wilde pulled Blondie into the shade alongside a tall wooden building, so close that Alabama had to scoot over and hop out his side.

"Where do we start?" she said.

Wilde looked around.

"It doesn't matter," he said. "Wherever we start, we won't find her until the last place we look."

Alabama punched him on the arm.

"Bad, even for you." She got serious. "What are you going to do to this lawyer, now that you know he's the pinup killer."

"I'm not sure yet but it will happen tonight," he said.

"Tonight?"

"Right. I'm not going to give him an opportunity to move the timetable up on Senn-Rae."

He pointed at an abandoned metal building three stories high. The first floor windows were covered with plywood. The upper level windows were busted out.

"Let's try that one."

All the ground level doors were locked and chained. Wilde pried the plywood off a window, cupped his hands, boosted Alabama up and then muscled through. The air smelled like a thousand years of bad dust. They found the interior stairway at the north and headed up. When they got to the roof, the latch was chained shut.

"Strikeout," Alabama said.

"Not necessarily."

"You think there's another way up?"

"Probably not."

"Then it's a strikeout," she said. "The chain would have stopped him."

"Not if he put it on after he left."

Wilde spotted a bar and tried to bust the lock. It wasn't in the mood. "Where's my gun? In the glove box?"

"No."

"Are you sure?"

"It's in your desk drawer. I saw it there this morning."

"How come it's never where I need it?"

"Karma. That's my best guess."

He tried the bar again, this time with all his strength, and didn't budge anything except maybe a few bones in his back.

"Let's try another building."

Outside he noticed a ladder bolted onto the side of the building that started ten feet off the ground and led all the way to the roof, something in the nature of a poor-man's fire escape.

"Well that's interesting."

Alabama studied it.

"I thought you didn't like heights."

"I don't," he said, "but I do like you."

She shook her head.

"You're not getting me on that thing, no way."

"Just don't look down."

"*You* just don't look down."

He got under it and cupped his hands.

"Put your foot in," he said. "I'm going to shoot you up. See if you can grab the bottom rung and get up."

She cocked her head.

"I'm keeping score of all this stuff, for your information. You're going to walk in one morning and find a list and an invoice sitting in the middle of your desk."

"I'll be on the watch for it. Put a chocolate on top. Be careful of those rungs, they're going to be hot."

She turned out to be the slowest ladder-climber in the world but eventually made it to the top and disappeared over the parapet.

A few heartbeats later she leaned over and shouted, "You

better get up here."

112

The coyotes came within five or six steps of Fallon, then spread out and put her in a circle, howling and barking with a greater and greater frenzy. They were so close they actually took shape; she could see them, blackish-gray shapes in an even blacker night. She spun, facing one way then another, not wanting to leave her back too long in any one direction.

She wanted to drop to the ground and curl up in a ball.

That was the absolute worst thing she could do and she knew it.

Don't fall.

Don't fall.

Don't fall.

If she fell she was dead.

She raised her arms and swung 'em.

"Go away!"

"Go away!"

"Go away!"

They backed up, not far, but a little.

She continued screaming, even louder, then took a step towards one as if charging. It actually scampered back. Then it turned and bounded off.

The others followed.

As soon as they left the barking stopped.

She was alone.

There wasn't a sound to be heard other than the air passing in and out of her own lungs.

She knew to get out while the getting was good but no longer had any idea which way to go.

She was totally and irretrievably disoriented.

All she could do was pick a direction, walk in a straight line and hope she got lucky.

She should have left the parking lights on.

How could she be so stupid?

She walked for ten minutes, then another ten and yet another.

No asphalt appeared.

All she got was more bushes and dirt and scratches and ankle twists and doubts.

She was pointed the wrong direction.

She was making things worse.

Her heart beat.

The realization that she could actually die out here was starting to take a more deadly hold.

She needed to change directions.

She turned left ninety degrees and started all over.

She walked for half an hour without changing course and didn't come to a road. Her feet were heavy, her legs were on fire, her brain was thick with fear.

Then something happened she didn't expect.

Headlights appeared far off to the left, a half-mile distant, maybe more, barely visible over a crest.

She headed directly for them.

They were moving at a fast clip.

In a few seconds they'd disappear.

Once they did, she needed to keep a straight line without veering.

That was critical.

Suddenly the headlights slowed and came to a stop.

They backed up and pulled behind something.

It was her car they pulled behind.

Someone was checking it out.

113

When Mojag told Shade to prepare herself for what he was going to tell her, she knew Visible Moon was dead. She opened the door and walked off, not strong enough to hear the words. It was almost as if a last resort defense mechanism had taken control of her; if she didn't hear the words, Visible Moon wouldn't be dead.

A door slammed behind her.

Strong arms grabbed her from behind.

"Shade, stop."

She looked into his face.

He had nothing good to tell her.

"We tried," he said. "We did everything we could."

He pulled her close.

She fought as if he was the enemy, then she surrendered and buried her face in his chest. Her body shook and her eyes watered.

"It's okay," Mojag said. "It's okay."

London ran over.

"What's wrong?"

"Visible Moon's dead."

They got in Mojag's pickup and took off, not needing to be a visible target for some lucky cop.

"I spotted the guy yesterday afternoon walking down the street," Mojag said. "I followed him to that tall building on 16th Street, the one with the clock at the top."

"The Daniels & Fisher Tower," Shade said.

Mojag shrugged.

"Whatever," he said. "The building has an elevator operator. I got a ten-dollar bill out of my wallet and held it in my hand and said a man just dropped it on the street and I wanted to give it back to him. I described the guy. I said he just came into the building a couple of minutes ago."

"That's Baxter Fox," the guy said. "He's an attorney up in Browne, Denton & Savage on the ninth floor." He held his hand out. "I'll give it to him if you want."

Sure.

Thanks.

"I got his address and paid a visit to his house while he was still at work," Mojag said. "Tehya's scalp was tacked to his bedroom wall like some kind of trophy. When I saw it, it was all I could do to stop myself from going down to where he worked and shoving it in his mouth until he choked to death on it. Instead I left it where it was and marked the mailbox. You never showed up last night."

"You know why," Shade said.

"No I don't."

"You haven't heard?"

"No. Heard what?"

She told him about the encounter with Jack Mack.

"You need to get out of Denver," he said. "We should just leave, right now."

She shrugged.

"Maybe."

They drove in silence.

Mojag continued.

"When you didn't show up I decided to just take care of him myself," he said. "It was about midnight. He was sound asleep in his precious little bed when I yanked him out and punched him in the face. I pulled Tehya's hair off the wall and said, *Where'd you get this?* At first he tried to get out of it. He said he bought it from someone. I had to lay pain on him, lots and lots of pain, before he finally admitted it."

"He admitted it?"

Mojag nodded.

"Right to my face," he said. "He even told me the woman worked at some dive Indian bar down in New Mexico. *Where's the other woman? What'd you do with her?* That's what I said. When I said that, he knew exactly what I was talking about. He didn't say anything like, What other woman? What he said was, *She's dead.*"

He pulled a pack of Marlboro's out of his shirtsleeve and tapped the pack.

There was only one left.

He lit it, took a long drag and handed it to Shade.

"When he said, *She's dead,* I lost it. I stuck my thumbs in his throat and choked the life out of him with every muscle in my body. He shit in his pants before he died. I never smelled anything so good in my life."

114

Natalie Levine's body was staged in pinup fashion behind the roofing ductwork, exactly like Stuart Black's macabre memoirs described. She wore the same clothes as the painting from Dames in Danger. "This proves the lawyer's our man," Wilde said. "This body's never been found. The fact that she's here isn't public knowledge. Only the killer would know it."

"And now us," Alabama said.

"Right. And now us."

"We should call the police and let them handle it from here on," she said.

Wilde already knew that wouldn't work.

"He knows someone broke in," he said. "I left the files on a table near the back door. He's undoubtedly spotted them there, not to mention he would have seen the bottom drawer of the file cabinet jacked open. Those files are history. They're up in flames by now."

He scouted the skyline.

Everything was small and distant.

Nothing seemed important.

He took one last look at the body and said, "Come on, we're going to Senn-Rae's."

When they got there, Alabama dialed Stuart Black's office and held the receiver between her ear and Senn-Rae's. The man actually answered.

"Is this Stuart Black?"

"Yes."

"Mr. Black, my name's Katie White. I had a little run in with the police."

"What kind of run in?"

"They think I stole a car," she said. "I'm out on bail. Is this the kind of thing you handle?"

'Yes, but not today. Stop by Monday."

"I will."

He gave her directions.

She said she'd be there at nine and hung up.

Wilde looked at Senn-Rae.

"Well? Is that your mystery client?"

She wrinkled her brow.

"I'm not positive."

"I need a yes or no."

"I can't give you a yes or no," she said. "It sounds like him but I can't say for a hundred percent that it is."

"Well what percent would you give it?"

She tilted her head.

"Eighty or ninety."

Okay.

Eighty or ninety.

Close enough.

Wilde headed for the door.

Before he stepped out he said, "He knows someone's on to him. You're his next target. The pressure might make him move his timetable up. Keep your door locked and don't open it for anyone. Until further notice, the law office is closed."

He waited for an argument.

She didn't give him one.

Heading down the stairs Alabama said, "Hey, I forgot to tell you something. Do you remember when we were in Jennifer Pazour's house the second time and you stuck her checkbook in your pocket?"

Right.

He remembered.

Jennifer Pazour was the pinup girl from the shed.

"I flipped through it," Alabama said. "There was something a little bit weird in there."

"Like what, a dead fly?"

"No, not a dead fly."

"A dead what, then? Don't tell me a dead elephant because it wouldn't fit. If you tell me a dead elephant I'm not going to believe it."

"Get serious for a minute, Wilde," she said. "You're impossible sometimes. There were two large deposits into her account."

"How large?"

"Five thousand."

Wilde was impressed. "That's a lot of money."

"Times two," Alabama said. "Two deposits of five thousand. Ten thousand total."

"You could buy a house with that," Wilde said.

"Right."

"She was a cab driver."

"That's my point," Alabama said. "Where'd the big bucks come from?"

Wilde shrugged.

"Maybe she had a sugar daddy. She was pretty enough."

"That's a lot of sugar."

"Maybe she was worth it."

"No one's worth it," she said. "And remember, her raven-haired friend and the dog were buried out there behind the shed. Something was going on."

They came out of the building.

The Denver sun was bright and hot.

Wilde opened the passenger door so Alabama wouldn't acrobat over it and screw up the springs.

"You're such a gentleman," she said.

"Right. We'll go with that."

He walked around and got in.

"Ten thousand, huh?"

Right.

Ten thousand.

"Is it still in there?"

"Most of it," she said. "Why? Are you thinking we should take it?"

115

A bright sun forced its way through the window covering with such intensity that it pulled Fallon out of a deep sleep. Alone in a soft bed, she rolled onto her back and stretched. The events of last night jumped into her brain. Whoever stopped at her car wasn't there when she got there. She didn't know if the person wrote her plate number down or not. She made it home without incident shortly before sunrise, told Jundee what she'd done then crashed into the sheets and closed her eyes.

The world immediately disappeared.

She swung her feet over the edge of the bed to find she was still in the same clothes as last night. She stripped them off as she headed for the bathroom, took a long hot shower, then found Jundee in the kitchen making pancakes and eggs for her.

He handed her a cup of coffee.

"Afternoon sleepyhead."

She yawned.

"What time is it?"

"Three."

It was dark in the house.

All the coverings were closed.

"What's with the windows?"

"Just a precaution," Jundee said. "I got a bad phone call a little while ago."

She took a sip of coffee.

"About what?"

He peeked outside, saw nothing of importance and let the

blind fall back.

"Do you remember that PI I hired?"

'Whitecliff," she said.

"Good memory, I'm impressed," he said. "Anyway, I gave him another assignment, to see if the Vampire woman had contacted the guy you stole the car from. He did some snooping around. The Vampire woman must have written down the license plate of the car you were driving out there in the desert, because when Whitecliff called the owner to see if he'd been contacted, he had."

"By Vampire?"

"No, by an investigator down there in Santa Fe by the name of Randy Richardson," Jundee said. "Whitecliff knows the guy pretty well and called him to see if he'd tell him what was going on. Richardson was pretty cooperative. He said he was hired to find out who stole the car. He did a little snooping around and found it was taken from a restaurant parking lot, the same restaurant where you worked and never showed up at that morning. He told his client that the person who stole the car was probably a young woman named Fallon Leigh."

She shoved a forkful of pancakes in her mouth.

"That's my name."

"Yes it is," Jundee said. "Richardson stopped being cooperative when Whitecliff asked him who his client was. That information, he wouldn't divulge."

"It has to be Vampire," Fallon said.

Jundee shrugged.

"Whitecliff had the impression it was a man."

"Vampire's not a man."

"True," Jundee said. "The bottom line is this. Someone's looking for you, someone who wants to find you bad enough to throw money at a PI, enough money to make him drop everything he was working on."

"It's the briefcase," Fallon said. "They don't want me, they want the briefcase."

"That may be but their sights are on you," he said. "They know your name. They probably know what you look like."

Fallon frowned.

"What we should do is just take the damn briefcase, put it on Vampire's doorstep, ring the bell and run."

Jundee shook his head.

'No. They're all spies or something," he said. "If they get that briefcase, they'll have the complete package. I guarantee you it will be in the hands of the Russians by this time next week."

"So let's just destroy it."

"Can't," he said. "It's our only bargaining chip if they capture you or me."

He rubbed her shoulders.

"Thanks for doing what you did last night."

"Sure. Do you really think Vampire's a spy?"

"Look at it this way," Jundee said. "She was out there in the middle of nowhere when the guy went off the cliff. She was out of her car waiting for you when you came up. She wrote down your license plate number, we now know that in hindsight. She went down to the wreck and got the second briefcase."

"If that's true then why didn't she just confront me when she had the chance?"

"You had the guy's gun, remember?" he said. "That probably saved your life." He exhaled. "Either she's a spy or someone found out about her after the fact and is getting her to cooperate with them."

"Why would she?"

"Maybe they're pretending to be FBI or CIA or something," he said. "I don't know. My money is on her being a spy all along. One thing I do know for sure, you're a serious target."

"Then so are you," Fallon said. "Vampire's seen you. She's seen us together. Sooner or later she'll put a name to your face."

He nodded.

"That's why the blinds are closed," he said. "We need to get that briefcase out of your hotel room and find a new place to hole up."

116

With Visible Moon dead, Shade had no more business in Denver. The CIA was in town hunting her down. The cops were after her in connection with the shooting of Jack Mack. The only rational course of action was to get out now while she could.

Mojag couldn't stress that enough.

"Don't go back to your hotel, don't flash your face around for even one more minute, don't do anything except get in my truck and head back to the reservation with me," Mojag said. "You'll be safe there. Let things cool off and then decide what you want to do." He nodded at London and said, "You can come too, darling. You're more than welcome."

London looked at Shade.

"He makes sense."

A cop car rolled through the intersection up the street.

Mojag flicked his cigarette into the street.

"I need to beat feet before that lawyer starts stinking up a storm and the cops start wondering who got him that way." He walked towards the truck and said over his shoulder, "You can come or not, your choice, but I'm not hanging around to see what the local jail looks like."

Shade stood there and watched him.

Mojag got to his truck, hopped in, slammed the door and fired up the engine. In the rearview mirror, he watched them for a few seconds, then jammed the clutch into reverse and squealed the tires until he got back to them.

The brakes went on, hard.

The truck jerked to a stop at the curb.

He leaned over and stuck his head out the passenger window.

"Last chance."

"We're wanted," Shade said. "You'll have a better chance without us."

He shook his head.

"Your funeral."

Then he was gone.

117

Driving back to the office, Wilde couldn't get the sight of Natalie Levine's dead body out of his eyes, he couldn't get the stench of her death out of his mouth, and he couldn't get the injustice of her killer walking around free and easy out of his heart.

He lit a cigarette and paced by the windows.

Alabama sat on the desk, keeping him in the corner of her eye, not saying anything, letting him work through whatever it was that he was working through.

He stopped and looked around.

"Where's Tail?"

"I told you," she said, "when I got here this morning Shade and London were in here. They said the door was open when they got here. Tail wasn't around when they came in." A pause. "Want me to go out and look for him?"

Wilde shook his head.

"You'll never find him," he said. "He's probably being served up for lunch over at Wu's."

He lit another cigarette.

The cupboard door from the shed where Visible Moon had been held prisoner had been leaning in the corner. In it were the scratches that replicated the markings on the floor under the mattress. Wilde pointed and said, "What happened to the wood that was over there?"

Alabama shrugged.

"Shade must have taken it."

Wilde blew a smoke ring.

Suddenly he mashed the butt in the ashtray, grabbed one of the red matchbooks out of his desk, dipped his hat over his left eye and headed for the door.

"Where you going?"

"To close in on our little killer friend," he said. "The time's come."

She fell into step.

"I'm coming with you."

"No you're not."

"Why not?"

"Because you got the looks," he said. "I don't want you on the guy's radar screen."

"Wilde—"

He put a finger on her lips.

"It's not open for discussion. While I'm gone, follow up on Shade's issue. Find out how much the cops know about that Jack Mack incident. Talk to Jacqueline White at homicide. Tell her the information's for me."

"She hates you."

"Only 75 percent of the time," he said. "Call her four times if you have to."

He headed down the stairs two at a time and pointed his shoes towards the lawyer's office, the same office he broke into earlier today.

Hopefully the man was still there.

Wilde needed to get a look at him.

He needed to figure out how he was going to handle things.

He needed answers.

Two blocks, that's how far he walked at a brisk pace, before he even once looked behind him. When he did he saw something he didn't expect.

Alabama was fifty steps behind.

He stopped and waved her over.

"What are you doing?"

"Watching your back."

"You don't take directions very well, do you?"

"Apparently not."

"Tell me again why I put up with you."

She ran a finger down his nose.

"Because you know that sooner or later you're going to flop me on my back."

"No I'm not."

"Yes you are. You said it yourself that I got the looks."

"I didn't mean it that way."

"Relax, Wilde. It's destiny. Just accept it."

When they got within sight of Stuart Black's office, the man was in the process of swinging the front door shut and heading for the sidewalk.

He was about thirty, tall and powerful.

Wilde didn't know if he could take him in a fair fight.

Wilde had only planned to get a feel for the man, not have an encounter. When he saw him though, something built up in his throat.

"Stay here," he told Alabama.

Then he headed over. The man was walking now, going the same direction. Wilde caught up from behind and put a hand on his shoulder. It was ripped with muscles. The man stopped and turned.

Wilde handed him the matchbook, the red matchbook with the gold B on the front, the one he found in the dirty clothes. As he did, it dawned on him that the B stood for Black.

"You dropped this," he said.

The man looked down at the matches then into Wilde's eyes.

118

After retrieving the briefcase from under the bed at Fallon's hotel, she and Jundee drove south until they got into the sticks and booked a room at a one-story dive called the Dangling Donut. They had no idea how the place got its name and didn't care.

Jundee was tense.

Something was wrong.

When Fallon asked what it was, he said, "I keep thinking about that car that stopped by yours last night. Your license plate is EZ3."

"It is?"

He nodded.

"The point is, I never noticed," she said.

"It's easy to remember," he said. "If someone concentrated on it, it would still be in their brain. If the body shows up and gets in the paper, whoever stopped there might remember that night and call the cops. He might remember the plate number. If he does, the cops can trace it to the rental agency and from there to me."

"So what do we do?"

He exhaled.

"It would be dangerous to go back there," he said. "Real dangerous. It might be more dangerous not to, though. I think we need to move the body."

Fallon laid face down on the bed and closed her eyes.

"Hey, hey, hey," Jundee said. "This isn't your fault."

"Yes it is."

"No it's not," he said. "It's just one of those things. I'd rather have the body where you put it than have it out there on the lawn. You did good, real good. We just need to make it a tiny bit better."

"Okay."

He rubbed her shoulders.

"We'll do it tonight," he said. "We'll do it right at the edge of darkness while there's just enough light to find it. We'll bring it back, put it in the trunk and find a new place for it another fifteen or twenty miles down the road."

"It gives me the creeps," Fallon said.

"What, the body?"

"Right. The body."

"It's just a body," Jundee said. "It can't hurt you."

He straddled her ass and massaged her back.

She rolled over, put her arms around his neck and kissed him.

"Come here, you," she said.

"Me?"

"Yeah, you."

Jundee took his time with her.

She'd never been loved that much, that thoroughly, that infinitely.

Afterwards, Jundee stood naked in front of the mirror and raked his hair back with his fingers as he studied his face.

He was gorgeous.

Beyond gorgeous.

Fallon had never seen a more perfect man.

"After we move the body, we'll pay a visit to the Vampire," he said.

Fallon sat up.

"You're kidding?"

No.

He wasn't.

Not even a little.

"We have to get that other briefcase out of her hands," he said. "Once we get the pair of them, we'll burn them to ashes, every single piece of paper. Then it will all be over. At that point they'll leave us alone." He paused and added, "She won't go to the police. She can't. She's a spy. That's where she got the money for that mansion. She must have been involved in some heavy things."

Shade frowned.

"That PI guy—"

"—Whitecliff—"

"—right, Whitecliff, he said he thought the person who hired the other PI was a man."

Jundee nodded.

"Right."

"If that's true then Vampire's working with someone," she said. "She has backup, or co-conspirators or whatever they are. They might be staying at her place."

"That's a chance we'll have to take."

She came over, wrapped her arms around his stomach and laid her head on his back.

"You scare me sometimes."

"Why?"

"Because you're not afraid of anything."

He shook his head.

"Trust me baby, I'm scared of every piece of this. I'm more scared than you could ever know."

119

Shade and London headed to Wilde's office to find the door locked and no one answering. A white cat with a black tail bounded up the stairs and rubbed against Shade's leg. They took it to the Ginn under Wilde's office, ordered beer and a bowl of milk, and kept one eye on the street and the other on Tail.

"So what now?" London said.

Shade shrugged.

"If I were you, I'd just get out of town. You really don't have a dog in this fight."

"That's actually a good idea. Come with me."

"Can't."

"Why not?"

"I made a promise to catch a mole," she said.

London wrinkled her face with disapproval.

"That's history," she said. "It would have been a long shot getting the goods even when you were on the inside. Now it's impossible. Just call your contact. Tell them it didn't work out. Let them go to Plan B."

"Can't," Shade said. "I need to nail whoever it is that's framing me."

"Penelope Tap."

"Probably but I'm not positive."

London took a swallow of beer.

It was cool but not cold, not frosty.

"I hate warm beer."

Shade agreed.

"Warm beer's only okay if it's your fifth or sixth," she said. "We should have gotten wine." A pause, then, "There was something wrong with Mojag's eyes."

"What do you mean?"

"I don't know. They were different."

"Eyes don't change," London said. "They looked the same to me. I didn't see anything different."

Shade patted the woman's knee.

"Thanks for being here. I really screwed your life up."

"Don't worry about it," London said. "It was time."

Suddenly an image jumped into Shade's brain. It must have registered on her face because London said, "What's wrong?"

"I just figured something out," she said. "Remember when we went to Wilde's office this morning and the door was open?"

Yes.

She did.

"There was something wrong, other than the door being open, but I couldn't figure out what it was. It's been nagging at me all day. I just now figured out what it was."

"So what was it?"

Shade didn't answer.

Instead she stood up and gathered Tail. "Come on, I want to get back into Wilde's office."

"He's not there."

"That's his problem."

They headed for the door.

"Wait a minute," a man said.

The words came from the bartender, a gruff man with a

raspy voice and too much vein pollution in his eyes.

"You might be interested in this," he said.

He handed them a newspaper.

Composite sketches of their faces were on page 5 in connection with the shooting of a man named Jack Mack on Market Street last night.

"I don't know if that's you two or not," the man said. "If it is though your secret's safe with me. I'm not a big fan of the cops."

Shade gave him a kiss on the cheek.

"Thanks.'

"No problem."

Wilde's office wasn't overly hard to break into. He really needed better locks. Inside, Shade pointed to the corner, the empty corner.

"There was a cupboard door leaning against the wall right there," she said.

"So?"

"So, that's what's wrong, it's gone. Help me look for it."

They searched.

As they did, Shade explained how it came from the shed where Visible Moon had been kept. Wilde had used it to scratch a replica of the marks on the floor under the mattress.

It didn't show up.

"Maybe Wilde took it home or something," London said.

Shade shook her head.

"We'll ask him but he'd have no reason. Someone stole it, that's my guess."

"Who?"

"I don't have a clue."

120

The lawyer showed no reaction to the matches. He didn't take them out of Wilde's hand nor did he say they weren't his. Instead he looked directly into Wilde's eyes and said, "Are you the one who broke into my office?"

"Maybe I am."

"That's a serious offense."

"There's a lot of offenses that are serious," Wilde said. "Take murder, for example. That's a pretty serious offense."

"I can't argue with you about that."

"I'd think not," Wilde said. "Did you file a police report on the break-in?"

"Not yet."

"Why not? Do you have something to hide?"

Black put a stoic look on his face.

He walked away and said over his shoulder, "Don't do it again."

Wilde let him get three steps and said, "Hey, Black."

The man turned.

Wilde blew him a kiss.

"That's from Senn-Rae. See you around."

"Maybe you will."

Wilde watched him walk away.

Then something happened that he didn't expect.

The front door of the office building opened and a woman stepped out. She locked the door behind her and headed up the street in the opposite direction of Black.

A briefcase swung from her hand.

Wilde intercepted her twenty steps down the sidewalk when she stopped to light a cigarette. She was about thirty. Tan legs and arms were framed in a white sundress. Her eyes were green and her hair was thick.

"Are you Stuart Black's secretary?"

She took a deep drag, pulled the cigarette out of her mouth and blew smoke.

The filter was red with lipstick.

"Maybe, why?"

He smiled.

"What's your name?"

"Jackie." A beat, "Jackie Fontaine."

Wilde shook her hand.

"Nice to meet you Jackie Fontaine. I'd like to talk to you about a few things if you have a couple of minutes."

"What kind of things?"

"Bad things," Wilde said. "Very bad things. Things that will make you wish you never met me."

"Well that's pretty mysterious," she said. "Am I supposed to be intrigued?"

He nodded.

"That's what I was hoping for. Can I buy you a cup of coffee?"

She studied him.

Then she smiled, not much but a little. The smile was slightly crooked; one side went up a little farther than the other.

It was very sexy.

"I like whiskey better than coffee," she said.

"Then whiskey it is."

Wilde put his arm around her waist and steered her towards Larimer Street.

She didn't protest the arm.

"My questions are about the Shadow file," he said.

As they cut down 16th Street, something happened that Wilde didn't expect. In the crowd up ahead, Senn-Rae walked directly towards him.

She was preoccupied, looking in windows.

Then she spotted him.

Her eyes went from him to the woman to him.

Wilde got busy thinking of what to say but never got the chance. Senn-Rae turned at the corner and walked briskly out of sight. When Wilde got to the street and looked up, Senn-Rae was running.

"A friend of yours?" Jackie asked.

"Yes."

"Sorry about that."

"It's not your fault."

They walked in silence.

Then Jackie said, "It doesn't bother me if you're a player. I'm just looking to rent, not own."

"Good to know."

121

Wilde and his new friend Jackie ended up at a cozy table in the back corner of a dark bar called Whiskey Snake. He felt bad about what he was doing. The woman was looking forward to getting him into bed and that wasn't going to happen. As bad as he felt about it, he felt worst about all the bodies piling up.

To his credit, he was honest with her.

Her told her there were pinup murders taking place.

He told her his theory that her boss, Stuart Black, was the

person doing them. Black's number was written on a piece of paper that Wilde found in the house of Jennifer Pazour, one of the victims. Black also did legal work for Jack Mack, who got shot to death last night. Most importantly, Black had files on the pinup victims in his office, hidden in the bottom drawer of his filing cabinet, in an expandable file marked Shadow.

The Shadow file.

Inside that file was information that only the killer would know.

"I'm putting myself out on a limb here telling you all this," Wilde said. "The reason I'm doing it is because I need you to help me."

"How?"

"I want to know if he's after the woman we just saw back on the street," he said. "Her name's Senn-Rae. She's a lawyer."

"What if he is after her? Are you going to kill him?"

Wilde lit a cigarette.

"If he somehow ends up dead, I'll be sure you get another job somewhere. You have my promise. If you have rent payments or something you're worried about, I'll cover 'em until you get on your feet."

She looked into his eyes.

"You're not going to take me to bed, are you?"

Wilde blew smoke.

"In different circumstances, if I wasn't already with someone, I would," he said. "There's something between us. We both know it. It's not something I can act on though."

She frowned.

"You shouldn't lead a girl on like that."

"You're right. I'm a jerk."

She didn't loosen up until the third drink. Then she started to talk.

"Stuart's a good man," she said. "He's not the killer you're looking for. His client is."

"His client?"

She nodded.

"The guy calls himself Shadow," she said. "We don't know his real name. After he does a kill, he calls Stuart up and tells him about it."

"Why?"

"In the end if he gets caught, he's going to have Stuart represent him," she said. "That's the official reason, anyway. Between you and me, I just think he needs to talk to someone about it. Stuart's the perfect guy. He understands defects and doesn't pass judgment. Plus he's not at liberty to tell anyone about it, attorney-client confidentiality and all that."

"So he doesn't know the guy's name, huh?"

"Negative."

Wilde slammed the whiskey down and ordered two more.

His head spun.

He didn't care.

In fact it felt good.

He hadn't been drunk for a long, long time.

Maybe this was it.

He was on that edge where he could go either way.

Something wasn't right.

Something didn't fit.

At first he couldn't figure it out but then he did.

"What you said explains the files," he said. "What it doesn't explain is why his phone number was written down on a piece of paper in Jennifer Pazour's house."

"She was a victim, right?"

He nodded.

"She was dumped on top of a shed way down south, out in the sticks."

"Poor girl."

Right.

Poor girl.

"So what do you think? Why was Stuart's number in her house?"

Jackie didn't know.

"The only thing I can figure is that someone must have referred Stuart to her for some reason," she said. "She never became a client though. She never even called him as far as I know. Maybe the guy who killed her wrote it down, Mr. Shadow. Maybe he was playing some kind of twisted game."

"Like what?"

"I don't know," she said. "Maybe he wanted the cops to find it and call the number. Maybe he wanted Stuart to get a call from the cops about a pinup murder and then not be able to talk to them about it. Maybe Shadow was testing Stuart somehow."

Wilde chewed on it.

He didn't swallow it though.

It was too farfetched.

Five minutes later Jackie got a strange expression on her face and said, "I just had a weird thought."

"How weird?"

"Freaky weird."

"That's my favorite kind."

"I'll bet it is," she said. "Anyway, Stuart has a client named Tessa Tanglewood. The last time she was in the office, me and her were talking while Stuart was finishing up with someone else. Anyway, Tessa told me that she had a girlfriend who was blackmailing someone and things were starting to get scary. Tessa told her to contact Stuart because she'd be able to talk in confidence and maybe he'd have some advice for her. Tessa was telling me this so that I'd relay it to Stuart when and if this other woman called. To my knowledge, no one ever called in with an issue like that. But what I'm wondering is whether this pinup victim—"

"—Jennifer Pazour—"

"—right, Jennifer Pazour, what I'm wondering is whether she was Tessa's girlfriend, the one she was talking about. Maybe she had the number written down because Tessa gave it to her."

Wilde was impressed.

It was a long shot but it was still a shot.

"You're a pretty amazing woman."

She leaned across the table and put her arms around his neck. She kissed him on the mouth then took his hand and put it on her breast.

"Amazing enough to get friendly with?"

122

Wilde's office was as good a place as any to be, so Shade and London hung out and waited for him to return. London turned on the radio to a jazz station. Tail hopped up and stuck his head right by the speaker, then rubbed his face on it. Ordinarily Shade would be impressed and make a comment.

Right now she was too preoccupied.

Words were stuck in her mind; namely the words spoken by Mojag, *He said he bought it from someone*, referring to Tehya's scalp.

She lit a cigarette, flicked the burning match out the window and immediately hoped no one was underneath catching it with the top of a head. She looked out just to be sure and saw it on the top of a man's hat, still burning. The man wasn't aware yet. She shouted out, "Hey, your hat's on fire," then ducked in before the guy could look up. Hopefully that did the trick.

She blew smoke and said, "Mojag said that the guy who killed Visible Moon first tried to claim that he bought the scalp from someone."

London nodded.

She remembered.

"What if that was the truth?"

"That was just a ploy," London said.

"How do you know?"

"Think about it," London said. "It doesn't even make sense. What do you think, that someone commits a brutal murder to the point of even scalping someone and then risks his entire life to sell something that ties him to the crime? For what, five dollars?" She shook her head. "He didn't buy it. Not in a million years. That was a lie. Don't even give it two more seconds of thought."

Shade paced by the windows.

London was right.

Still, something nagged her.

"Mojag shouldn't have killed the guy," Shade said. "Not without making him take her to Visible Moon's body first."

London shrugged.

"He snapped," she said.

"He shouldn't have," Shade said. "We don't have any proof that she's dead. What if she's still alive chained somewhere like she was in the shed, rotting to death even as we speak?"

London put her arm around Shade's shoulder.

"Look, I know this is hard," she said. "The last thing the guy would have done is tell Mojag he killed Visible Moon if he didn't. If she was alive, he would have played on it. He would have told Mojag she was alive and that he'd show him where she was. That would have given him a chance to escape. Or he would have tried to make a trade, his life for information as to where she was." She shook her head. "He wouldn't have said he killed her unless he did."

Shade blew smoke.

"I want to find her body," she said. "I need to be sure."

"You want some advice?"

"No."

"Good because here it is," London said. "Just let it go."

"The guy scalped Tehya."

"So?"

"So, don't you think he'd do the same thing to Visible Moon at the end?"

London shrugged.

She didn't know.

"There was only one scalp on his wall," Shade said. "Only one." She exhaled. "We need to get to his house and pick up the trail."

123

Mean charcoal-gray clouds rolled off the Rockies Saturday evening and threw a thick blanket over Denver. A breeze kicked up. Rain was coming. Blondie's top was up. Wilde sat behind the wheel parked in front of Tessa Tanglewood's house, waiting for her to show up from wherever she was.

His head buzzed from the whiskey, but not much.

The more he thought about Jackie Fontaine's theory that Tanglewood was referring to Jennifer Pazour when she talked about a blackmail that was getting scary, the more it made sense.

That would explain the mystery deposits into Pazour's bank account.

They were blackmail payments.

If this was a dead end then he didn't know where to turn next.

He was running out of ideas.

Alabama leaned over, pulled the pack of Camels out of Wilde's coat pocket, lit one and handed it to him.

"Here. Smoke. Calm down."

Right.

Good idea.

"I know you're all sweet on that secretary Jackie Fontaine, since she gave you all that information and wanted to screw you," Alabama said, "but I'm not so sure if she's as naïve and innocent as you think."

"What's that supposed to mean?"

"What it means is, maybe the whole thing was staged. Maybe the whole story was a big charade, orchestrated by the lawyer and played out by her."

Wilde blew smoke.

"Are you saying she's covering up for Black?"

"I'm saying I wouldn't necessarily rule him out. The matchbooks have a B on them; his last name's Black. Don't forget that."

"I haven't."

"That's not all," Alabama said. "According to your new love Jackie-girl, the files were just notes that Black took while talking to Shadow—right there, that's a clue something's wrong. It's a stupid name. Shadow. Who calls a client Shadow? No one, that's who."

Wilde smiled.

"Right," he said. "So?"

"So, it's one thing to take notes," she said. "But there were pages torn out of the magazines in there to. So what happened? Are we supposed to believe that Black got the reports from his so-called Shadow client, and then independently went out and dug up the magazines—most of which were out of print by that time and no doubt hard to find—just so he could rip the pages out and make the files a little more complete? That seems like a lot of work. It seems like a lot of time consumed by someone who really doesn't have a lot of time to spare."

Wilde chewed on it.

He gave it fair consideration.

Still, it didn't fit.

"I don't think Jackie was lying to me."

Alabama rolled her eyes.

"Wilde, here's a problem," she said. "Women lie to you all the time and you never have a clue."

"How do you know?"

"Because I do it myself."

"You do?"

"All the time," she said. "God, you're so cute."

He wrinkled his forehead.

"What do you lie to me about?"

She was about to answer when a cab appeared from out of nowhere and pulled into the driveway. The back door opened and legs encased in a tight red skirt swung out, followed by a young woman about twenty-two. She was tall, five-ten or five-eleven, with the body of a tennis-player. She paid the driver and fumbled in her purse for her keys as she headed for the front door.

Wilde and Alabama hopped out and followed.

"Hey Tessa, wait up," Wilde said. "We want to talk to you about Jennifer Pazour."

"You know Jennifer?"

"Sort of. I hate to tell you this and don't know how to do it except to just do it. She's dead."

Over the next thirty minutes, they learned a few things.

"Jennifer dropped a fare off one night way up on the north edge of the city and ended up getting flagged down by a man and a woman just as she was starting to head back," Tessa said. "They were sort of out there in the middle of nowhere with nothing really important around. The guy had blood on his hands, not a lot and not obvious, more like he'd been pretty bloody at one point and then wiped it off but didn't get it all. They were both pretty tipsy. Anyway, they had her drop them off at a bar on the west side, almost in the foothills, a place called Senior Frogs. She knew the bar. It wasn't their kind of place. A younger crowd went there."

"Okay."

"Anyway, the next day she's reading the paper and comes across an article about a woman being run over the night before," Tessa said. "Accordingly to the article, someone named Mary something-or-other got a flat tire. She was changing it when a car came speeding down the road and took her out, the side of her car, too. This all happened at night, after dark. Are you following me?"

Yes.

He was.

"It turned out that Mary got run over not far from where Jennifer picked up the man and woman. She started to wonder if they were the ones who did it."

Wilde nodded.

"That makes sense."

"That's when things went bad," Tessa said.

"How so?"

"She didn't go to the police like she should have," Tessa said. "Instead, she hired a PI to find out who the man and woman were. Somehow, the investigator actually figured it out.

Then Jennifer blackmailed the guy, doing it anonymously, just being a voice on the phone. I didn't know any of this was going on. You believe me, right?"

"Sure, why not?"

"It's the truth, I didn't know," Tessa said. "Anyway, the guy she was blackmailing was starting to close in on her. She got scared and told me everything that was going on. That's the first I knew of it. I told her to contact my attorney, Stuart Black, who might be able to arrange some kind of a standoff between the two. She said she would and wrote the number down. That was the last I saw of her."

"Who was the guy she was blackmailing?"

Tessa didn't know.

"She never told me."

"Why not?"

"Probably because she wanted exclusivity but I don't know that for a fact."

Outside, walking to Blondie, Alabama said, "Whoever she was blackmailing caught up to her."

Wilde said nothing.

"You're supposed to say, Right," Alabama said.

"Maybe that's right, maybe it isn't."

"What do you mean?"

"Maybe she did call the lawyer like she said she would."

Alabama wasn't impressed.

"If she did, your little love Jackie-girl wouldn't tell you about Tessa. There'd be too big a risk that you'd run it down."

Wilde lit a cigarette.

"Maybe she didn't know about the call," he said. "Maybe she wasn't at work when the call was made."

"Interesting."

"Isn't it?"

"So we're back to Black again."

"Not necessarily," Wilde said.

Alabama punched his arm.

"Make up your mind," she said. "Is he the guy or not?"

Wilde blew smoke and said, "You never answered my question before. What do you lie to me about?"

She kissed him on the cheek.

"Got you curious, don't I?"

He fired up the engine.

"Where we going now?" she asked

He took off and said, "Got you curious, don't I?"

124

Saturday evening, Fallon and Jundee drove south under a windy, blackening sky. A storm was moving in and it wouldn't be pretty. Fallon sat in the center, next to her man. Jundee had his left elbow out the window and a cigarette in his left hand. His right hand alternated between the steering wheel and Fallon's knee.

"Maybe it would just be better to let the body be," Fallon said.

"We're already en route."

"We can turn back."

"It'll be fine," Jundee said. "Don't worry about it."

They got to their destination exactly when they wanted, at the edge of darkness.

The road was deserted.

The last car they crossed was fifteen minutes back.

Jundee stepped out, closed the door and stuck his head through the window.

"If I don't get back before dark, turn the headlights on for three or four seconds every minute or so." He ran a finger down her nose. "See you soon."

"I'll be here."

She watched him as he headed into the terrain. Before long he was nothing more than a black silhouette. Then the thickening darkness swallowed the silhouette.

Five minutes passed.

Rain came, light at first then mean and nasty.

It blotted out the little light that was left.

Fallon slid over until she was behind the wheel, flashed the headlights for three seconds then shut them down.

"Come on, Jundee."

Minutes passed.

Lightning exploded overhead simultaneously with a deafening slap of thunder. Then something bad happened; headlights appeared in the rearview mirror, still distant but definitely heading this way.

What should she do?

Think.

Think.

Think.

If she just sat there the person might stop. It would be too suspicious if she didn't at least roll down the window. He'd see her face. More importantly, he'd want to know what she was doing out here. What would she say? Moving a body that me and my boyfriend killed?

The other option would be to lock the car, head into the terrain out of sight and wait for him to pass.

That would be better.

It still wouldn't be good though.

He might stop.

What if he turned out to be the guy who stopped last night? Now he'd really think something was strange. If he didn't write the plate number down last time, he definitely would this time.

Damn it.

This was bad.

Wait.

There was another option.

She could drive down the road a quarter mile or so with the lights out, turn around, put the lights on and then drive back this way.

That way they'd be nothing more than two cars passing each other.

That was the best option.

She cranked over the engine and looked ahead.

The road was nearly invisible.

She'd have to be careful.

"Don't go off the road. The last thing you need is to get stuck in the squish."

She shifted into first and took off.

125

Baxter Fox—the man Mojag killed—wasn't listed in the phone book. He should have been easy to track down, being a lawyer. How the hell did Mojag find his house yesterday? Did he follow him home from the office?

"I can't believe this is so hard," Shade said.

"Maybe he does divorce law," London said.

"Meaning what?"

"Meaning a lot of those types lay low out of the office. That makes it harder for mad husbands to hunt 'em down."

Shade smiled.

It was a joke but there was probably some truth in it.

As a last resort, they went over to the Daniels & Fisher Tower to see if there was anything there to be gained. The building was locked and the lobby was dark. They knocked on the door next to the revolving door until someone came and cracked it open.

It turned out to be a middle-aged woman in a blue cleaning uniform.

"We're trying to find Baxter Fox," Shade said.

"The building's closed."

Shade pulled a five-dollar bill out of her purse and dangled it in her fingers. "I'm supposed to pick something up from his office. I'm running late. It's important. If you could let me in it will only take a second."

The woman hesitated.

"I'm not supposed to do that."

"Help me out there, please, or I'm going to end up getting fired."

She studied Shade's eyes for a second, looking for danger or exaggerations, then opened the door and let them in. She took the bill and handed over a key.

"His office is on the ninth floor, No. 904. The elevator's shut down. You'll have to walk up."

"Thanks."

"Lock his door when you leave. I'll probably be gone before you get back down. Put the key over there in that flowerpot," she said pointing. "To get out of the building use that back door over there. Be sure it's closed tight. It locks by itself from the inside."

"Will do."

"Don't tell anyone I let you in."

"I won't."

Rain pelted against the building.

"Be careful of the ghosts. There are a lot of ghosts in here, even on a nice night. On a night like this you never know what you're going to get." She wrinkled her face. "I don't like the guy, personally."

"Who?"

"Baxter Fox. I don't like him."

The stairwell wasn't just dark, it was pitch-black. There were no emergency lights, no after-hours lights and no other lights. They may as well have been a mile under the surface of the earth, blindfolded.

"This is creepy," London said.

"Don't talk, you're going to wake the ghosts."

"Do you think she really believes in them?"

"No. She was just messing with us."

"I don't know," London said. "You don't see her in here with us. Maybe she really does know something we don't."

"Are you trying to freak me?"

London laughed.

"Maybe a little."

"Well stop it, it's not funny."

They came to a landing.

"This is floor five if I'm counting right."

"That's what I have too."

"Four more then. Four more to go."

They continued up.

"At least we don't have to worry about running into the cops here," London said.

"Right."

"Unless of course the ghost-lady recognized us from the paper and is calling them as we speak."

"Stop talking. You're not making things better."

126

From Tessa Tanglewood's house, Wilde headed for the first public phone he could find. A black rain pelted out of an even blacker sky. Blondie's wipers swung at full speed and still only delivered a blurred mess. The ragtop would start leaking if this kept up.

He spotted a phone but it had no booth.

He'd just have to get wet.

Luckily no one had ripped off the phone book. It was sopped though. The pages stuck together. He opened the yellow pages to Private Investigators. There were six numbers listed, one being his. The names were familiar. He reached in his pocket, found no coins and trotted back to the car.

"I need change."

"You didn't check before you went over there?"

"Apparently not."

Alabama found some in her purse. Wilde dialed the first number, got no answer and remembered it was Saturday night. He looked up the man's name in the white pages and dialed. His question was direct. "This is Bryson Wilde," he said. "Did you do any PI work for a woman named Jennifer Pazour?"

"No."

On the fourth try he got the answer he needed, "Maybe, why?"

"She's dead," Wilde said. "I don't know if you knew that or not."

"I didn't."

"I have time for details but I need information and need it

now. You were trying to find out the name of a man she picked up in her cab one night."

"Right."

"What was the guy's name?"

A pause.

"That's confidential, Wilde."

"Do you think I don't know that? Let me repeat, the woman's dead. I'm in the middle of a mess here. I need to know the man's name and need it now."

Hesitation.

"You never heard it from me. His name is Parker Trench. He's a lawyer in a law firm downtown."

"Parker Trench?"

Right.

Parker Trench.

"Thanks."

"You owe me a referral."

"You'll get it."

"Make it two."

"Fine."

He hung up and dialed Senn-Rae. She answered with wine in her voice.

"Do you know a lawyer named Parker Trench?"

No.

She didn't.

"Who was that woman you were with this afternoon? The one in the white sundress?"

"No one."

"It looked like someone to me."

"I don't have time for this right now," he said. "I'm coming over. I'll be there in five minutes. Don't go anywhere."

"Why, what's going on?"

"Just stay there."

Six minutes later he turned the knob of her door and walked in.

"This is supposed to be locked," he said. "I thought we had an understanding. Where's your phone book?"

She got it.

He flipped to the T's, got the number he wanted and dialed. As it rang he got Senn-Rae's head by his and stuck the receiver between their ears. "I'm calling Parker Trench," he said. "Listen to his voice and tell me if he's your client."

A man answered.

His voice was deep.

Strong.

"Trench," he said.

"Who?"

"Trench."

"I'm trying to get Robert."

"There's no Robert at this number."

"Are you sure? Robert Brown, that's who I'm trying to get."

"There's no Robert Brown here. You dialed wrong."

The line went dead.

Wilde hung up and looked at Senn-Rae.

"Is that your mystery client?"

"Yes."

"It is?"

"Yes, I can't believe it."

"Are you positive?"

"Absolutely positive. How'd you find him?"

Wilde headed for the door.

"It's a long story. I have to run. Keep your door locked."

"Okay."

"I mean it."

"Okay I said."

He was three steps down the stairs when he heard, "Bryson!

Come back here."

He did.

"You didn't kiss me."

He did it.

"Better?"

"Yeah."

He turned.

"There'll be a lot more later. For right now just keep your door locked."

He got all the way to the ground level then headed back up, turned the knob and found it locked.

"It's me, Bryson."

She opened.

He grabbed the phone book, turned to the T's and looked up Parker Trench again, not for his number but his address. "Next time I forget something, tell me," he said. "Lock your door."

Then he was gone.

Outside it was storming even stronger than before. He fired up the engine, waited for the wipers to make a clean spot and squealed out.

"Where we going?" Alabama said.

"To see the pinup killer, Parker Trench."

"That's nuts."

The words shocked him because they were so absolutely true. It was nuts to bring her with him. It was nuts to put her in danger.

He slammed on the brakes.

"Get out."

"No."

"Do it."

"Bryson—"

"Do it I said."

She stepped into the storm and slammed the door.

"This isn't fair!"

She smacked her fist on the trunk as Wilde pulled off. She also shouted something, he wasn't exactly sure what it was but it sounded something like, "I hope you get shot!"

127

Sometimes things happen exactly the way they're supposed to even when the likelihood of them happening that way is minimal. So it was with Fallon's plan to drive down the road with the headlights off, do a one-eighty and then swing back. It worked perfectly. No encounter took place other than two pairs of headlights passing each other in the middle of a storm.

That's where the perfection stopped though.

Jundee showed up five minutes later with a heavy breath and said, "The coyotes ripped him apart."

"Really?"

He cracked the window and lit a cigarette.

"He's basically just rags and bones."

Halfway back to Denver flashing lights appeared in the rearview mirror.

Jundee checked the speedometer.

He wasn't speeding.

His headlights were on.

"What do these yo-yo's want?"

He pulled over, shifted into neutral and left the engine running.

Two cops approached, one on each side.

Flashlights sprayed in.

Fallon whispered in Jundee's ear, "Those are the same cops from yesterday."

"The ones who stopped you?"

"Yes."

The butt of a flashlight rapped on the driver's side window.

Jundee rolled it down halfway and said, "What's the problem?"

The cop put on a hard face.

"What are you doing out here? Are you looking to settle a score?"

Jundee looked straight ahead.

His heart raced.

Then he looked directly into the cop's eyes.

"Here's your choice," he said. "You and your friend can drive back to the station right now, this minute, and quit your jobs. If you do that, the score's settled."

The cop laughed.

"Did you hear that?" he said over the roof.

"Yeah, I heard it. It looks like we have a comic on our hands."

"It sure does."

He hardened his face.

"I don't think we're interested," he said. "Why don't you step out of the vehicle?"

Jundee stepped out.

The weather assaulted him.

The rain was cold.

It hit like needles.

Five minutes later he got back in. His face was a mess, his body was a mess, his lungs were on fire. Fallon slipped in the other side and scooted over to the middle, not as badly battered but breathing just as heavy if not more so.

Two asshole cops were on the ground, not moving, not breathing, not bothering anyone. Jundee ran over the one in front of the car as he pulled away, the one Fallon managed to grab by the eyes as he straddled her and beat her face with his fists. The body caught up on an axle, dragged for fifty yards and spit out the back.

Jundee pulled up an image of human hamburger and said, "Nice knowing you."

Fallon laid her head on his shoulder.

"I'm sorry you got pulled into that."

"I'm not."

128

Something thick and heavy hit the back of Shade's head. She knew she'd been attacked but crumpled to the floor in a black fog before she could turn to see who was responsible. A sharp pain radiated briefly and then everything disappeared. She regained consciousness sometime later not knowing if she'd been out two minutes or two hours. She was on the floor face down. Her hands were tied behind her back. Her ankles were tied together. The room was dark except for a sliver of light that crept through the windows. Rain pelted the building. Her brain throbbed and wouldn't let her remember where she was.

Then it came to her.

She was in Baxter Fox's office.

"London!"

"Well who's finally awake."

The voice belonged to a man.

She'd heard it before.

Suddenly a strong hand grabbed her face and tilted her head up. She found herself looking into the eyes of Mojag. They were intense, bordering on insane.

"You wouldn't let it go," he said. "No matter what happened, you wouldn't let it go. I gave you every chance but you wouldn't let it go. That's why you're here right now. You have only yourself to blame."

"Mojag—"

"Shut up!"

He pulled a sock off her foot, shoved it in her mouth and wrapped tape around her head.

"There, better?"

She mumbled something.

"What was that? London? Is that what you said, London?" He slapped her ass. "London can't hear you anymore so don't waste your breath."

He paced.

Then he lit a cigarette, squatted down and blew smoke in her face.

"Do you know what it said on the floor under the mattress? It said, Mojag killed Tehya," he said. "Do you know what it said on that cupboard door where you copied what was under the mattress? It said, Mojag killed Tehya. Do you know what it said on that piece of paper you copied from the cupboard door? It said, Mojag killed Tehya. Do you know why it said that? Because Mojag killed Tehya. Do you want to know why I killed her? Because she was turning five-dollar tricks in the back room of that stupid fucking bar. I told her to quit a hundred times. She never did. That night I got drunk, way drunk, beyond stupid drunk. I told her she was going to quit the tricks, it was over, she wasn't going to do it again, not even one. She told me to fuck off. She pushed me on the chest and ran out. That's when my brain exploded."

He punched the wall with his fist.

Something fell off.

Glass shattered.

"I killed her. She had it coming and I'm not sorry about it. I didn't take Visible Moon though," he said. "I scalped Tehya because no one in a million years would picture me doing that. They'd picture a white man. The reason I came to Denver with you was to help you find the person who took Visible Moon. It wasn't to rescue her though. It was to plant Tehya's scalp in his house. It was to make him the one who killed her, not me."

Lightning exploded.

The room lit up then returned to blackness just as quickly.

Thunder slammed against the building so hard that the windows shook.

"I made you take me to the shed to show me what was under the mattress, not because I needed to see the original but so I would know where the shed was and be able to burn the fucking thing down," he said. "I stole the cupboard door out of Wilde's office. I scraped the face to a pulp, busted the wood into a hundred pieces and threw them in ten different places. While you were passed out I took the paper out of your purse and burned it to ashes. All the evidence is gone."

Gone.

Gone.

Gone.

"The only other evidence that was left was Visible Moon herself," he said. "I pretended like I had spotted her killer. I pretended that I found Tehya's scalp tacked on his wall. I pretended that he said he killed Visible Moon. I pretended that I killed him in a rage. All that was to get you to stop trying to find her and get you to the reservation where I could keep you from saving her. You didn't do it though. That's why you're here right now. You wouldn't stop. You'll never stop as long as you're alive."

He flipped her onto her back.

He straddled her.

His weight was enormous.

She tried to wiggle but couldn't.

"Goodbye," he said.

Then he sunk his thumbs into her throat and bore down with an insane pressure.

She couldn't breathe in.

She couldn't breathe out.

Her brain turned to fire.

Seconds passed.

Then more.

Then more.

Her struggle got weaker and weaker.

The world got blacker.

Then she slipped into the darkness of death.

129

Parker Trench lived in a fancy house on a tree-line boulevard just off Colorado Boulevard on the west side of town. Wilde sat in Blondie three doors down, smoking a cigarette and contemplating exactly how to handle things. Half of him wanted to go in, make him confess and then kill him. The other half balked at the seriousness of that. Rain battered down so thick that the ragtop dripped.

Headlights swung around the corner and passed him.

Then the car stopped and backed up next to him.

It was a cab.

Someone gave paper to the driver and hopped out.

It was Alabama.

She ran around Blondie and hopped in the passenger side.

"It's raining," she said.

"What are you doing here?"

"Helping," she said. "What's the plan?"

He exhaled.

"I don't know yet."

"Is he home?"

"Yeah, I see a shadow move every now and then."

"Let's go in and get him."

"If I go in I'm going to end up killing him," he said.

"So?"

"So, that's serious."

"I'll do it then," she said. "You hold him."

He pictured it.

"We need to think it through."

Suddenly Trench came out the front door and trotted through the weather to the garage. Headlights came on and moved down the driveway.

Wilde fired up the engine but left the lights dark.

"I'm going to follow him. You go in and snoop around. Find out if he's after Senn-Rae. After fifteen minutes, get out of there whether you've found anything or not."

"Okay."

"I mean it," Wilde said. "Fifteen minutes tops. Promise me."

"Wilde, I always do what you say."

She hopped out and ducked into the shadows.

Wilde followed Trench who was already at the corner turning right.

In the city it was easy to hang behind and just be an anonymous car in a sea of cars. As they got farther south though the traffic thinned and Wilde's headlights got more pronounced. If they went much farther it would be obvious what was going on.

What to do?

Maybe he should just ram the guy and force a confrontation.

No.

Hold on just a little longer.

Find out where he's going.

Traffic got almost non-existent.

Suddenly Trench pulled to the side of the road.

They were in the sticks.

The place was deserted.

If Wilde stopped, it would be obvious he was following.

It was already obvious though.

He slowed down and came to a halt fifty yards back.

Nothing happened for ten seconds.

Then a gun fired and his windshield exploded.

More shots came.

Bam!

Bam!

Bam!

He opened the door, dove to the asphalt and rolled into the shadows. The bullets continued to hit Blondie. Wilde got to the far side of the road and sprinted through the blackness towards the gun. All he could hope was to stay invisible for as long as it took.

He closed the gap in no time.

Trench never saw him coming.

In a heartbeat Wilde had the man on the ground, pounding his face with every ounce of strength he had.

"This is for Jennifer Pazour!"

130

Vampire's house was dark. Not a light was on inside. Either she was sleeping, out, or laying a trap. Fallon and Jundee broke a window in the back and climbed in. Jundee grabbed the largest gourmet knife of several displayed in a wooden holder in the kitchen and headed upstairs with Fallon in tow.

Vampire was asleep.

Jundee flipped her over and put the knife to her throat.

"All we want are the documents," he said. "Be smart and you'll live."

The woman stared at him.

Then she said, "Okay."

131

Wilde's fists pounded into Trench's face over and over and over. He was killing the man but couldn't stop. "You're the pinup killer!"

"No I'm not"

"Bullshit."

"I'm not."

"Bullshit I said!"

"I can prove it," Trench said.

Wilde stopped his fist in mid-swing.

"I killed Jennifer Pazour," Trench said. "I'll admit that. I didn't kill anyone else though."

Wilde punched him again.

"You're lying!"

"I have a woman captive," he said. "If you kill me she'll rot to death. Her blood will be on your hands."

Wilde punched him again.

"You're lying."

"No I'm not," Trench said. "She's an Indian girl."

The words jerked Wilde's rage to a stop.

"What's her name?"

"Her name's Visible Moon. She's real, I swear to you."

Wilde grabbed the man's shirt with two fists and pulled him to his feet.

"Take me to her, now."

They got in Trench's car with Wilde behind the wheel.

"Go straight," Trench said.

They rode in silence.

"Here's the deal," Trench said. "I'll take you to her but you have to let me go. Nor can you ever tell the police about what I did to Jennifer Pazour."

Wilde leaned over and punched the man's face.

"That's your deal."

"You'll never find her," Trench said. "If I don't tell you where she is you'll never find her. I guarantee you that."

Wilde's instinct was to break his fucking nose a hundred different ways.

He didn't though.

He held his fist in check.

"Look," Trench said. "I was drunk one night and ran into a woman who was changing a tire. It wasn't entirely my fault. She didn't have the car lights on and she was partly in the road. But

I hit her nonetheless, plus I sideswiped her car. I was driving a friend's car at the time, a female friend's. She was with me that night."

"I don't care."

"Just hear me out," Trench said. "We ditched the car, walked a half-mile and got lucky enough to spot a cab. We flagged it down. We told the driver—who was Jennifer Pazour, in hindsight—to take us to a bar on the west side of town. We drank there for a couple of hours. Then we came out and pretended like the car had been stolen out of the parking lot. We called the police and they made a report. They found the car three days later and eventually tied it to the accident where the woman got run over. They never challenged our story though that the car had been stolen. We were off the hook."

"Good for you."

"Right, good for us," Trench said, "but not for long. The cab driver figured things out and hired a detective to find out who we were. Then the blackmail started. We paid her twice, $5,000 each time, but it was clear she'd never stop. We had no choice except to kill her."

"That's a coward talking."

"Be it as it may, that's what we decided to do," he said. "I decided it, actually. The woman I was with on the night in question wasn't involved. She didn't have the deep pockets, I did."

He put a finger to his face.

"You broke my nose."

"Fuck you. I'll break it again."

"Right, fuck me," Trench said. "Anyway, being a lawyer I have lots of lawyer friends. One of them is a man named Stuart Black. Over lunch one day, Stuart told me about a man who referred to himself by the name Shadow, who kept calling Stuart up and telling him about these pinup murders he was committing. I decided to duplicate that MO when I killed Jennifer Pazour. That way the blame would fall on someone else."

"Clever."

"We can go to a phone and call Stuart right now," Trench said. "He'll verify that my voice isn't the voice of the Shadow. He'll also verify that he told me about Shadow over lunch."

"So who's Shadow?"

"I don't know," Trench said. "Stuart doesn't know. No one knows. I'm telling you what I'm telling you so you'll understand that I'm not the pinup killer. I killed Jennifer Pazour but I'm not Shadow. I'll tell you more, the part about Visible Moon, but only if we strike a deal."

"There are no deals."

"Then there's no Visible Moon."

132

Wilde was stuck and he knew it. Sure, there was a chance he could find Visible Moon on his own; she'd be somewhere remote, like the shed. He could check every remote place he could find in this part of the universe. But there was a risk he'd never find her. That wasn't a risk that sat good in his throat.

Over the next five minutes driving through the relentless storm, he hammered out a deal with Trench.

Trench, for his part, would tell Wilde where Visible Moon was. He would also tell him why she was there.

Wilde, for his part, would let Trench go. Also, he'd never tell the cops or anyone else anything about the tire-changing accident, the murder of Jennifer Pazour or Trench's involvement with Visible Moon.

"Visible Moon has seen my face, many times," Trench said. "She'll talk to the police. That's fine. I'll be on the run and I deserve it. But I don't want you telling the police some of the other things I'm going to tell you, things that Visible Moon doesn't know."

They shook.

They had a deal.

There was one additional agreement though. They would leave each other alone for a week. After that week was over, Wilde was free to hunt Trench down and kill him if he chose to, and Trench was likewise free to hunt Wilde down and kill him if he chose to.

Wilde, for his part, didn't know if he'd ever act on that option. It was worth having it though even if that meant giving Trench the same thing.

"Okay, talk," Wilde said.

"I was with the CIA for a number of years," Trench said. "A couple of the higher-ups slowly brought me into their confidence. One was a man named Kent Harvin. Another was a woman named Penelope Tap. They were selling confidential information to the Russians. They recognized me as a money-oriented man and brought me into the fold."

"They were moles?"

"Moles, double-spies, whatever you want to call them," Trench said. "They sold secrets to the enemy. I was one too by the end, the number three man. I made a lot of money. I don't regret it. There came a point where I didn't trust my luck to run forever. I got out, moved to Denver and started a law practice. On the side, though, I still do an occasional project for my two friends."

"Okay."

"One of the biggest things going right now is the nuclear arms race," Trench said. "We're ahead, Russia's behind. We've been developing an H-bomb for some time now. The project is spearheaded in Las Alamos, New Mexico. One of the foremost scientists is a man named Richard Zephyr. He was a pretty straightforward man but had a little quirk. There was an Indian bar that he stumbled on one day while driving. The bartender was a woman named Visible Moon. Zephyr developed a little thing for her, and to his credit, got a similar reaction from her. They began seeing each other more and more frequently. Are you following me?"

"I'm following you."

"Good," Trench said. "The information on the H-bomb was worth a fortune but the CIA didn't have access to it. Kent Harvin and Penelope Tap came up with a plan. The plan was to kidnap Visible Moon and then give Zephyr an ultimatum, either turn over the plans for the H-bomb or kiss his little Indian friend goodbye. My part in the plan was to be the one who kidnapped Visible Moon. I went down there, waited outside in the shadows for the last drunk to leave the bar where the woman worked, then kidnapped her and brought her up here to Denver. The scientist, Zephyr, actually chose his girlfriend over everything else. He was in the process of driving to Denver to deliver the documents. Unfortunately, he ended up missing a turn and driving over a cliff. The documents disappeared."

"Interesting."

"Right, that's one word for it," Trench said. "This is where it gets strange. Unknown to anyone, a CIA agent named Shade de Laurent turned out to be a half-sister of Visible Moon. She started a search, first down at the reservation then getting a lead that brought her to Denver. My two contacts—Kent Harvin and Penelope Tap—didn't want her on the case. She was too good. Kent Harvin, believe it or not, was actually her immediate supervisor. He knew what she was capable of."

"Small world."

"Small world indeed," Trench said. "Anyway, they set her up to look like she was a mole. They broke into her apartment and planted evidence that made it look like she was selling confidential information to Russia through her contacts in Cuba."

"So she's not a double-agent?"

"No," Trench said. "With the so-called evidence in place, Penelope Tap through her underlings hired a freelance woman named London to bring Shade in dead or alive. Somehow Shade converted her. The next move was to hire a local named Jack Mack to kill the both of them. That failed. Another person was hired to file a police report saying that he was in the vicinity the night Jack Mack got murdered. He gave the police composite sketches of Shade and London. All the while, another hitman was sent and is probably in town even as we speak." He exhaled and said, "We're almost there."

Wilde slowed down.

"Here."

Wilde pulled to the side and stopped.

"Down that way a half mile," Trench said, pointing to something that might have once been a dirt road. "That's where you'll find Visible Moon. I can already tell you it's not drivable."

Wilde pulled the keys out of the ignition.

"You're coming with me," he said.

"No I'm not," Trench said. "Give her a kiss for me."

Then he was gone.

Wilde got out with no intention of chasing the man.

The storm pelted his face.

He dipped his hat lower and braced it with his hand against the wind.

"Hey, Wilde."

The words came from behind him.

He turned.

Trench walked over.

"One more thing for your information," he said. "After

Zephyr died, Visible Moon had outlived her usefulness. My two friends at the CIA wanted me to kill her. That wasn't my thing though. I told them I'd keep her off the streets until they sent someone else to do the job. That person is scheduled to arrive in town tomorrow. So your timing's good."

Wilde headed down the road.

Then he turned and said, "Trench, come back here a second. I have one more question for you. You hired Senn-Rae, right?"

"Yes."

"I don't get why you did that."

"Because I wanted her to find the pinup killer."

"I don't understand."

"The pinup killer had just struck," Trench said. "He killed a woman and left her on top of a boxcar. Stuart Black got his customary call about it and I learned about it from him. I went out there, saw the body and knew exactly where the guy had been. I told Senn-Rae that I had accidentally killed a woman during a bondage scene and buried her in a place that wasn't too far from the boxcar. I told her that the body had been dug up and I had been blackmailed by someone. All that was a lie. I never killed anyone, I never buried anyone and I never got blackmailed by anyone."

"So why'd you tell her that?"

"Because I knew she'd sniff around the area for who might have seen me burying the body," Trench said. "I knew she'd eventually make her way over to the boxcar. I knew she'd figure that whoever killed the woman there was the same person who was blackmailing me. I was hoping that she'd be able to track the guy down."

"Why?"

"I took some of Jennifer Pazour's personal things from her house," Trench said. "Once Senn-Rae found out who the pinup killer was, I was going to plant those things in that guy's house. At that point he'd be connected to physical evidence. I'd be a hundred percent off the hook."

"You put her at risk," Wilde said. "That wasn't very nice."

"Does that mean I'll see you in a week?"

"You might."

"I'll be watching for you."

"That's a good idea."

133

From Vampire's mansion, Fallon and Jundee went straight to Jundee's house, bandaged up their cuts, changed into non-bloody clothes, picked up the other briefcase and drove to a dilapidated industrial park east of the South Platte River. There they broke into an abandon building, collected a pile of wood, cardboard and combustibles, and set the two briefcases on top.

"You want the honors?" Jundee asked.

"Sure, why not?"

He handed her a book of matches.

She tore a stick off, struck it and held it under the edge of a box.

It took the flame nicely.

Within minutes the fire was five or six feet high.

They watched it from as close as the heat would let them.

"No H-bomb for you, Russians," Fallon said.

"Maybe next time."

She laughed.

"Right, maybe next time."

She stuck the matchbook in her purse and said, "I'm going

to keep these forever. A souvenir."

134

The path was muddy and filled with potholes but it was also choked with weeds which kept Wilde from sinking in. The enemy wasn't the mud so much as the darkness, which was absolute. It was all he could do to figure out where the road went. It would be easy to get off course and veer into the wild.

A half-mile up, that's where Visible Moon was, assuming Trench was telling the truth.

Wilde didn't even know what he was looking for.

He didn't know if it was a structure, a 55-gallon drum or what.

Something unexpected happened behind him.

The vehicle started up, the headlights turned on and then disappeared down the road.

Wilde felt in his pocket.

The keys were there where he put them.

Trench must have had a spare key under a mat or up in the visor.

A terrible thought jammed into Wilde's throat—he'd been set up. Trench outsmarted him. He dumped him out here in the middle of nowhere and tricked him into walking off into mud.

He kept walking, hunched against the storm.

Every square inch of his body was soaked. He couldn't be more wet if he'd fallen off a bridge into Clear Creek.

It was hard to judge how far he'd gone.

His pace wasn't steady.

He had no point of reference.

He kept going.

That was his only option, to keep going.

If there was even a remote chance Visible Moon was out here, he'd walk all night.

Ten minutes passed, then ten more, then ten more.

He must have gone at least a half-mile by now, maybe even a mile.

He stopped.

What to do?

Keep going?

Head back?

His legs were numb.

His body was loosing temperature. The rain was too cold to keep fighting.

Damn it.

Damn it to hell.

He kept going.

Then something strange happened.

He bumped his head on something metal.

What the hell?

"Visible Moon!"

No one answered.

He called again—"Visible Moon! I'm a friend. I'm here to help you."

Silence.

He felt the structure and found it to be smooth and round. As he edged down it started to take a shape. It was the fuselage of an old plane. He worked his way to the end and felt a jagged edge, no doubt where the body broke. He stepped inside.

"No!"

The word came from a woman at the other end.

"I'm not going to hurt you," Wilde said. "I'm a friend of Shade's. I'm here to take you home."

"You're tricking me."

"No, I'm not."

He inched towards the voice, slowly, moving his hands back and forth in front, not knowing what jagged edges were waiting in the dark to grab his face.

He got to the woman.

She was curled up in a ball at the farthest end.

She smelled like urine.

Wilde got down next to her.

She recoiled.

"I'm a friend," he said.

Then he got her in his arms and held her.

Her ankle was secured in a metal cuff. A chain ran from that to the framework of a seat where it was attached with a solid padlock.

"Do you know where the keys are?"

"The man takes them with him."

"Do you have a flashlight?"

"No."

Wilde pulled a matchbook out of his pocket and tried to light it. It was too soaked. He did the same with all the others. None of them worked.

He settled down next to the woman and rocked her.

She laid her head on his chest.

"It's okay," he said. "We'll wait until morning. Then I'll get you out of here."

DAY SEVEN

June 15
Sunday

135

Shade woke up in a hospital bed. Her brain was foggy, her vision was blurred and her tongue was dry. A face appeared in front of her. It was Visible Moon's face.

"I hear you've been looking for me."

It was her.

It was actually her.

Visible Moon kissed her on the forehead.

"You're going to be okay but you're under medication," she said.

"Mojag killed me. He choked me to death."

"Mojag's dead."

"He is?"

"Your friend London killed him," Visible Moon said.

They talked for a long time, quietly, and made plans to go to the reservation together.

They'd get to know each other again.

They'd let everything that happened wash off.

They'd be born again.

London came in and Visible Moon gave the two women their privacy.

"I heard you killed Mojag," Shade said.

London nodded.

"It seemed like the right thing to do."

"Remind me to thank you some day."

London laughed.

"I will."

"Because you deserve a good thanks."

"I'll be waiting for it."

London had some interesting information.

Shade's boss, Kent Harvin, and another CIA uppity-up, Penelope Tap, were uncovered as moles in connection with a plot to sell H-bomb information to the Russians. They were out. It was also discovered that they tried to frame Shade as being a double-agent.

Shade was in.

She frowned.

"I lied to you about something," she said. "I told you I was helping the white house catch a mole. That was a lie. There was no such assignment. I told you that to get some breathing room to find Visible Moon. I told you a second lie too. I told you that I was being framed as a double-agent."

"You were being framed."

"Okay, I was, but that's not the complete story. The other part of the story is that even though I was being framed, it was in fact true. I was a double agent."

"You were?"

Shade nodded.

"I've been selling confidential information to the Russians through my Cuban connections for years."

"Damn."

"Right, damn," Shade said. "I didn't just get money, though. I got information too, information that I passed on for the good of the order. That's the way I structured my deals. When you added it all up and subtracted it down, I got more than I gave. That was my logic, for better or worse. If you want to get right down to the guts of it though, I liked the thrill of being on both sides. I liked the risk, I liked the danger, I liked the rush. I liked being places I shouldn't, seeing things I shouldn't, knowing things I shouldn't, being something I shouldn't. It was a drug."

"I guess the question now is whether you're going to continue."

"I don't know," Shade said. "But if I do, I could use a partner."

"Me?"

Shade nodded.

London looked into the distance.

Then she refocused and said, "This is crazy talk."

"Is it?"

DAY TEN

June 18
Wednesday

136

Wednesday evening Jundee took Fallon to a dive bar on Larimer Street called the Whiskey Snake. They sat in the next-to-last booth in the back and drank wine. "Baby, I did something and I don't want you to be mad at me," Jundee said.

She ran a finger down his nose.

"What'd you do you bad boy?"

"Remember when we burned those briefcases?"

"Yes. I remember.'

"Well, the original document's weren't exactly inside them."

She wrinkled her brow and moved back.

"What do you mean?"

"Well, I thought they might come in handy for something," he said. "So I switched them out. Over the past few days I've been negotiating with Vampire to return her briefcase back to her, plus ours. This afternoon we reached a deal." He smiled. "We're rich, baby. That's what I'm trying to tell you. She's already delivered the money. I have it stashed in a hotel room."

"Did you deliver the briefcases to her?"

"Well, not the originals, they burned," he said. "I delivered the documents. Yes, she has them."

"I thought we went through everything we did so we could destroy them."

He kissed her.

"Well, change of plans," he said. "We're rich beyond our dreams. What's the matter? You don't look happy."

She worked a smile onto her face.

"No, I'm thrilled. I'm just in shock."

"You're not in shock, you're in rich shock. Filthy-rich shock."

"I got to pee."

"Then go do it, girl."

In the bathroom, she took a long look at her face in the mirror.

Then she opened the window, hiked her skirt up and climbed out.

At the first phone booth she called the police.

"There's a woman named Rebecca Vampire who lives in Capitol Hill. She's a spy and she has documents about the H-bomb in her house. She's going to sell them to the Russians. If you get there quick you can probably stop her."

"Who is this?"

"This isn't a joke," she said.

"Have you been drinking?"

"Yes but that doesn't mean I'm lying.'

She hung up and walked down the street.

137

Wednesday evening, Wilde got Senn-Rae drunk on white wine, put her over his shoulder, carried her into the bedroom and threw her on the mattress. He pinned her arms above her head and gave her a long kiss.

"You're so evil," she said.

"You have no idea."

He took his time with her, peeling off one precious layer of impediments after the other, bringing her to a slow, deep boil.

Then his phone rang.

He froze.

"Don't answer it," Senn-Rae said.

He chewed on it then got up.

"It could be something. Give me five seconds."

On the other end of the line was someone he didn't expect.

"Bryson?"

Right.

Him.

"This is Jackie Fontaine. I'm Stuart Black's secretary. Do you remember me?"

He pulled up the image.

Nice face.

White sundress.

Hot for him.

"Of course I do."

"You're not going to believe what just happened," she said. "I'm down on Larimer Street at the Whiskey Snake. That's the same place you took me. In fact, I'm sitting in the exact same booth."

"Look, this is bad timing," he said.

"No, no, let me finish. There's a guy in the next booth, he's drinking with a girl. She just went to the bathroom. He's sitting there by himself. He's Shadow. I recognize his voice."

"Are you sure?"

"I'm positive," she said.

"How positive?"

"A hundred percent. It's him, I'm telling you. It's him. I'd recognized his voice anywhere. It's definitely him. The girl calls him Jundee."

"Don't let him leave."

He slammed the phone down and shouted into the bedroom, "I got to go."

"Wilde! Don't you dare—"

He didn't answer.

He was already out the door with pants in one hand and keys in the other.

138

Blondie was in bad shape thanks to Trench's gun Saturday night. The windshield was gone, bullet holes had destroyed the hood and fenders, both headlights were shattered and the interior was trashed from the rain. She still ran though. Wilde pulled her out of the garage into the night. He hadn't gotten a block before a drizzle dropped out of the sky and flew horizontally into his face.

He didn't care.

There was no room in his mind for anything except what would happen.

He brought the vehicle to a skidding stop in front of the Whiskey Snake, jumped out and ran inside.

The back booth where Jackie Fontaine should be was empty. So was the one next to it.

Wilde reached over the bar, grabbed the bartender by the shirt and said, "There was a woman sitting back there. Where is she?"

"She left."

"When?"

"Fifteen minutes ago."

He bounded out the front door and looked up and down the street.

Jackie was nowhere.

Think.

Think.

Think.

Where'd she go?

Did she do something stupid and tip her hand?

Did the guy stick a knife in her ribs and say, "We're going for a little walk?"

He paced back and forth, not sure what to do.

Suddenly a woman came running up the street.

It was Jackie.

"You're here," she said. "I was hoping you wouldn't leave."

"Where'd you go?"

"The guy's girlfriend went into the bathroom and never came out. The guy left. I followed him. He went to the Kenmark hotel and got in the elevator. It stopped on the fourth floor."

"Let's go."

They ran too fast to talk.

At the hotel, Wilde grabbed Jackie by the arm, pulled her over to the reception desk and said, "What was he wearing?"

"Black pants. His shirt was blue. It had long-sleeves."

To the guy behind the counter, "That guy came in here ten or fifteen minutes ago. What room is he in?"

The man hesitated.

"I'm not supposed to—"

Wilde slapped his hand on the counter.

"Just tell me!"

"407."

"Thank you."

They bypassed the elevator and took the stairs two at a time to the fourth floor. They walked down the hall to 407 and Wilde knocked on the door.

"Who's there?"

Wilde pulled Jackie aside and whispered, "Is that him?"

"Yes."

"Are you sure?"

"Positive."

He slapped her on the ass.

"Get out of here, now."

"But—"

"Go I said."

Wilde stepped back in front of the door and said, "I have a message from your girlfriend."

The door opened.

A man stood there.

He had a bad-boy's face and a taut chest. There was anger in his eyes.

"Who the fuck are you?"

Wilde reached in his pocket and pulled out a red matchbook with a gold B, the one he found on the ground by the boxcar.

"She wanted me to give you this."

The man snatched it and looked it over.

"What the fuck's going on?"

Inside on the bed was an opened briefcase filled with money.

"You're the pinup killer," Wilde said. "I'm here to take you to the police."

The man punched him in the face, cat-quick, landing a solid blow before Wilde could cover. The impact sent him onto his back. He landed on his tailbone and pain shot up his spine.

The door slammed.

Wilde already knew what was happening.

The man was grabbing the briefcase and heading for the fire escape.

Wilde got up, tried the knob and found it locked.

He kicked the door.

It didn't budge.

He kicked it again.

It was solid.

The door to the adjacent room opened and a head looked out to see what the commotion was. Wilde ran over, pushed the person out of the way, ran through the room and pulled the window up.

He shot through the opening onto the fire escape.

The killer was out there heading directly for him.

The man froze with surprise.

Then he ran the other way.

There was no down, only up.

That's the way he went.

Wilde followed.

The man was fast, faster than Wilde but he had nowhere to go. The fire escape dumped them onto the roof. It was flat and filled with obstructions.

The man set the briefcase down and rolled up his sleeves.

"So, you want to play? Let's play."

Wilde didn't advance but he didn't back up.

"It doesn't have to be this way. Just let me take you in."

"Sure, no problem."

The man charged.

It took ten minutes to kill him up there on the roof, ten bloody minutes straight out of hell. After he threw his final punch, Wilde didn't have enough strength left to get to his feet. He rolled onto his back and felt his chest pound.

The rain fell.

He kept his eyes closed.

The rain felt good.

It felt like it was washing everything bad away.

139

Fallon sat on a curb in the rain.

Cars sped by.

They smashed puddles at her.

She kept going over it until she was positive she was making the right move. No matter what angle she looked at it from, the result was the same—she couldn't trust Jundee.

Without trust there could be no love.

Without love there could be no oxygen.

They had history together but that wasn't enough.

She got up, stuck a cigarette in her mouth and reached in her purse for matches. She pulled out the red book with the gold B. That was the pack she'd been saving as a souvenir, the ones she used Saturday night to set the briefcases on fire.

She tossed it into the gutter.

"Don't need you anymore."

She fumbled around until she found the other pack, struck a match and lit up.

The smoke felt good in her lungs.

She inhaled deeply then blew out.

New York.

That's where she'd go.

New York.

Five minutes later she found a beat-to-death pickup truck with the keys in the ignition. Ironically, it had New Mexico plates. She slipped in, fired it up and said, "Whoever owns this, I'm sorry."

Then she took off.

About the Author

Formerly a longstanding trial attorney before taking the big leap and devoting his fulltime attention to writing, RJ Jagger (that's a penname, by the way) is the author of over twenty hard-edged mystery and suspense thrillers including the Nick Teffinger, Bryson Wilde and Nicole Stone novels.

In addition to his own books, Jagger also ghostwrites for a popular bestselling author. He is a member of the International Thriller Writers and the Mystery Writers of America.

www.rjjagger.com

CPSIA information can be obtained
at www.ICGtesting.com
Printed in the USA
BVHW030807180520
579803BV00020B/14/J

9 781937 888404